What the critics are saying...

ಶು

About Dallas Heat:

"Ms. Jacobs skillfully weaves a heartwarming story between these two injured souls." ~ *Just Erotic Romance Reviews*

About the Black Gold series:

"Ann Jacobs' scorching tales sizzle with a combination of heat, sensuality, passion and romance." ~ *Cheyenne McCray, USA Today bestselling author of Forbidden Magic*

"Ann Jacobs shines bright amongst the rising stars of erotic romance." ~ *Jaid Black, USA Today bestselling author of Deep, Dark and Dangerous*

"Darkly erotic and emotionally fulfilling stories to capture the imagination. Ann Jacobs has penned a thought provoking series..." ~ *Kate Douglas, bestselling author of Wolf Tales*

Ann Jacobs

DALLAS Heat

Ellora's Cave
Romantica Publishing

An Ellora's Cave Romantica Publication

www.ellorascave.com

Dallas Heat

ISBN 1419954717
ALL RIGHTS RESERVED.
Dallas Heat Copyright © 2003 Ann Jacobs
Cover art by Syneca.

Electronic book Publication September 2003
Trade paperback Publication August 2006

With the exception of quotes used in reviews, this book may not be reproduced or used in whole or in part by any means existing without written permission from the publisher, Ellora's Cave Publishing, Inc.® 1056 Home Avenue, Akron OH 44310-3502.

This book is a work of fiction and any resemblance to persons, living or dead, or places, events or locales is purely coincidental. The characters are productions of the authors' imagination and used fictitiously.

Warning:

The following material contains graphic sexual content meant for mature readers. This story has been rated E–rotic by a minimum of three independent reviewers.

Ellora's Cave Publishing offers three levels of Romantica™ reading entertainment: S (S-ensuous), E (E-rotic), and X (X-treme).

S-*ensuous* love scenes are explicit and leave nothing to the imagination.

E-*rotic* love scenes are explicit, leave nothing to the imagination, and are high in volume per the overall word count. In addition, some E-rated titles might contain fantasy material that some readers find objectionable, such as bondage, submission, same sex encounters, forced seductions, and so forth. E-rated titles are the most graphic titles we carry; it is common, for instance, for an author to use words such as "fucking", "cock", "pussy", and such within their work of literature.

X-*treme* titles differ from E-rated titles only in plot premise and storyline execution. Unlike E-rated titles, stories designated with the letter X tend to contain controversial subject matter not for the faint of heart.

Also by Ann Jacobs

❧

A Mutual Favor
Awakenings
Black Gold: Firestorm
Black Gold: Forever Enslaved
Black Gold: Love Slave
Captured *(Anthology)*
Colors of Love
Colors of Magic
D'Argent Honor: Eternally His
D'Argent Honor: Vampire Justice
Dark Side of the Moon
Enchained *(Anthology)*
Gates of Hell
Gold Frankincense and Myrrh *(Anthology)*
Haunted
Lawyers in Love: Bittersweet Homecoming
Lawyers in Love: Gettin' It On
Lawyers in Love: In His Own Defense
Lords of Pleasure: He Calls Her Jasmine
Love Magic
Storm Warnings *(Anthology)*
Tip of the Iceberg

Books In Print
A Mutual Favor
Black Gold: Another Love
Black Gold: Firestorm
Black Gold: Sandstorms
Enchained *(Anthology)*
Lawyers in Love: The Defenders
Lawyers in Love: The Prosecutors
Mystic Visions *(Anthology)*

About the Author

ଚ୬

First published in 1996, Ann Jacobs has sold more than thirty-five books and novellas. A CPA and former hospital financial manager, she now writes full-time except, of course, for the hours she devotes to being a wife and mother to seven kids. A transplanted midwesterner, she's lived in west-central Florida all her adult life.

Ann loves writing Romantica—to her, it's the perfect blend of sex, sensuality, and happily-ever-after commitment between one man and one woman.

Ann welcomes comments from readers. You can find her website and email address on her author bio page at www.ellorascave.com.

Dedication

*To everyone who's ever overcome a disability or had a loved one who has triumphed over his or her demons and come out on top, Dan and Gayla's story is for you.
I hope you enjoy DALLAS HEAT.*

Ann Jacobs

DALLAS HEAT
ಶು

Prologue

The Ghosts

ಐ

"You think that's bad? That Sophia's going to marry Davey Brown? I'd ask nothing more if my son would find a nice girl to marry. Danny, all he does is work, work, work. If I hold my breath waiting for him to make me a grandchild or two, I'll die."

"You're already dead, Ruthie. And you got what you wanted — your son the doctor. God knows, you've told us how wonderful that boy of yours is so many times I think I may be sick if you say it again. Make up your mind. You want Danny should be famous or that he should be the greatest lover west of the Mississippi?"

Ruth Newman set down her cards and riddled her sister, Toni Schwartz, with a disdainful stare. "I want Danny to be happy."

"Maybe he is. Who are you to say?"

"I'm his mother."

Toni shrugged. "And I'm his aunt. Look, there's that woman, Sylvia something-or-other. I hear she's from Dallas, too. Maybe we should ask her to play a rubber of bridge with us, if you think you can keep your bragging mouth shut so as not to drive her away."

"What do you think, Nana?" The last thing Ruth wanted to do was upset the ghost of her long-dead, acid-tongued mother-in-law. The old woman nodded, and Ruth beckoned the newcomer to join them.

As they played bridge, conversation drifted toward the ones they'd left behind. Toni gushed on and on about her two insipid girls, and mousy little Sylvia Harris preened over her own two daughters. As usual, Nana contributed an occasional acerbic remark. Ruth preened every time she boasted that her only son had become a doctor. But she couldn't squash her concern that Danny had buried himself too deeply in his work. So deeply that he was going to deny her the vicarious joy of seeing him produce a new generation for her to worry over.

"You say your daughters live in Dallas, too?" she asked Sylvia after dinner that night, when she finally got the woman alone.

Sylvia smiled. "Both of them live there now. Tess and her husband have a nice place out in Plano. She's the older one. Gayla's not married."

"She lives at home with your husband the doctor?" It had annoyed Ruth when she'd learned there was someone else in their little group who could boast a doctor in the immediate family. Still, that could be an opening for her to push Danny into meeting a prospective bride.

"No." Sylvia's eyes brightened as if she were holding back tears. "They don't get along."

"Why not?"

"Gayla had some problems—she's better now—but Eli had no heart for accepting my baby unless she was perfect."

Ruth's mind churned that information around. Her Danny wasn't perfect either—not that any decent woman would reject him because of... She couldn't bear to think about that, not even now, after twenty-five years had gone by. At least she hadn't lost him.

Ruth forced a casual tone. "So where does Gayla live? What does she do?"

"She coaches swimming at a country club in Dallas. She almost made it to the Olympics six years ago," Sylvia said wistfully. "Has her own dollhouse of an apartment, right there on the golf course." The look on the woman's pretty face revealed a lot. Ruth guessed that this not-so-perfect little girl had been her mother's favorite. "Look. That's Gayla, standing at the edge of the pool. She's wearing the blue print swimsuit. What do you think?"

"She's pretty." Ruth watched Sylvia's daughter putting a group of young swimmers through their paces. "Tiny?"

"Five feet two. About a hundred pounds."

Good. Only five feet ten himself, Danny needed a small woman. Ruth had always hated to see women towering over their men. On the other hand their children would likely be shrimps. She shrugged away that thought—bigger wasn't always better.

The more Sylvia said about Gayla, the more Ruth became convinced a match between the girl and Danny would be ideal. Pity that matchmakers were a thing of the past. They'd have to make the children think getting together was their own idea.

"What's Danny like?" Sylvia asked, her gaze still glued on her daughter—Ruth's future daughter-in-law if all went well.

"To die for. Girls have been chasing him since he started high school." Ruth told herself she was exaggerating only the tiniest bit. *"He's smart, kind—everything you could possibly want in a husband for your daughter."*

"I'm surprised he's thirty-four years old and still single."

"He's been busy with his work. All those years of school and training—he has only had his own practice for the last few years." Ruth paused, shaking her head. *"Of course, if I hadn't died just as he was finishing up his residency..."*

"I think we should arrange for them to meet." The other ghost's tone was diffident, almost as though she was afraid to ask for what she wanted.

As Sylvia was watching Gayla, Ruth peeked in on Danny. As always, her heart beat faster when she saw him—her and Bernie's only child. *Oh, no.*

She'd caught up with him in the locker room at the hospital gym, getting ready to work out. Ruth watched her precious boy strip off the top of ugly green scrubs and untie the string that held up his baggy pants. Not a good time to show him to his future mother-in-law.

Sylvia smiled. *"Shall we make some plans?"*

"Tell me more about Gayla," Ruth said as they settled down on a bench in a sheltered alcove of heaven to set their plans in motion.

Later, after they had agreed how to arrange the young people's first meeting, Ruth fretted for hours. As she floated back and forth above the carpet in her bedroom, she hoped she was setting Danny up for love, not heartache.

Chapter One

Every bone in Dan Newman's body ached. After a marathon operation where everything that could go wrong had, he was tempted to forego his daily workout, but if he did he knew he'd regret it later. Willing himself to put one foot in front of the other, he turned the corner in the hospital corridor and...

"Are you blind, mister?"

Recovering the breath that the collision had forced from his lungs, Dan glanced down at the furious heap of feminine hostility sprawled out on the floor of the deserted corridor. "Sorry. Are you all right?" He went down on his knees to check out the damage he'd inflicted. Judging from her expression, he figured this tiny virago just might kill him.

"No thanks to you!" She grimaced as if in pain when she tried to push herself up.

"You hurt your arm. Let me see."

She jerked it back. "Don't you think you've done enough already?"

"Look, I said I was sorry. Let me see how badly you're hurt. I'm a doctor."

She glanced at the ID badge clipped to the collar of his lab coat. "You may have 'M.D.' after your name, Doctor Newman, but as far as I'm concerned, you're just the hundred seventy pounds or so of irresistible force that sent me sprawling onto the floor."

"One fifty-five."

"Whatever. My arm's okay, but I could use a hand here. You knocked the wind out of me. Just help me up and I'll be on my way."

Dan got up, then bent to take his victim's outstretched hand. "Easy, now. Where do you hurt?"

"Where do you think?" With a disgusted look she rubbed at her left hip. Then she met his gaze. "Don't look so worried, Doc, I'll live. You'll be safe from a lawsuit this time." Her grim expression belied the humor in her retort.

"That's comforting." God, she was gorgeous. Suddenly he wanted to touch her again, to soothe away the bristly veneer and learn more about the woman hidden behind it. Then he noticed she had no nametag and assumed she was visiting the hospital. "May I help you find something?"

"Someone."

"Who?"

"Dr. Eli Harris."

Old Ironsides? The chief of surgery? The slave driver who had been the bane of every resident's existence for as long as Dan could remember? "You want to see Dr. Harris?"

"He's my father. I need to drop this by his office." She fished a large manila envelope out of her tote bag and waved it in front of Dan's nose. "Know where Daddy hangs his shingle these days?"

Did he ever. He doubted if he'd ever forget having spent several uncomfortable hours in that office eight years ago, trying to persuade her old man his so-called handicap wouldn't keep him from succeeding as a surgery resident. Why wouldn't Harris's own kid know where to find him? "I'll walk you there."

"All right."

"This way." When he touched her elbow, the sudden crack of static electricity made them both jump back.

"Ouch." She shot a suspicious look his way, as though she thought he'd intentionally created the sudden current that passed through them.

Dan's hand still tingled. "Ouch, yourself. You're a walking hazard to a guy's health." And his sanity. Deliberately he assessed Old Ironsides' daughter from head to toe. She must take after her mother, because nothing in the small but sexy-as-hell package reminded him of Eli Harris.

"Are you going to take me to Dr. Harris's office?"

"Yeah." Dan could barely resist reaching out and taking her hand again. "I think we should introduce ourselves since we keep causing each other bodily harm. My name's Dan Newman."

"Gayla Harris."

Harris? Dan glanced down and saw that her left hand was bare of jewelry. They rounded the corner and entered the wide corridor that led to Old Ironsides' chamber of resident horrors. "Could I take you to dinner after you finish up with your dad?"

Her hand on the polished brass of the door, she tilted her head back to meet Dan's gaze. "You're wrong if you think taking me out will get you brownie points with my father, *Doctor*. Besides, I make it a point to stay as far away as possible from everybody in the medical profession." With that Gayla stepped inside the door and left the mysterious envelope with a sour-faced woman at the reception desk. Then she came back into the hall and closed the door behind her with a louder-than-necessary thud.

She looked up at Dan and smiled. This time he noticed a twinkle in her dark eyes. "I can find my way out. No need for you to waste any more time trying to make amends for being abysmally clumsy and running into me."

Clumsy? It had been a long time since someone had called Dan that. It had also been a while since a woman had made him obsess about darkened bedrooms and tangled bodies. "It's no bother." Deliberately he matched his gait to hers. "I'm headed your way anyhow. Why not pretend I'm anything but a doctor and give us a chance?"

"Because I'm not a masochist. I have no desire to punish myself by trying to please somebody who thinks he's less than one step away from being God. I've been there, done that, thank you very much!"

He couldn't help the grin he felt spreading across his face. "I found a cure for the God complex, honey. Perfect I'm not. Far from it, unless I'm working on someone in the OR. Come on, give me a chance." He bent down to whisper in her ear. "Please?"

For a minute she appeared to consider what he'd said. Then she propped her hands on her hips and looked him in the eye. "Okay. You want a date, fine. But you're going to have to prove on my turf that you don't have a latent God complex. I'm not about to let you take me to some fancy restaurant where they're going to fawn over you and…"

"Wherever you say is fine, honey." *A bedroom. A sofa. Hell, the backseat of my car would do just fine.* For the first time in his recent memory, Dan's cock began to throb at the idea of having sex with a specific woman.

"Tomorrow. Seven o'clock. Bluebonnet Country Club. We're going to see how your ego fares, doing something you probably don't do as well as I do."

He grinned. "Golf? Sounds like fun." The idea of being beaten by a woman didn't put him off. Years ago he'd accepted just being able to hold his own.

"Swimming. Bring your suit. You do swim, don't you?"

"Yeah." He tried hard to sound casual. As soft and cuddly as Gayla Harris looked, it wasn't fair for her to have her old man's piranha-like talent for finding and attacking the vulnerable areas of a person's psyche. But apparently she did.

"Well, I was a two-time national champion. Think your ego can take being beaten by a woman half your size?" Her evil grin added a silent "Gotcha!"

The tension drained from Dan's neck and shoulders. So she simply wanted to beat him at her own sport, fair and square— not take advantage of the disability he doubted now that she'd even noticed. He smiled.

"Well?" she prodded.

"I'll be there." He opened a door and followed her outside.

"Here's my card. It has my phone number at the club in case you decide to chicken out." Again their fingers connected as she handed him an aqua business card—and he felt a pervasive, unfamiliar heat.

As he watched Gayla get into a beat-up compact sedan, he glanced down and thought for the second time in as many minutes about his very imperfect self. Then he shelved those unproductive thoughts and headed to the gym. Once there, Dan tortured his exhausted body unmercifully, as if by sheer force of will he could turn carbon graphite, molded polyurethane, and a bunch of synthetic skin into living, feeling flesh.

At least he'd learn right away how this woman would react to the reality of his missing lower left leg. By meeting her challenge he'd show her a hell of a lot more than he'd ever revealed in words to women he dated when he told them he was an amputee. The prospect both intrigued and terrified him.

* * * * *

Back at her apartment on the club grounds, Gayla wondered what on earth she'd done, inviting Dan Newman over for a swim. She couldn't kid herself. The gorgeous young doc took her breath away, made her nipples tighten and her mouth water. Before she'd walked away she'd felt hot slick fluid dampening her panties.

But she wasn't ready to play at another male-female relationship. Maybe she never would be. Her therapists had told her time would heal the pain. Four years had passed, though, and she still hurt as much as she had the day her world had tumbled down around her.

She still pictured her family the way they'd looked that day in the hospital, standing over her bed when she came to. Tess and their mother had sat silently on one side of the room, their expressions hooded. Her father had scowled down at her from the other side while Marc had stood at the end of the bed, wearing a guilty look while he shifted his weight from one leg to the other. She'd known as soon as she saw their faces that she'd blown it badly.

They hadn't had to tell her the baby was gone—that she'd never hold him in her arms or watch him grow up into a strong, sturdy child. Or that she'd missed out on the best chance she'd ever had to make them proud. She'd guessed right away that that her wedding set for less than a week away was off. And she'd learned soon enough that her father would turn his back on her and give the affection he'd denied her to Marc. Marc, his fair-haired resident—the man who apparently didn't want a loser for a wife.

Gayla tried desperately to erase the memories—forget the past four years. She wished she could deny the escape she'd made after those painful losses, forget that shadow world where only alcohol and drugs had dulled the memories. Each day she relived the slow, hard climb back to a life her mother had escaped by dying. A world where she found that to her father she, too, had died. Now she forced herself to concentrate on the kids she was coaching at this struggling country club that couldn't afford to delve too deeply into its employees' past mistakes.

Going to the hospital today had opened all her old wounds. Gayla had known it would be hard before she went, but she'd never have dared to risk tossing out the mysterious envelope someone had sent to her father, in care of her. While he hadn't spoken to Gayla in years, Eli Harris would expect her to deliver the envelope promptly—and Gayla knew he was not a man to thwart. She'd learned that lesson at age nine, when she'd dared not to win an event on the one day he'd cleared his schedule to watch her compete.

So she'd braved her demons and delivered the envelope. And literally collided with a good-looking young doctor with a killer grin and gorgeous dark eyes—a doctor who swore he didn't think he was God. Gayla figured tomorrow she'd get the last laugh. Or would she? She certainly wasn't at her world-class best, and for all she knew, Dan Newman could be a national champ himself, chuckling right this minute over the prospect of putting her in her place.

Much later, as she lay in bed, Gayla wondered who on earth had delivered that envelope marked "Confidential" and "Urgent," addressed to her father in care of her. Whoever it was must not have known Eli Harris had disowned her years ago.

Her mind drifted, then settled on Dan Newman. Why had he of all people nudged her long-dormant hormones into overdrive?

Chapter Two

"Damn!"

Every time Dan closed his eyes, he saw that prickly, almost defiant look Gayla had shot him when she proposed they meet for a swim tomorrow. He glanced at the digital clock on the nightstand. Not tomorrow. Today. It was one o'clock, and he had to be in the OR before seven.

He'd never had trouble sleeping. Never, not even when he'd been recovering from his amputation or the stump revision he'd submitted to before beginning his residency. Not until he'd collided with a tiny brunette with flashing dark eyes who scrambled his brain. Pounding his pillow into a misshapen ball, he gave it one last punch with his fist before burrowing his head into it and trying again to get some sleep.

How much more comfortable he'd be if he could rest his head against Gayla's high, firm breasts—wrap his arms around her and feel her hips nudge gently at his cock. How easily he'd fall asleep if he fucked her until they both collapsed in a sweaty, orgasmic heap.

The woman had bewitched him. Hell, he must have spent too many hours in surgery and not enough seeing to his own needs. Otherwise he wouldn't be lying here, his balls ready to explode and his cock harder than stone. Harder than when he'd been a teenager too scared of being turned down to seduce his girlfriend and relieve his sexual tension. Dan tried to erase the erotic images in his brain by concentrating on the delicate reconstructive surgery he had scheduled.

It didn't work. Disgusted with his inability to control the usually dormant libido Gayla had jump-started hours earlier, Dan rolled to the side of the bed and reached automatically for his prosthesis. Rolling the silicone suspension liner up but not bothering with a sock for the short trek he had in mind, he slid his stump into the socket and made his way to the shower.

He sank onto the plastic seat in the corner of the shower stall and released the suction valve that held the prosthesis in place, setting it outside the shower stall before rolling off the liner and turning on a prickly blast of cold water. When he wrapped up in a towel minutes later, he was shivering and his skin had shriveled—but at least his problem had shrunk to a manageable dull ache.

Dan glanced at the clock. *Too late to try to sleep.* He'd dress and pour a gallon or so of coffee down his throat. By then it would be time to head to the hospital.

After putting on his clothes he shuffled to the kitchen and thumbed through a new medical journal while he waited for the coffee to brew. Articles he normally would have tackled with enthusiasm failed to capture his interest. All he could think about was Gayla.

And that he was going to see her tonight. While he chatted with members of the surgical team later that morning, her image kept flashing through his head. Still, he was grateful when two orderlies wheeled in their first patient, a teenage girl whose car had lost a battle with a utility pole out on I-20 the day before. Focusing on her and the delicate repair job he was about to do took all his concentration.

That operation and the ones that followed went well. For once no emergencies presented themselves to complicate his day. Whistling as he left the hospital at four o'clock, Dan decided his unusually routine day at work must have been a good omen.

As he slid out of his car in the parking lot of the country club where Gayla coached, he grinned. Grabbing a battered gym bag, he headed for the pool.

* * * * *

He came. Gayla hadn't been at all sure Dan would show up, but here he was, striding across the pool deck and looking good enough to eat. The late afternoon sunlight bounced off his thick, wavy hair, brightening some of the dark brown strands to burnished gold. In a polo shirt the color of the Texas sky, loose-fitting gray cotton slacks, and white canvas deck shoes, Dan Newman looked more like a college boy than a doctor—but then looks often deceived.

Up close now, he grinned as he took off the aviator-style glasses that had shielded those dark, mesmerizing eyes from her view. Tearing her gaze away, Gayla reminded herself she wasn't ready to risk caring for any man just yet. She'd never be ready for another one whose ego had to be as impressive as the rippling biceps that stretched the short sleeves of his shirt.

"Hi." His gaze settled on her face after he'd made a lazy visual inspection of her from the ground up. When he reached out and clasped her hands, it was as though lightning had struck.

"Hello. I'll be finished here in just a minute." Forcing her attention to the few teenagers still doing warm-down laps in the pool, she tried hard to deny the pull she felt toward Dr. Dan Newman.

"I'll go change."

Gayla, what have you let yourself in for? "You can use my office," she told him, fighting down a desperate need for this man to keep his clothes on. What had she been thinking of, suggesting an activity that required them both to be as close to naked as the law allowed?

"Thanks."

When he was out of sight—not out of mind—Gayla hurried her young athletes along. The last thing she needed was to have them watch her making a fool of herself. By the time she'd all but pushed them out the swinging doors that led to the parking lot, she'd managed to sweep away most of the crazy urges that came over her every time she thought of those brief, electrically charged moments yesterday when she and Dan had touched.

When she turned around, he was already sitting at the edge of the pool, his dark gaze practically scalding her skin. Gayla fought the urge to run the opposite direction and instead went to join him. God, he was gorgeous, all well-developed muscle cloaked in golden skin only slightly marbled by dark body hair. It was all she could do to keep from running her fingers over his chest to learn if that hair felt as silky as it looked.

Gayla had to squash these wayward feelings—quickly. Stripping off the sarong that matched the competition suit she wore, she shot an appraising glance his way. "Ready for a beating, Doc?"

He glanced up at her, grinning. "Give me a minute. I've got to take this leg off."

Gayla tried hard to hide the shock that engulfed her. Against her will, she looked past his flat, ridged abdominals—past the impressive bulge of male flesh barely restrained by taut navy swim trunks—at the limb in question.

Apparently he wasn't kidding. She watched the lower part of his left leg pop off, revealing some sort of skin-toned covering that he was peeling down and off the limb that ended abruptly maybe six inches below his knee.

It couldn't be. But it was. Before she remembered the manners her mother had drilled into her, Gayla gaped at the limb Dan had set on the deck, and at the empty place on the deck where his leg should have been. "I—I'm sorry. I didn't mean to stare."

"It's okay." Dan's smile didn't quite reach his eyes. "Kind of shocks people when they see it for the first time." That apparent vulnerability didn't lasted more than a few seconds.

"Yes. It does," she said when she recovered her voice, managing a smile when she met his questioning gaze.

"Come on, I'll race you." The water splashed softly as he slid into the pool.

"Okay." Gayla jumped into the lane next to Dan, needing the cooling water on her burning cheeks more than the opportunity to prove she could swim faster than a man with just one leg. "We don't have to do this, you know. I'd never—"

"Have suggested a race if you'd known?" Letting go of his left-handed hold on the lane rope between them, Dan gestured toward his damaged leg. "Princess, I may not beat you but I'll give you a run for your money. Ten laps okay?"

All Gayla could do was nod as she fitted goggles over her eyes, and when they pushed off together a few seconds later she set a steady pace. Only when she noticed him passing her on the sixth lap did her competitive instinct take over and force her arms to move faster, her legs to pound out a six-beat sprinting cadence. Her out-of-shape lungs began to scream in protest.

She finished half a pool length ahead of him, winded but exhilarated. Dan had pushed her hard. While trying to catch her breath, she critiqued his powerful freestyle pull. *He could have been a champion.* She gave herself a mental shaking. *Stop it, Gayla. The last thing this man must want is sympathy. Besides...*

"Congratulations. You weren't lying when you said you were fast. I owe you dinner. Gayla, are you all right?" Disappearing under the water, Dan resurfaced at her side.

I'm staring again. What on earth has come over me? "Yes. Just the coach in me, I guess. I was admiring your stroke while I tried to catch my breath." Nervous as well as embarrassed half to death, Gayla met Dan's endearingly lopsided grin with a smile of her own. "You weren't wrong when you said you'd give me a run for my money."

"I try to get in a few laps almost every day. Now how about dinner?" Apparently not stressed at all from the five hundred yard race, Dan levered himself out of the pool and sat on the edge, legs dangling into the water. Gayla noticed him giving her a visual once-over that could have been payback for her blatant staring at him—or maybe it was simply appreciative masculine interest.

She hoped it was the latter, because Dan turned her on like no one had for a long, long time. She might not be ready for a relationship, but she wouldn't be averse to exploring the sexual attraction that fairly crackled between them.

"Gayla?"

"What? Oh, dinner. Sure. As long as we go someplace close. And casual."

Dan grinned. "I've got just the place. Need some help getting out?"

She didn't, but wanting him to touch her, she took his outstretched hand and let him lift her and onto the deck beside him. Her skin tingled where his hands had been. "Thanks."

"You're welcome. Go on, princess, winner gets the first shower."

They could do it together. A shower and much, much more. Her cheeks burning at the images of them clinging together, warm water raining over their naked bodies, she came back down to earth. "I'll use the girls' locker room. Make yourself at home in my office. There's a clean towel over the shower curtain." She struggled to her feet, afraid that if she didn't get away she might actually suggest they live out her wayward fantasy.

When she emerged from the locker room wearing a tropical-patterned brown, rust, and black sundress that set off her deep golden tan, Dan was waiting outside her office door.

* * * * *

"McDonalds?"

Dan chuckled as he pulled into a parking space outside the fast-food restaurant not a mile from the country club. "You said casual. And I doubt we'll find any fawning waiters here." He shut off the engine of his red BMW convertible and unfastened his seat belt.

By the time Gayla found her voice, Dan had walked around and was opening her door. "We could go someplace else if burgers aren't your thing."

"I didn't think they would be yours." When she slid out of the car, her body brushed briefly against his, setting off sparks that shot straight to her pussy. "Hope you don't mind being around kids," she commented as they strolled past a high-tech children's playground on the way to the door.

"Not at all." While they stood in line, he held her hand. Involuntarily she pictured those strong, slender fingers working magic all over her body...holding a baby like the man in front of them was doing...saving someone's life in the operating room.

Oh, no. This man is a doctor. A surgeon, if those green scrubs he was wearing yesterday weren't figments of your imagination. Like your father. Like Marc.

"Gayla, what would you like?"

To get out of here, run as fast as I can. "A burger and fries. And a chocolate shake," she murmured, forcing herself to meet his questioning gaze.

Dan paid for their order and picked up the plastic tray, detouring by the self-service drink machines to pour them each some water. When they'd settled down at a corner table, the smile he shot her took her breath away.

God, every time he looked at her she got wetter and hotter. Determined not to climb across the table and jump him, Gayla concentrated on squeezing catsup onto her French fries. He might make her sizzle more than these fries had when they were bubbling in hot oil moments earlier, but she dared not let her hormones drag her into a situation where she'd be certain to get hurt.

Dan's fingers touched hers briefly, as if to get her attention. "What's wrong?"

"Nothing."

"Look, if it's my leg..."

"What kind of monster do you think I am?" Gayla couldn't believe he thought she'd reject him because of something he obviously couldn't help.

His half smile tore at her heart as much as the hollow sound of him tapping on his prosthesis. "Not a monster at all. Some people just get turned off, seeing disfigurement as obvious as this."

"Well, I don't. Dan, what kind of doctor are you?"

"A neurosurgeon." From his expression Gayla could guess that her abrupt change of subject puzzled him.

Gayla laughed until tears ran down her face, aware of Dan's quizzical stare as she struggled for self-control. "Oh, great! Just great. A blasted brain surgeon! My father thinks he's God because he's able to fix and replace hearts. And now I've had to go get the hots for a guy who has an ego big enough to let him tinker with essential body parts that *can't* be replaced!"

Now it was Dan doing the laughing, huge guffaws that made Gayla want to hug him and strangle him at the same time. When he settled down enough to talk, the expression on his face would have lit up the place if it suddenly lost electrical power.

"You're priceless. Having met your dad, I understand why you might think all doctors are a bunch of egomaniacs. But let me set your mind at ease. I haven't opened up anyone's brain since I was a resident. Even then I had a lot of help. My specialty is the peripheral nervous system—little nerves that when I fix them will make my patients' lives more pleasant. Very little life-and-death kind of stuff."

"Oh." Gayla couldn't help returning his smile. "Then I guess we can be friends."

"And lovers?" His tone was low, insinuating. Downright seductive.

Her heart beat faster, and when she spoke she sounded almost as breathless as she'd felt when she finished their race. "No. Maybe. Dan, you're coming on too fast."

"Yeah. There's this weird chemistry. It made me hard for you the minute we collided in that hallway. And my hormones don't generally kick in before my brain."

His gaze scorched her, made the juices gush out of her pussy onto her thighs. "Me, neither. But this is insane. We don't even know each other."

"So what's to say we can't remedy that? Ask me anything."

"Anything?"

"Anything at all."

"Your…"

"Leg. Don't be shy, honey. I don't mind talking about it. I should have told you first—then it wouldn't have come as such a shock."

"Do you usually tell and show instead of the other way around?" She loved the way he looked at her, amusement plain in his twinkling eyes.

"Yeah. You're only the second person I can remember having shown first, told later."

"And the first?" Gayla wondered how the other woman had reacted.

Dan's expression sobered. "A patient. A little boy, seven years old. He thought his life was over when he woke up from surgery a few months ago and learned we'd had to amputate his leg."

"Oh." Her father never revealed anything really personal to his family. She couldn't imagine him ever confiding in a patient. "That must have been hard for you."

"Yeah. Our team had been working to save his legs for close to four years. Both legs were almost completely severed in a car accident. We reattached them, then had to put him through four more surgeries. Great little kid, though. He never complained, and he suffered some god-awful pain. Showing him I manage pretty well was the least I could do."

Impulsively Gayla reached out and covered one of Dan's hands with her own. "Why did you show me?"

"There was no way in hell I could go swimming with you and *not* show you. But I'd have told you before accepting your challenge if you hadn't made me so damn mad, acting as if I were a pariah because you've got a thing against the way I earn my living."

"What happened to you?" Gayla asked just as a bunch of rowdy preteens started yelling at each other from tables directly across the room.

"Come on, let's find somewhere quieter, and we'll talk," Dan suggested, gathering up the wrappers from their meal and sliding out of the booth.

Should I have noticed? While they walked back to his car Gayla hung back a step, looking for any signs she should have seen while she'd been drooling over his killer smile and yummy shoulders. She didn't detect a limp or any other outward sign that his left leg was not all his own. All she saw was one compact, gorgeous example of fit, male *Homo sapiens*. Dan Newman took her breath away.

In a quiet park not far away, they sat at a picnic table overlooking a deserted playground and talked. While Gayla hurt for Dan when he told her how his doctors had found cancer when he was nine years old and taken his leg to save his life, she felt no pity, just admiration for the man he'd become.

He laughingly said he'd been lucky to lose part of his left leg instead of his right, thus saving the expense of getting hand controls installed in his cars. That, and the casual way he related funny incidents that had to do with his being an amputee made Gayla realize how comfortable he must feel with himself.

And why shouldn't he be content? Dan Newman had taken a nasty hand fate had dealt him and forged ahead. He'd made chicken salad out of chicken shit—as one of her coaches had been fond of telling some of her hapless teammates could not be done.

On the other hand, she'd taken the best parts of the chicken and turned it to barnyard droppings. As her father had taken apparent pleasure in telling her before writing her out of his life, she'd tossed away every opportunity she'd been given and ended up with nothing. "I think I'd best be going home," she said as she fought back tears. Dan's hand stilled against her shoulder as if he thought he'd caused her distress.

"What's wrong?"

"Nothing." She hoped he wouldn't question her further. Her wounds had healed too imperfectly for her to talk about them without making them bleed or fester.

* * * * *

For a while Dan had thought he was overcoming the obstacles that stood in the way of beginning a relationship with Gayla. Now, as he drove her home, her silence gave him second thoughts.

"Turn right here," she told him as they approached a gravel driveway. Then she clammed up again until he walked her to the stairway to her tiny apartment above the golf cart storage garage. "There's no need for you to come all the way to the door."

"I don't mind." Tucking a hand beneath Gayla's elbow, Dan accompanied her up the steep, narrow steps. Taking her key, he opened the door.

Strong light framed her face when she turned and looked up at him. A soft breeze ruffled her dark hair and filled Dan's nostrils with her clean, feminine fragrance.

Her wistful, yearning expression made him want to wrap her in his arms and never let her go. "Kiss me," she said, so softly he wouldn't have understood if he hadn't been staring at her, trying to memorize her features.

"Like this?" Gently drawing her closer, Dan bent and nuzzled at the silky strands of her long, dark hair before moving his lips down her cheek and placing nibbling kisses at one corner of her mouth.

"No, Dan. Like this."

Desire slammed straight through him when she turned slightly and deepened the contact. When she slid her tongue back and forth across his lips, his cock came instantly alert. Damn it, every cell in his body was screaming for him to take her inside and fuck her until they both collapsed in a sweaty, satiated heap. From the way she held onto him he got the idea she wanted that, too.

But it was too soon. He wasn't an out-of-control teenager anticipating his first taste of pussy, and he liked her too much to treat her as though she were nothing but a handy piece of ass. Still, it took all his will power to stand there hard as stone, doing nothing more than invading her mouth with his tongue. Wishing it were his aching cock slamming into the hot, wet softness of her pussy.

He took the sweet torture as long as he could before gently pushing her away. "We've got to stop unless you want to continue this inside." His words came out roughly between labored gasps for air. Her heavy breathing hinted that she, too, was close to the edge. But when Dan looked into her eyes, he saw glistening tears.

"Gayla." Her name escaped his constricted throat, half plea and half prayer.

"Y-yes?"

"May I call you?" Dan watched a teardrop trickle down a satiny cheek flushed, he guessed, from the kiss that had his balls aching with need.

"No! You don't know me. If you did you wouldn't want... Please, just go. Don't make me want more than I can ever have." She pulled away and practically leaped through the door, slamming it shut behind her.

Disappointed, he turned away from the door. Then he remembered the tears in her eyes and the pained look on her face. As he made his way down the stairs and to his car he sensed that she was watching him. He'd be calling her again, trying to beat down the barriers she'd put up. He had no choice.

Chapter Three

The Ghosts

"Shall we look in on Gayla now?" Sylvia asked.

"Oh, all right. Did you never let her out of your sight when you were alive?"

Ruth's question, delivered in a voice fairly dripping with sarcasm, made Sylvia wince. Sometimes the other ghost reminded Sylvia of Eli, the way she insisted on doing everything her way. Not wanting to stir up an argument, Sylvia forced a smile at Ruth as she checked on her child. The other ghost might think she fretted too much—but Ruth didn't know all her poor baby had gone through.

Fully expecting to see Gayla enjoying a pleasant evening with the man Ruth seemed to think was perfection itself, it shocked her that her daughter was alone in her tiny apartment, sobbing quietly in the darkness as she clutched a thick album to her chest—the photo album Sylvia had made for Gayla before she left home for college, she realized.

"He's hurt her!" It was easier to blame Ruth's son than admit that too many people, including herself, had made her baby cry.

"Not my Danny." Ruth scowled, her fingers curled into fists. *"Sylvia, look at him. Does this look like a man who has just made your daughter cry? It seems to me as if Danny is the one who is suffering."*

Sylvia got her first really close look at the man she was hoping would become Gayla's husband. When she'd seen him before, he'd always been in some operating room, with a mask hiding half his face—and, Sylvia had suspected, some imperfection it might not suit his doting mother to reveal. She'd been wrong. In addition to being a respected doctor, Ruth Newman's only son was handsome enough to be a matinee idol.

Danny *did* look sad, she decided after watching him settle into an easy chair with some sort of medical journal. His frustration showed when he heaved the magazine all the way across the room and buried that gorgeous face of his in his large, well-shaped hands. Surgeon's hands, like Eli's. Hands meant for performing all kinds of delicate surgery.

Sylvia glanced down at Gayla, who was up now and apparently getting ready for bed.

"Sylvia, my Danny looks as devastated as Gayla. Maybe even more. She must have said something that hurt him."

"Gayla? She's always been the soul of kindness. Most likely your Danny's feeling down because she didn't jump at the chance to let him into her bed. She's a good girl, my Gayla."

Ruth riddled Sylvia with a look that would have killed her—if looks could kill, and if she weren't already dead. *"My Danny's a good boy, too. Look, my friend. If we want our children to fall in love, we've got to work together. Now let me see…"*

Having spent her entire adult life being bossed around by Eli, Sylvia had no intention of spending eternity being ordered about by the mother of her future son-in-law. *"Well, Ruth, I want my daughter to stop looking like somebody just crushed the life out of her. I wish your Danny would send her some flowers or something. That would make her smile, I think."*

"You don't think at all, Sylvia. You just wished your girl would get a few blossoms. What will that accomplish? How will that get them together?" Ruth scowled again, and Sylvia found herself trembling—the way she had when she was alive and had displeased Eli.

"What should I have wished for?"

"You should wish for something that would get them together. Like this. I wish Danny would take Gayla to that big banquet the hospital will be giving later this month."

Horrified, Sylvia gaped at Ruth until she found her voice. *"What? You want him to take her where she's bound to run into her father? After I told you they don't get along?"*

"Danny needs to go to these social affairs. I wish his partners would make him go. I told you, didn't I, that he works with a team whose success at reconstructive surgery brings them patients from all over the world?"

Sylvia didn't recall Ruth's having mentioned a team before. She had the distinct impression from this overbearing woman that her precious son—the one who had made her Gayla cry—performed all the miracles his mother talked about incessantly all by himself. *"I don't remember your mentioning him working with a team..."*

"Of course I did. Didn't I?"

"I don't think so."

So what if Danny needs help to make him God? Sylvia could imagine arguing all night with Ruth about this particular detail—and she wanted to watch Gayla's face light up when her bouquet from Danny arrived sometime within the next few hours. *"Don't you need to rest?"* she asked, hinting for Ruth to float away.

Ruth shrugged. *"Not really. No more than you do. But I'll leave you to your Gayla-watching."* With that parting comment she floated off toward the game room.

What am I doing, trying to saddle poor Gayla with the mother-in-law from hell? Sylvia asked herself as she watched her overbearing partner in crime disappear around the corner. Then she laughed out loud. Ruth was dead—as dead as she! Her baby could have the boyish-looking doctor with the killer smile and not have to put up with his domineering mother.

Sylvia would be the one to have to deal with Ruth, and that would be a small enough price to pay for Gayla's happiness. Satisfied, Sylvia settled comfortably on the sofa and watched her little girl.

Chapter Four

ಬ

"Hey, I'm lookin' for Gayla Harris." The gruff voice came from behind a veritable garden of roses.

"Yes."

"Here. These are for you."

Gayla found herself holding a crystal vase brimming with of roses of every imaginable color as she looked at the retreating back of the delivery man. Overwhelmed by the flowers' sweet fragrance, she set the vase on a poolside table. With trembling fingers, she slit the envelope and pulled out an ivory business card. She strained to read the bold scrawl on the back of it:

"Gayla—they tell me red's for passion, blush for innocence. To me you're both. Sorry if I came on too strong last night. The last thing I wanted was to scare you off. Dan."

Tears stung Gayla's eyes. Why couldn't she have met this man who seemed to be perfect in every way that mattered years ago, before she'd screwed up her life? If he found out the truth about how she'd spent the past four years, he'd take back the feelings he'd put into those sweet words on the back of his fancy engraved business card.

Vaguely she noted the tear that fell onto a perfect blossom as she carried the bouquet to her office. When she composed herself, she called the number on the front of the card that held Dan's note and left a thank-you message with the woman who answered the phone. She didn't dare ask to speak to him in person. Her resolve to stay away from him wouldn't hold up if she had to listen again to that deep, sexy voice.

* * * * *

"Hey, this one's personal. Sending flowers to some chick, Danny?" Grinning from ear to ear, Kelly Simpson-Taylor handed over a pink phone message slip.

Dan snatched the paper and quickly scanned its content. "Yeah. What's it to you, Kel?" Why the hell had the team's pain management specialist taken it upon herself to sort through the morning's accumulation of phone messages?

"I can't believe it. Newman holding up surgery to order flowers!" Jamie Turner, their prosthetist, could be counted upon never to miss a chance to dig at him or one of the other doctors.

"I didn't hold up surgery. They forgot to give the patient his pre-op meds up on the floor, so I decided to take advantage of the extra time. Why did you decide to show up an hour early, anyhow? That has to be a first."

"Dan, florists take orders over the phone," Jamie pointed out with an evil grin.

Dan shrugged. These team members were as close to a family as he had. They meant well, even if the women on the team did sometimes act as if their only pleasure in life was teasing him or the other guys in the group. "I wanted to write the card myself, oh nosy one."

"Is she pretty?" That was Kelly again, fueling the gossip flame.

"Knock it off, honey. We've got real problems to go over." Their plastic man, Jim Taylor, sounded forceful, but he diluted the effect of his words by caressing Kelly's hand. Suddenly Dan envied these colleagues. Kel and Jim had managed to stay in love—and married to each other—through med school, residencies, and the stress of working together since the team had formed five years ago.

All of them were here, except Michelle Smith, the physical therapist—and Frank Grogan, the orthopedic surgeon they'd chosen as chief of their group. Sifting through some patient notes he planned to discuss, Dan jumped reflexively at the sound of slamming doors. When he looked up he saw Frank stomping into the room.

"Who rattled your cage?" Jim asked mildly, his attention apparently fixed on the back of his wife's small hand.

The scraping sound of the chair Frank yanked back across ceramic floor tiles made Dan shove the notes he'd been reading back into a manila folder, while Frank took his usual seat at the head of the small conference table. "What's up?" Dan asked, treading lightly so as not to exacerbate his partner's obvious ill temper.

"What's up is that the damn new hospital administrator's on the warpath. Thinks we bring in too many no-pay cases. The son of a bitch says we've got to capture some big-money grants, or he's going to cut off our admitting privileges."

Dan met Frank's angry gaze. "They've already done that, Frank. We've always had to put off scheduling secondary reconstructive surgeries until patients can come up with whatever deposit the hospital requires."

"Dan's right. The guy's just blowing off steam," Jim said.

"Wrong. I just listened while he shoved spreadsheets and graphs under my nose, showing me how much precious cash we lose for this moneymaking machine—the same one that charges us five grand a month to hang our shingles in a cramped suite of offices and do our thing in their state-of-the-art surgery suites. He's going to block transfer admissions of 'financially questionable' primary trauma cases. That means, my naive friends, that unless the folks who need our services happen to have killer insurance or Texas-big wallets, they're going to be out of luck."

"Unless they're admitted here in the first place." Kelly always could come up with the bright side of a coin, no matter how tarnished it might be.

"Kel, I doubt if five percent of our reconstructive trauma cases drop in on us courtesy of our own ER," Jim told her.

Frank eyed them all with a disgusted look. "Three and a half percent. Look. I've spent all morning talking this issue into the ground. Here's the bottom line. We troll for money or we're out of business."

Jamie grinned. "No problem. Gary and his team just dropped a few hints and came up with nearly ten million dollars to cover charity care for their patients."

"Your fiancé and his team have life versus death to sell, Jamie. All we're peddling is a chance at a better life," Dan told her gently before Frank could open his mouth and really cut her down.

Frank rapped a fist on the table. "Dan's right. It won't be easy. While I was walking here from Scrooge's office, though, a plan came to me — almost as if by magic."

Dan imagined that Frank's plan would involve them all doing things they would prefer not to, such as putting the bite on wealthy former patients and their families. "Let's hear it, Frank."

"The bash the hospital gives every year for the medical staff and all the big contributors. We're going."

"We always go," Kelly said sweetly.

Frank shot her an intimidating scowl. "You and Jim always go. Well, this year we're all going. I stopped by and reserved a table. Cost ten thousand dollars, for God's sake. For just one night we're all going to be the politicos we aren't." He tossed eight beige envelopes with gilt lettering into the center of the table. Dan assumed they held the "invitations" the ten grand had procured.

"I assume we're supposed to zero in on potential victims the way vampires go for blood?" Jim asked.

"You and Kelly are supposed to be your sweet, loving selves. You're the nearest thing to high-society respectable this team has to offer. Jamie, bring Gary and have him introduce you to some of the fish he snared for his cancer research. Whatever we do, we have to make folks think we're mature, respectable, responsible members of the medical establishment."

Jamie snorted. Kelly visibly held back a twitter. Jim shrugged as if this quest would be defeated before it could take shape. And Dan stared at Frank, incredulous. This idea had to have popped into his partner's head through some kind of paranormal phenomenon, because if any one of them was less than "high society respectable," it would have to be Frank himself. Not to mention that Frank had literally sworn off using what few social graces he'd ever had after Erica had taken their little boy and left.

"Well?" Frank said silkily.

"We'll do what we have to." Dan wished to hell he knew where this conversation was leading.

"Fine. You'll all be there early for the cocktail hour, and you'll make as many contacts as you can. Look sharp. Successful. All that shit. Dan, you can come up with a decent date, can't you?"

Immediately a picture of Gayla came to mind. "I can try. Does this mean you're going to find a date, too, and get that mop of hair chopped off?" He looked pointedly at shoulder-length blond hair he doubted Frank had cut since Erica left, then eyed a scruffy, three-day growth of stubble on his partner's chin.

"I'll take Michelle. There are just eight seats to a table. But one of you jerks can make me an appointment with your high-dollar hairstylist, and I'll let him do his thing." Frank ran nervous fingers through his unruly hair.

Dan doubted if Frank would go out and find a real date even if the damn table seated a dozen, but he figured it would be safer not to voice that thought. While one part of him resented letting his partners force him into taking a woman to what most certainly would be an evening of business instead of pleasure, another part rejoiced that he now had the perfect excuse to get Gayla to go out with him again.

* * * * *

"You're asking *me* to go with you to some fancy medical staff banquet? I told you taking me wouldn't get you any points from my father. You don't want…"

"Gayla, give me credit for knowing what I want." Dan's voice on the phone sounded restrained, as if he didn't want to attend this bash—but Gayla believed he really wanted her to be with him there. "Will you go with me?"

She glanced at the beautiful bouquet she'd brought back from her office and set next to the photo album on the table by her bed. More than anything she wanted to say yes, to much more than a boring evening together, dressed to the nines and making small talk with Dallas's finest. But she couldn't. Could she?

"Go with him, Gayla. Show your daddy you're not afraid."

Who said that? It sounded like her mother's sweet voice, but it couldn't be. Gayla looked around the room but saw nothing and no one.

"It's me, baby. You can't see me, but I'm here."

"Gayla?" Dan sounded as if her long silence had confounded him. "Will you go with me?"

"Why not?" Her psychiatrists had persuaded her she wasn't a monster or even a total failure. She could be anything she wanted to be. Perhaps confronting her father on his own turf was a task she'd put off long enough. Maybe the decent woman she'd painfully reconstructed from ashes of her former self might even be worthy of a good man like Dan.

"You mean you'll go?"

"Yes." Relieved to have agreed to face her demons head-on, Gayla smiled into the phone. "The roses are beautiful," she murmured as she lifted one perfect ruby bud from the water and rubbed it gently against her cheek.

For a few minutes they chatted, small pleasantries about their respective activities since they had parted the night before.

When she set the phone in its cradle, Gayla let herself imagine her mother really was somewhere out there, knowing and caring—even though she knew she'd broken her mother's heart.

* * * * *

For nearly two weeks Dan had pictured Gayla, imagined what she'd wear and how she'd fix her satiny sable hair for the banquet. The reality of her in shimmering deep red silk that hugged every tantalizing inch of her from shoulder to ankles except for a side slit that gave glimpses of one long, silky leg, nearly took his breath away when she let him into her apartment.

"I'm almost ready. Let me get my shoes. Would you like a drink or something?"

Her smile faltered a little, as if she were no more used to going to the glitzy kind of banquet Frank had sentenced them to for the evening than he was. "I'm okay," he told her, wishing he could get out of this monkey suit, strip off her dress, pull those glittering pins out of her elegantly upswept hair, and haul her into the small bedroom he could see from her living room.

* * * * *

"Do you do this often?" she asked after they had driven into the city and Dan handed his keys to an attendant at the downtown hotel where the banquet was being held.

He took her hand, as much to reassure himself as to guide her. "No. I'm here because someone bewitched the chief of our group into believing we can reel in enough donations here so we can keep helping patients who can't afford rehabilitative surgery or therapy. Given the choice, I'd be taking you somewhere quiet—private. How about you?"

Dan felt Gayla's almost imperceptible shudder as she glanced around the ballroom. "It's been years since I've gone to an affair like this one."

"Smile, princess. We'll make this fun." In the ballroom now, Dan searched for familiar faces. His hand at Gayla's waist, he maneuvered her through the crush of elegantly clad guests, making his way to the table.

Introductions went quickly, and before long it seemed Gayla was right at home with Dan's colleagues. Her self-deprecating humor, the easy way she fit in with the members of the team—the twinkle in her dark brown eyes when she looked at him—combined to help him have fun and ignore the serious reason he'd come.

Gayla squeezed Dan's hand as they walked onto the dance floor. He made being back among the Dallas medical community seem easy. Resting her cheek against the crisp black wool of his tuxedo jacket, she let herself move with him, in time with the slow, dreamy song the combo was playing. She liked the partners he'd introduced as his family, and felt as if she belonged when they included her in their irreverent, shamelessly self-serving conversation about finding donors to placate the hospital and keep their program alive.

"I like your friends," she murmured as she watched Jim and Kelly showing off with intricate dance patterns. "Especially Michelle. Frank doesn't seem comfortable, though." The striking blond who looked more like a pro football player than a doctor had uttered maybe ten words other than when he was wooing a potential contributor.

"This is even less Frank's kind of party than it is mine. Since his wife left and took their little boy to California, his whole life is our rehab program. Nothing other than the threat of losing hospital backing could drag him to a function like this."

"Then he and Michelle aren't…"

"He more or less ordered Michelle to come with him. Since she's part of the group, she had to be here anyhow. Frank swore off women after Erica walked out." Dan increased the pressure of his hand at Gayla's back, and instinctively she snuggled closer.

He moved with an easy, natural rhythm that made her melt inside. With him she felt beautiful...protected from the spirits of her past that she'd thought would haunt her tonight.

As they walked back toward their table, the most fearsome of those ghosts appeared, and it looked as though he was heading their way. She grasped Dan's hand a little harder. Maybe, if she concentrated hard enough, she could call on his strength as well as her own.

"It'll be all right, princess." Obviously Dan was as aware of her father as she was. Gayla wasn't sure if the tension that radiated from his hand all the way to her constricted throat was all her own.

She forced a smile and made herself look at the man she'd idolized—the one who had bitterly denounced and disowned her, she reminded herself when she suddenly had the urge to run to her father and throw her arms around him. "Dad," she murmured when they came within arms' length of each other.

"Newman." Her father gruffly acknowledged Dan's presence but not hers. The lump in her throat grew.

Dan squeezed her hand as if he knew she needed the contact to realize she wasn't alone. "Dr. Harris. It's good to see you."

"It would seem that my wayward daughter has surfaced."

Her father looked not at her but straight through her. When had been the first time she'd turned his stern features icy cold like this? Gayla couldn't remember. All she knew was that this encounter was almost more than she could bear. If Dan hadn't been at her side, an anchor in this emotional storm, she'd have turned and run as far and as fast as she could.

Dan cleared his throat. "If you'll excuse us, sir, we'll go back to our table."

"I want to talk to you, Newman. Alone." Her father locked gazes with Dan, making Gayla shudder again as she turned to walk away.

After she sat down at the table beside Michelle and Frank, Gayla watched her father herd Dan into a secluded alcove. Her father's angry gesticulations and Dan's horrified expression gave her a good idea that she was the subject of the tirade. When Dan came back to the table, he seemed shell-shocked.

"I'm sorry about that, princess. I'd have liked to tell your father we'd have to postpone that talk, but with the power he has as chief of surgery, I didn't dare. Shall we dance?" he asked, his expression so earnest she wanted nothing more than to feel his strong arms around her again.

She couldn't, though. She couldn't put him in a position where her father would want to destroy him. "Please get me out of here, Dan." She tried to suck in a breath despite the excruciating tightness in her throat.

Chapter Five

The Ghosts

ಬ

"Sylvia Harris, you're nothing but a fraud!" Ruth practically slammed down her empty wineglass before whirling around and drilling Sylvia with an accusatory gaze.

Sylvia tried to choke back her tears. Her baby wasn't the monster Eli had portrayed to Dan. Gayla was good enough for any man, let alone a cripple. *"What about you, Ruth? You never mentioned this disability my husband talked about to your boy."*

"It's nothing. Nothing at all. You try to tell me your Gayla's all sweetness and light when she's nothing but a lush and a dope addict, and you dare accuse me of deceiving you?"

"Gayla's not a lush. Or an addict. She had a problem for a while, but she's been well now for a long time. At least she's not a cripple."

Ruth snorted. *"Danny's no more crippled than you are. There's nothing my boy can't do."*

"What's this disability Eli was talking to him about, then?"

"Danny lost part of a leg to cancer when he was nine years old. You'd never know it to look at him now."

"Oh, God." Sylvia couldn't imagine her little girl with someone who couldn't share her interest in sports and outdoor activities.

"Exactly my thought! The last thing Danny needs is a woman who might go off the wagon and humiliate him any minute."

"The last thing Gayla needs is a cripple who can't play golf or tennis — or even swim with her."

"Danny can do all those things — as well as or better than most. I told you, he's not a cripple, you narrow-minded ninny! And he doesn't

need a woman who needs a keeper. He's too busy with his work. Important work."

Sylvia's temples throbbed, the way they had when Eli had gone on the rampage at her when she was alive. She couldn't take any more of Ruth's vicious diatribe right now. She had to get away from the other ghost. *"I'll see you in the morning, Ruth."* She squared her shoulders and floated away, deliberately ignoring Ruth's parting shot.

In her room Sylvia stared out into the clouds, silently cursing Eli and Ruth and all the others through the years who had thoughtlessly hurt her baby. She cursed Danny Newman for not being all his mother had claimed him to be, even as she hoped for Gayla's sake that Ruth's son would make her little girl happy again—bring back the joy in living that Gayla's father and that rat Marc Solomon had so cruelly wrenched away from her.

Chapter Six

☙

"What did my father say?" Gayla asked as soon as Dan started the car, determined to face the demons the way her psychologist had said she must.

Dan shrugged. "Not much. I'd really rather forget it."

"But you can't, can you?"

"No, I can't. Let's go somewhere private where we can talk."

"All right."

"My apartment? It's closer than yours." His fingers gripped the steering wheel so hard Gayla thought it might shatter.

The knot in her throat kept her from speaking, so she simply nodded and laid a hand on his muscular thigh. While he drove, she tried to prepare herself for facing truths she'd foolishly hoped would remain buried and forgotten.

As she'd done many times since she thought she'd heard her mother's gentle voice two weeks earlier, Gayla tried in vain to make contact with her again. If she'd ever needed a mother's comfort it was now. The only sound she heard, though, was her own pulse pounding in her head like a hundred tiny hammers.

* * * * *

"You have a nice place," Gayla said when Dan opened the door and let her into the condo he'd called home for the past four years.

Did she *really* like the beige-black-and-white color scheme and the stark contemporary furniture his mother had picked out for him before she died? Somehow his place seemed cold and dull when he compared it with Gayla's vibrant beauty.

"Make yourself at home," he said conventionally, indicating the sunken conversation area just to the right of the foyer. "Would you like a drink?"

"No!"

Damn it. He should have realized she'd know her old man had spilled the story of her abusing drugs and alcohol. He reached over and squeezed her hand. "I meant a soda or something. Or I could make coffee." What was it about Gayla that made him act like a clumsy teenager instead of the respected surgeon who often got compliments on his bedside manner?

"Nothing, thanks."

Nearly lost in the cushions piled at the corner of the sofa, Gayla looked like a child who needed comforting...except that no child had the kind of hot body she did. He wanted to join her, strip off that sexy red gown, and love her until she forgot that scene with Old Ironsides. Instead he sat on a leather lounge chair, not at all certain he could keep his hands to himself if he didn't maintain a bit of distance. "Let's talk, princess."

Suddenly her head came up and she met his gaze. "Don't call me that. I'm more a screw-up than a princess, as I'm sure Daddy wasted no time letting you know."

"He definitely tried to scare me off."

"What did he say?"

"He mentioned something about you having a problem with alcohol and drugs."

"I did. Still do, according to the counselors. I imagine he also told you I wasn't good enough for you."

Dan shrugged. "Your father has never cared for me. It could just as easily be that he was trying to protect you from getting involved with me." No one else but Eli Harris had ever flat-out told Dan he'd never make it as a surgeon because of his leg. Dan imagined the older man still smarted when forced to admit to himself that his prediction had been wrong.

Gayla laughed, a brittle, tinkling sound that spoke more of pain than joy. "Not in a million years. Daddy vowed four years ago that he'd make sure no colleague of his ever got involved with me again. I should have expected it."

"What happened?"

With her gaze fixed on her trembling fingers, Gayla began to talk, her voice so soft that Dan had to strain to hear. As she talked, he got the picture of a college girl desperate for her dad's approval, certain she'd won it when she qualified for the Olympic trials and accepted a proposal from Marc Solomon. Dan recalled him slightly—a pompous, self-serving asshole who'd been Ironsides' golden boy a while back.

"Marc came to see me at school two months before the trials. I guess it was then that I got pregnant. I found out just three days before I had to swim. I couldn't have backed out even if I'd wanted to. It shouldn't have hurt the baby. After all, I'd been swimming three miles every day before that." Gayla choked back a sob, then cradled her head in her hands.

Dan wished he could give Gayla the comfort she obviously hadn't received from the people who'd professed to love her. When she started talking again, he heard her anguish in each word.

"I didn't make the Olympic squad. Two days later, though, I lost the baby. Marc said I cared more about the damn Olympics than I did about him. Daddy said I couldn't do anything right, that I'd proved what a screw-up I was. For over a year I tried to prove him right."

Suddenly Dan felt as if he were the one choking. He loosened his tie and slipped off his jacket and vest. Then he moved to the sofa and took Gayla in his arms.

"No. Daddy was right. I'm an alcoholic. And a coke addict. I haven't used either since I nearly overdosed three years ago and started rehab—but this minute I'd kill for a drink or a snort."

"Painkillers." Dan rubbed his hand gently down Gayla's back, willing her to relax. "You don't want to undo three years' hard work, do you? You'd be proving to your father that you don't have the strength you've shown to me."

Soft strands of Gayla's hair tickled his neck, and her subtle fragrance filled his nostrils. "I made him hate me."

"Sounds to me as if your dad expected you to be perfect. That he blamed you for something no one but God could have prevented. No one ever had a miscarriage because they took a swim." Though he could have gladly wrung Eli Harris's neck, Dan spoke quietly, stroking Gayla, soothing her. Hurting for her and wishing he could take her pain away.

Gayla lifted her head and met Dan's gaze. "It wasn't the miscarriage that bothered Daddy. It was that I didn't make the Olympic squad."

Dan's own memories of dealing with Old Ironsides paled in comparison with what the son of a bitch had done to his own child. It didn't make sense, though. "If you'd made the team you wouldn't have been able to compete, anyway."

"He thought I would. He and Marc had already talked, agreed that then wasn't the time for me to be having a baby. If I'd have made the team, they would have insisted I..." She looked down, apparently trying to concentrate on the third stud in his tux shirt.

"They hadn't told you they wanted you to have an abortion, had they?"

"No. They hadn't even said anything to Mom or Tess. They didn't tell me until after I'd miscarried. Marc left, and Dad disowned me."

Gayla's words had a hollow sound, as if she was talking about a tragedy that had happened to someone else. No wonder she'd fallen apart after losing her baby, her father, her fiancé, and her Olympic dreams in the space of two days. "Cry, honey. Get it all out."

"Y-you don't hate me?"

"No." I could very easily come to love you."

Wiping the tears from her eyes, Gayla met Dan's gaze again. "It feels so good when you hold me," she said, the barest hint of a smile at the corners of the soft lips Dan yearned to taste.

"I like holding you."

Gayla's hint of a smile faded as tears returned to her soft, dark eyes. "I'm no good for you."

"You feel good to me." Dan wanted nothing more than to loosen her hair and run his fingers through the silky tendrils that were tickling his neck. If only he could heal by touching her, he'd chase away her demons — demons far more daunting than any that had ever tormented him.

"Make love with me, Dan," she whispered, her gaze meeting his as her fingers burrowed inside the open collar of his shirt. "Bring me back."

Back? Back from a trip to the past that hurt so much she couldn't stand remembering? The immediate rush of blood to his groin suggested that he not ask questions but take her to the bedroom. But he couldn't. Making love with her in her present state of mind might ultimately do Gayla more harm than good.

"Are you sure?" he asked, pulling back slightly when her nipples tightened against his chest.

"You don't want me." Tears cascaded down Gayla's cheeks now, and she trembled as if with grief.

"Damn it, yes I do! I just..."

"It's all right." Standing up, Gayla smoothed her dress with unsteady hands. "I don't blame you."

Dan got up and dragged Gayla into his arms. "For what? For wanting to make sure this is really what you want?" Cupping her bottom with both hands, he brought her so close she couldn't possibly mistake the extent of his desire. "Do you want to make love with me? Or do you just want to use sex to forget? Because if you do, it won't work, any more than a drink or a handful of pills."

She snuggled even closer, her breath warm and damp against his shoulder. "I've wanted you, Dan, from the moment you walked onto the pool deck looking good enough to eat. I know I'm not good enough…"

"Shut up. Don't even think that. If you're sure…"

She lifted a hand and covered his mouth. "I'm sure."

When she looked up at him, her eyes glistening with tears, he saw desire for him—not for escape. She stroked his cheek, and when he turned and brushed her fingers with his lips she smiled.

A beautiful, come-on-to-me-baby smile no sane man could resist. And Dan considered himself fairly rational. "Okay, princess. Since you're asking, let me show you to my bedroom." His conscience beaten down by his aching balls as much as by her words, Dan lifted Gayla into his arms.

* * * * *

"Should you be carrying me?" Gayla asked when he started walking with her toward a darkened hallway.

"You feel good in my arms." Setting her down, he opened the door to his room and flipped on a light. "Any second thoughts?"

"None. How about you?"

Her soft smile did a lot toward allaying his discomfort, and the touch of her hand on his cheek set off a fresh burst of fire in his cock. "Come here." He moved toward the king-size bed that had never held quite the same appeal before he'd pictured her golden-tan body stretched across the stark black sheets.

Suddenly weak in the knees, he sat down, drawing Gayla between his legs and rubbing his cheek across the silky material that molded softly to her curves. He reached behind her and found the zipper, opening it to let the fabric slither slowly to the floor.

Dan had seen women before. Fucked them, too. Still his mouth went dry when he stared at Gayla's tiny, perfectly proportioned body, the slick satin bra and bikini panties that matched the dress that lay in a heap at her feet. While he unfastened the matching garter belt and skimmed pale silky stockings down her firm, silky legs, he tried to tell himself Gayla was just another woman, as far from perfect as he.

"One of us has on too many clothes," she whispered as she went down on her knees in front of him.

His hands went to the studs still in place on his shirt, but she brushed them away and worked them out one by one. Every time her knuckles brushed against the bare skin on his chest, Dan got hotter. The rasp of her knuckles against his belly made him jump, not as much from surprise as from the knowledge that the next thing to go would be his pants.

"Not yet, princess," he muttered when she tackled the button at his waist. "My turn again."

"Okay." Her gaze locked with his, Gayla got up and joined him on the edge of his bed.

"I've dreamed of seeing you stretched out across these sheets," he told her when she lay back and extended her arms behind her head. "The reality's more arousing than the dream."

His heart beat faster, and he was sure he'd burst if he got any harder, but he tortured himself by stroking her from head to toe, first with his hands and then with his mouth. Her skin was soft, so soft, yet her flesh felt firm and fit beneath his searching fingers. An athlete's body, perfect and compact and so damn responsive he thought he'd die. When he dropped open-mouthed kisses along her collarbone and down one tanned arm, she whimpered.

He treated the satin scraps that barely hid her breasts and pussy as obstacles, sliding his fingers beneath the taut elastic, shoving it aside with his nose so he could nuzzle the pale, fragrant flesh it hid. His balls ached and his cock throbbed, but he was in no hurry to finish undressing her.

When he did, he'd have to bare himself. The knowledge that Gayla had seen his leg before was little comfort. As he worshiped her physical perfection, his mind magnified his own flaws. Memories rushed to his head of another woman—of a time long gone but not forgotten when he'd allowed mindless lust to chase away the reality of what he was. What he'd always be.

Caught up in the memory of the first time a woman had asked him to make love and the instant cooling of her passion when she saw him naked, Dan hadn't realized his hands had stilled on Gayla's body until she guided his hand to rest between her legs. Realizing she was wet with wanting him had his cock so hard he could hardly stand it.

"Sleepy?" she asked, searching out one of his nipples and stroking it with her thumb.

"Hardly." *Scared stiff's more like it.* Shoving his anxiety to a far corner of his mind, he concentrated on getting her even more aroused—as hot as he was. Within moments he had her naked, writhing and moaning while he sucked her small, ripe breasts.

Her nimble fingers sent waves of fire through his body when she explored the contours of his chest and arms. The moist heat of her breathing against his neck made him want to tear off the rest of his clothes and bury his cock in her pussy.

He'd never ached for a woman the way he was throbbing for Gayla now. Taking a deep breath, he struggled to slow his pounding heart to match the languid pace he'd set. Nothing mattered as much as making this good for her. If it took all night, that was all right. His body could scream all it wanted for him to hurry, but the wait wouldn't kill him.

He kept repeating that in his head as he moved lower and lapped at her clit. Velvet and honey, the scent of some exotic flowers mingled with musk and sex and sweetness pervaded his senses. The sounds of her quick, ragged breathing and the feel of her nails raking lightly at his back fed the urgency he could barely restrain.

"Bleep."

That wasn't his fucking beeper. Couldn't be. God wouldn't be so cruel. If he ignored it maybe it would go away. He took her clit between his teeth and flailed it with his tongue.

"Bleep. Bleep. Dr. Newman, call 888-5251. Emergency."

Dan wanted desperately to toss the goddamn squawk box out the window and pretend it never had made the first strident sound. But he couldn't. Swearing under his breath, he rolled to the edge of the bed, picked up the phone, and punched a button on the automatic dialer.

Where Dan had warmed her, Gayla now felt chilled. She sensed another kind of urgency when he spoke to whoever was on the other end of the line. Sitting up and drawing the sheet around her, she waited for him to turn back into her arms.

"I've got to go," he said, a wry expression on his handsome face. "Wait for me?"

"Here?"

"Yeah."

Gayla let the sheet drop and snuggled up against his chest. "How long?"

"I don't know. Could be hours. Depends on how much we can do toward patching up a Dallas undercover officer."

"I'll wait."

Dan sounded so earnest, so concerned. So unlike Marc, who had talked about his patients as if they'd been rats in some research lab. Unlike her father, too.

"Good."

Brushing a gentle kiss across her lips, he gave her one last hug before getting up and taking off the tux pants she'd tried to get off him earlier. As if he didn't have a self-conscious bone in his body, he strode across the room, pulled jeans and a polo shirt out of a drawer, and put them on.

"Sleep, princess."

"I don't know if I can." Every fiber in her body ached to have him with, in, and around her every way lovers could be.

Dan brought her hand to his fly. "This isn't going to go away. Look, I..." His voice trailed off as though he didn't quite know how to say whatever was on his mind.

"Go on. Say it or get out of here so I can try to get some sleep."

He shrugged. "If we'd been together for years, maybe even months—hell, maybe weeks—we could have had a quickie and neither of us would be aching now. I don't want that for us, though. Not our first time."

That slightly crooked grin—the deep, lulling tone of his voice and the promise in his gaze—made Gayla want to drag him back to bed. But his patient was waiting. "You're right," she said quietly, pushing aside her own needs as she sent him on his way. "You're also special. Now get out of here and do what you can for that cop."

After Dan left it took a long time for Gayla to quit aching and fall asleep.

* * * * *

He'd done surgery when he was a lot of things, but this would be the first time he'd have done it horny. As Dan changed into scrubs, his mind was filled with Gayla. It was only when he picked up Zach Hamilton's chart and began to review it that he could focus his attention on the patient whose hand he was about to try to save.

When he examined the unconscious cop, he shuddered.

"Hell of a mess, isn't it?" Jim muttered from beneath his mask. "Want to start on that hand while I try to rearrange his face?"

"Yeah. Where's Frank?" The orthopedic man was usually the first of their team to arrive on a trauma case, since his apartment was less than a block from the hospital.

"On the way in from Michelle's place."

Settling onto a high stool and adjusting the focus on a microscope positioned over the mangled mess that was his patient's hand, Dan began to assess the damage to bone, muscle, and nerves. "I don't think I can wait for him."

"You can't. Frank will have his hands full with the guy's leg. Damn!" Glancing up when Jim swore, Dan immediately saw his colleague's problem—a small, gushing artery on their patient's forehead. "Suction!"

Dan turned back to his own task, and when Frank arrived fifteen minutes later Dan hardly noticed. Hours passed as he and the other surgeons labored to piece together the living jigsaw puzzle a bomb had created from a healthy man. When he'd done all he could to save the mangled hand, his shoulders and arms throbbed, and his head felt as if someone had crunched it in a vise.

As he trudged to the locker room to shower and change clothes, he remembered he'd left Gayla curled up in his bed. Despite his fatigue his balls tightened and his cock began to throb. There was also an unfamiliar, tender yearning. Gayla had definitely gotten under his skin.

It wasn't until after he got to the garage at his apartment building that Dan remembered his partner's whereabouts when he'd gotten the emergency call. Woman-hating Frank apparently had realized Michelle was more than just their dedicated physical therapist and command-performance companion at events that required a date. It would be interesting to see whether she'd try to cure Frank of the female phobia Erica had left with him.

Reminded that for once he was coming home to a woman instead of an empty apartment, Dan stepped out of the car and strode quickly to the elevators, forgetting for the moment how physically drained he was from the past six hours' work.

* * * * *

"You look awful." As glad as she was to see Dan again, Gayla couldn't help noticing the way his shoulders drooped and his eyelids fluttered over reddened eyes. Suddenly she wanted to take him in her arms and coax away his fatigue. She stood on tiptoe to brush a kiss across the faint lines at the corners of his mouth. "Want some coffee?"

"Yeah. I'm beat." His arms went around her as if to help him stay on his feet.

He sounded as tired as he looked but he felt oh, so good—too good to be real. "Want me to bring it to you in bed?"

"I want you to bring yourself to me in bed, princess. I just need a jolt of caffeine so I won't fall asleep before we take up where we left off."

Obviously Dan needed sleep at the moment, not sex, even though the hard ridge of flesh prodding insistently at her belly denied what his shaky stance and trembling hands did. "What you need now is rest," she told him as she broke their embrace and put an arm around his back.

"I need you."

"I'm not going anywhere. At least not until you deliver the loving you got me all primed for before you had to go."

"Promise?" He shot her that killer grin as he sank down on the edge of the bed.

"I promise." Suddenly she needed to touch him, do something to make him feel as good as he'd made her feel earlier. Settling next to him, she took his hand. "How about a massage?"

"Sounds great. Want me on my stomach?"

"For starters. Got any lotion?"

As if he'd suddenly realized the extent of his exhaustion, Dan flopped face-down across his king-size bed. "Medicine cabinet in the bathroom."

Gayla scrounged around in a cluttered cabinet until she found the brand of deep-heating rub she'd always used after a tough swim. Padding back to the bed, she positioned herself cross-legged at Dan's side. "You've got on too many clothes," she told him for the second time in less than twenty-four hours.

For a minute she thought he'd gone to sleep, before he rolled onto his back and pulled his shirt off over his head. His hand stilled at his belt as he met her gaze.

"Let me." Gently she brushed his hands away and unbuckled his belt before tackling the snap and zipper on his pants. "Lift up your buns, Doc," she quipped as she skimmed the material along fit, muscled flesh that she longed to touch.

"How much of me are you planning to massage?"

"Every inch."

"Promises, promises."

Gayla met his teasing gaze and replied in a deliberately casual tone when she'd worked his pants almost to his knees. "How do I get this thing off?" she asked, tapping gently at his prosthesis.

"You really want me helpless in your clutches, don't you?" While Dan spoke lightly, Gayla sensed his hesitation. Why, she wondered? She'd seen him minus the artificial limb before, but she decided to play it his way. "I've always thought having the upper hand in bed might be fun. Now, how do I take it off?"

He shrugged, then showed her the button hidden inside the cosmetic cover. When she pushed it, the prosthesis came off into her hands. "Now take off the socks and roll the liner back."

When she'd done that and set it all onto the floor, she heard him let out a big breath of air. Smiling, she turned back to face him.

"I'm yours. Do your worst." Meeting Gayla's gaze Dan lay back and rolled onto his belly, plain white boxer shorts and tanned, supple skin contrasting vividly with the black sheets on his bed.

Gayla's fingers tingled at the touch of pungent, heating lotion. They tingled more as she began to work the stuff into the warm, satiny skin that stretched across well-defined muscles in

Dan's shoulders and upper arms. Her lips curled upward with satisfaction when she felt tension draining out of him with each kneading motion of her hands.

"You could make a fortune doing this," he said as Gayla shifted her hands lower. "You've got magic in those pretty hands."

Magic? Maybe. Gayla knew she'd never gotten such pleasure before when she'd rubbed down fellow swimmers. She couldn't recall anyone feeling like this—silk over steely muscles whose definition she could trace with her fingertips, warm, responsive flesh she longed to touch with every cell in her own aching body. Dan was special. And he was hers, at least for now.

"Raise up a little." The waistband of his boxers hampered her when she tried to massage his tight, slightly rounded butt; so when he complied, she slid them down and off. Then she started to knead his glutes. "Feel good?"

"God, yes."

"This?" Her hands moved lower to stroke the backs of his muscular thighs.

"Mmmm. Harder. I feel as if I just ran a marathon. Six hours standing in the same place damn near did me in."

"How's your patient?"

"Better than he was before. His hand and wrist reminded me of a jigsaw puzzle my mom got me once. Damn thing must have had five thousand pieces—took me forever to piece them together. Only difference today was the guy today had about a third of the pieces missing."

"What happened?" Gayla kept up the massage, moving down to work on the knotted muscles in Dan's calves. Carefully, so as not to hurt him, she avoided touching the slightly reddened stump of his left leg.

"Car exploded as he was getting in on the passenger side. The driver was killed outright. Don't stop, princess. That feels great."

"You must ache all over."

He chuckled. "Some places more than others. My shoulders and neck. Legs. Head."

"Head?"

"Eyestrain. Hours of staring into an operative microscope takes its toll. Lower."

Tentatively Gayla stroked his right ankle and the blunt, muscular stump of his left leg. "Tell me if it hurts."

"That feels good. Hey, quit tickling," he complained when she rotated her fingers lightly over the tip of the stump.

"Like this?" Grinning, Gayla repeated the action on the bottom of his foot. "Flip over if you've got the energy."

Like a big, lazy cat, Dan stretched, then rolled onto his back. Reminding herself that he needed rest, she tried to ignore his impressive cock that jutted enthusiastically from a nest of soft, dark hair and beckoned to her hands and mouth. Instead she worked her way up his body, kneading and coaxing out the tension she still felt in the ridges of muscle cording his belly and chest.

"You're ignoring the tensest muscle of all." He opened his eyes and met her gaze. His lazy grin melted her heart.

With one finger she traced around his scrotum and along the length of his cock before sitting back on her haunches and putting the lotion on the bedside table. "I thought I'd leave this for later. After you've gotten some sleep."

Dan rolled to his side and held out his arms. "Come here. Nap with me, princess."

Gayla couldn't resist. Slipping off his shirt that she'd slept in and tossing it to the floor, she joined him, enjoying the way his soft chest hair tickled the skin of her back—and the feel of his velvet-smooth, rock-hard penis pulsing strongly between her thighs. His hand cradling her breast warmed and soothed her, and soon she fell asleep.

* * * * *

For a minute Dan thought he was dreaming, that the warm soft woman in his bed was only a figment of an overactive imagination. But she felt too real. Silken tendrils of her dark hair tickled his nose, and her small rounded breasts rose and fell against his hand as she breathed.

He opened his eyes, blinking at light too bright for early morning—even in summer. He'd have looked at his watch, but he dared not move his hand off her lest she fade away. Memories returned in bits and pieces...Gayla at the banquet...sobbing in his arms...here in bed with him. He remembered the hospital's untimely call and the battered cop, and coming home to Gayla instead of to an empty apartment.

With skilled hands, she'd coaxed his sore muscles to relax. Massaged away aches and pains that came with the territory when one chose to piece together nerves, bone, and muscle for a living. She'd curled up beside him, lulled him to sleep. Just thinking about her hands on him—and recalling that she'd promised him he could seduce her later sent blood surging into his cock.

Were those her thighs surrounding his rapidly hardening flesh? He moved his hand down from her breast until his fingers burrowed into the soft hair on her mound—then lower, into her slick wet slit. When he rocked his hips back and forth in a primal, mindless search for a mate, his cock slid between her silky folds.

"Mmmm. You're awake."

So his dream lover talked. Her husky tone got him even harder, and the way she wiggled her little bottom against him damn near made him come.

"Awake and horny." He freed the hand that had been trapped between them and slid it under her while he brought his other hand back up. Cupping both her breasts, he shuddered when her nipples hardened and poked insistently at his palms.

"I can tell." Raising one leg and draping it over his, she reached down and took his cock in her hand. Gently she guided him to her dripping, heated pussy. "I want you now, Dan." She shifted to take the tip of him inside her.

He couldn't recall ever having burned like this. Or having been so damn hard he thought he'd burst. Still he had enough sense to pull back. "Gayla, honey. I need to protect you."

She rolled to her back and met his gaze with passion-darkened eyes. "Hurry." Her urgent, almost desperate tone was driving him wild.

He knew he had some condoms somewhere. Suddenly he pictured a good-sized box of them, right where he'd put it on the top shelf of the bathroom linen closet. Dan started to get up, then remembered she'd taken off his prosthesis before they went to sleep. "You've got me pretty damn near helpless, princess. Unless you want to wait for me to put my leg back on, I'm not likely to be moving much, so be a good girl and fetch the box of condoms for me."

Her hand burned like fire when she stroked the length of his throbbing cock. "Where are they?" she asked, as if reluctant to wait another moment for him to join their bodies.

"In the bathroom. Linen closet." Why the fuck had he hidden the damn things away instead of stashing them within easy reach? "Top shelf."

"You must use lots of these," she teased when she set the box onto the nightstand and fished out one foil packet. "Lie back and let me put it on you."

No woman had ever made rolling on a rubber such a treat. Dan closed his eyes and let the sensations ripple through his body as she smoothed the condom over his heated cock.

"Well, do you?"

"What? Oh, you mean the condoms? You might say I was being optimistic when I got them from one of the medical supply salesmen." Optimistic hadn't been the word. If the salesman hadn't been peddling his overstock in front of his partners and half their office staff, he'd have declined the super deal on the gross of prophylactics. Occasions for which he'd required protection had been damn near nonexistent the past few years.

Suddenly all he could focus on was the need that surged through him when Gayla rubbed her cheek against his sheathed erection. "I'd say so, big guy," she teased. "What are you going to do with this now?"

"Make you feel good. Real good. Come here, and I'll show you." Clasping his hands around her waist, he drew her down on the bed, pausing to nip at the column of her neck before tasting the sweetness of her pebbled pink nipples.

"Fuck me, Dan. Now!" Gayla writhed beneath him as though she couldn't wait any longer. About to explode, Dan positioned himself between her widespread legs and drove into her steaming cunt, hard and deep. Damn. She was so tight and wet he had to struggle to keep from coming on the spot.

Chapter Seven

ಬ

The walls of her pussy stretched to take his thick, pulsating length. It felt so good. So right. Gayla wrapped her legs around Dan's muscular thighs, urging him to take her faster, deeper, harder. She loved the feel of his chest hair tickling her nipples, his warm breath moistening the hollow of her throat.

He trembled above her, as though he too fought to make this last. She wanted…to come. To hold out. To savor the sensations that had never been so good. Never felt so right. This was more than a great fuck, more than a man and a woman sharing a moment's pleasure. This was Dan loving her, giving himself into her keeping at least for now.

"Love me," she whispered, meeting his gaze—a gaze full of needing and wanting and something more. Could he care for her in spite of what he knew? Her fingers tangled in his chest hair, and she felt the wild pounding of his heart.

"I do." He sounded as though he could barely speak when he braced himself and began to move. "I am." He bent his dark head to her breast, and his tongue snaked out to tease her nipple, sending a wave of sensation deep into her belly that made her inner muscles constrict around him.

Tension built as he moved, the ebb and flow of his big cock within her so tantalizing that it overwhelmed every other sensation. The pressure built, threatened to implode. Desperate for release, she opened wider to him, wrapping her legs tighter about his narrow waist. Faster now, he slid in and out, his motion a driving rhythm that catapulted her toward her goal.

It began as a simple twinge, a tiny burst of sensation—an involuntary clenching of her internal muscles against the heat and hardness of him that stretched and filled her. Instead of diminishing, the sensation built until it burst and shot through every nerve in her body. Before the incredible feelings overwhelmed her, she heard Dan gasp her name.

The first thing she felt when she came to was Dan's strong arms surrounding her, his fingers lightly molding the contours of her bottom as they lay on their sides, face to face. Slowly she opened her eyes. His lips curved upward, revealing straight white teeth. Hair mussed, a silly grin on his perfect face, he looked like a mischievous little boy—one who had the world by the tail, at least for the moment.

"Wow!"

Gayla met Dan's gaze. "Yeah. Wow!"

"Want to try that again?"

She giggled. "Now?" Surely he couldn't be up for a repeat performance so soon.

"Gotta get my money's worth out of that box of condoms, princess," he quipped as he nibbled playfully along the junction of her neck and shoulders.

"Oh, God, the phone. Not again!" Gayla sounded more than a little annoyed. She sounded downright mad.

Automatically Dan snatched up the receiver. "Newman here," he said more harshly than he would have if the call hadn't come at such an inopportune time. "Today? Frank, did it occur to you that I might have something better to do than talk about raising money?" At least it wasn't someone at the hospital demanding his immediate presence, he told himself as he listened to his partner cajole him with promises of food and drink. "Just a minute."

He cupped a hand over the phone's mouthpiece and looked at Gayla. "Want to go with me to a barbecue at Jim and Kelly's place?"

"Sure. We've got to eat." Her lazy, sexy grin reminded Dan of what they'd been doing when the phone rang. After telling Frank they would be there, he hung up and rolled over, bracing himself with his hands to keep from crushing her.

"Now where were we?"

Gayla laughed. "You were about to tell me we needed to get your money's worth out of that giant economy-size box of condoms."

"Yeah. Can't let them go to waste!"

"No. That would be a shame. Come down here and kiss me." Playfully she tugged at his shoulders until he gave in and let himself down until his chest grazed her pert nipples and her heart beat a slow, regular cadence that matched his own. She tasted sweet, yet ever so sexy, her open mouth softly molded to his, her tongue dancing against his in a rhythmic pattern that sent blood rushing to his groin. Her nipples prodded at his chest, as though begging for the touch of his hands and mouth.

When she wrapped her legs tighter around his waist he nearly came again. Groaning, he reached for a foil packet and tore it open. Rolling to his back, he slid the condom on with more haste than finesse. "Ride me."

She fucked him like he couldn't remember ever having been fucked before, taking him along the path where he'd led her earlier. Her tight, dripping pussy gripped his cock, bathed his balls in her honey as she lowered herself, then raised up, her small, firm breasts swaying with every movement. Her inner muscles encircled his flesh. So hot, like a velvet glove caressing every inch of his cock. He wanted more. Wanted all of her. Arching his back, Dan met her with desperate thrusts that had his cock slamming into her G-spot, making her scream out her pleasure. Her inner muscles spasmed around him. Milked him. His balls tightened painfully, then relaxed as his cock pumped out wave after wave of scalding come.

* * * * *

"Dan, I don't have anything here that I can wear to your friends' barbecue," Gayla complained after they woke again from a nap.

Grinning, he rolled to his side and stroked a hand possessively over her silky body. "I like you just as you are, princess."

She laughed. "Are you planning to go naked too?"

"No. But then I don't have the attributes to show off that you do."

"I don't know about that, Doc. You look pretty awesome to me." Her finger traced a path along his right pectoral muscle.

"Thanks." For once Dan didn't resent the hours he put in every day, keeping what was left of him in shape. "If you keep looking at me like that, we're going to skip that barbecue and light our own fires again right here. But I'm washed up and hung out to dry for the moment. Want a shower? Afterward you can throw on one of my T-shirts and some running shorts, and we'll stop by your place so you can change."

"Together?" Gayla's eyes lit up with what appeared to be pure anticipation.

"Sure. Hand me my leg, would you?"

"You bathe with it on?"

He grinned. "No. But you haven't fed my ego enough that I'm ready for you to watch me hop around like an oversize rabbit—or a midget kangaroo. Give it here."

"It doesn't weigh much." She handed him the prosthesis first, followed by the suspension liner and two wadded-up wool stump socks.

"The better to use it for chasing you around the bedroom, princess," he told her, glancing up from his task of rolling the liner over his stump to shoot her a wolfish smile. "Actually this one weighs more than the one I use for active sports."

"Why?"

"Different foot. And the sports model doesn't have padding or a cover—just the essentials. Ready?" he asked, getting off the bed and holding a hand out to Gayla.

She came into his arms, her tiny body molding to his much larger frame. "You're forgetting something, aren't you?"

"Huh?" He had trouble thinking when she plastered her satiny body full-length against him. Parts of him had obviously forgotten they had been worked damn hard during the past few hours!

"These. Feels as though we may be needing them." Nodding toward the box on the nightstand, Gayla reached over and grabbed a couple of wrapped packages. "I've got some."

"Obviously you've never taken a shower with an amputee," Dan said with a chuckle. He felt ten feet tall, though, because she appeared to see him as fit and whole.

"Won't that seat I saw hold both of us?"

He felt the grin spread through each set of the small muscles in his face. "Don't know. Never have checked it out that way. Come on, oh insatiable one. I'm going to douse you with ice water before you kill me."

* * * * *

His ratty Stanford T-shirt hung nearly to her knees, and his running shorts hung precariously over her hipbones. As they walked to his car, the contrast between her Little-Orphan-Annie look and his put-together appearance made Gayla laugh.

In plaid shorts and a polo shirt that reminded her of pine needles in the spring, Dan could have easily been a model for Ralph Lauren—except for the prosthesis he'd hesitated before putting on in place of the one she'd taken off him earlier—his stripped-down model, he'd said with a smile.

This prosthesis didn't look like a real leg at all, with its exposed metal shaft that joined a foot wearing a Nike athletic shoe with the socket that held the stump of Dan's leg. It didn't, however, detract from the urgent pull Gayla felt toward the man who wore it. She smiled as he opened the passenger door of his car.

A quick stop at her apartment, a change of clothes, and a short ride through the quiet streets of suburban Dallas brought them to a new subdivision where luxurious new homes sat on lots the size of small ranches. Kelly met them at the door of a mock Tudor-style house and ushered them to the backyard where Jim had already started up a built-in gas grill.

"Where's Frank?" Dan asked after looking around and apparently noticing his other partner's absence.

Kelly shrugged. "He went to get Michelle. Why don't you and Gayla join Jamie and Gary in the pool?"

"No thanks. I want to show Gayla what Jim has done with your garden." Dan draped an arm casually over Gayla's shoulder, running his fingers lightly through the ends of her hair.

"Go ahead. Make yourselves at home while I go put together a salad." With that, Kelly headed inside.

Dan and Gayla walked around, admiring the native shrubs and the bright flowering plants. She enjoyed the now-familiar sparks that went off whenever Dan touched her.

"Nice place." *Very much like where Tess lives. Not so very different from the house where I grew up.* Jim and Kelly—and their new home—fit the image Gayla had always associated with successful physicians. They contrasted with the absent Frank, who had struck Gayla when they met as being the consummate rebel.

"They like it. Personally this place reminds me of some English manor house. My taste runs more toward good old Texas comfortable. What about you?"

"What would you say if I told you Victorian houses turned me on?" she asked, tilting back her head to meet Dan's gaze.

"That you're pulling my leg."

"Really?"

"Yeah, really. You strike me as one hundred percent the contemporary woman. One who'd like angles and brass and lots of open space and light. A woman who'd be satisfied to spread her living space out on one floor instead of stacking it up and joining it together with a bunch of stairs."

Gayla stared back at Jim and Kelly's house, noticing for the first time that it must have at least three levels of rooms. "You don't like stairs, I take it." She'd noticed that he took what looked like special care when they descended the steep staircase from her apartment earlier.

"Nope. Not so many of them. And not as a steady diet."

It suddenly struck Gayla that Dan had to work at things most people just took naturally, but that very little if anything stymied him if he wanted to tackle it. "What can't you do?" she asked, smiling as she met his gaze.

"There's not a whole lot I *can't* do. There are things I'd rather *not* do if I don't have to. Climbing a lot of stairs probably fits around the middle of my list of un-favorite things—behind skydiving, mountain climbing, and a few other daredevil activities."

Dan's grin warmed Gayla clear down to her toes, reminding her how close they had gotten—and not just in bed. "It really doesn't slow you down, does it?"

"Not anymore, for which I probably should thank your father. If it hadn't been for his raising hell about the hospital accepting me for a surgical residency, I probably wouldn't have summoned up the nerve to have that second surgery before starting my last year of med school."

"Second surgery?"

"Yeah. Frank revised my stump. The surgery changed living with a prosthesis from being a major challenge to just a minor inconvenience."

Gayla had no trouble at all imagining her father insisting that no one less than perfect in every way could possibly enter *his* perfect residency program. Tears threatened to spill from her eyes. "I'm sorry." She pictured Dan bearing the brunt of her father's cutting sarcasm.

"Hey, princess, don't cry. It isn't as if this happened yesterday. I had the revision over eight years ago. I got the residency in spite of your dad's objections, and I think I've proven him wrong."

"You have." Gayla would take Dan Newman any day, any way, and if she thought she was good enough and strong enough, she'd try her damnedest to hold onto him for the rest of their lives. She wasn't, though, and she knew it. Brushing her tears away, she reminded herself that with her history she had the potential of becoming too big a challenge to ask Dan—or any man whose family must uphold a sterling image because of his choice of profession—to take on.

Determined to enjoy whatever time she might have as Dan's lover, Gayla rose up on tiptoes and invited his kiss.

"Hey, you two! Steaks are cooking."

Gayla pulled back and felt the warmth of Dan's hands as they moved from her shoulders to rest comfortably at her waist. "Hello, Frank," she said, acknowledging his sudden appearance.

"Yeah. Hi, Gayla. Newman, has anybody told you it's broad daylight?"

Dan kept his hands at Gayla's waist and grinned down at her before replying. "Don't you have something else to do?"

Frank grinned. "Michelle's helping Kelly get the green stuff on the table. Meanwhile I've got nothing better to do than come harass—"

"Go drown in the pool." The twitch at one corner of his mouth and the twinkle in his eyes belied the venom in Dan's words.

"If I get in, I probably will. One of these days I'm going to learn to swim." Shrugging, Frank turned and headed toward the pool.

"He really can't swim?" Gayla didn't know many able-bodied adults who couldn't at least paddle around in water.

"No. Sinks like a rock. The first time we got together here, I shoved him in. It took Jim and me together to drag him off the bottom. After he dried out, Frank told us how he'd nearly drowned when he was a little kid, and that his folks had kept him away from water for the rest of his childhood."

Shaking her head, Gayla shot Dan an incredulous look. "You pushed Frank in the water without knowing if he could swim? You ought to have been shot."

"Damn it, Gayla, we were horsing around like we always do. How the hell was I to know Frank didn't at least know how to save himself?"

"You might have asked."

"If I'd taken the time to do that, he'd have tossed me in." Dan's expression turned contrite. "He *did* know *I* could swim. He sees me doing it often enough in the lap pool at the hospital's health club."

"There. As I said, you should have been ashamed of your bullyish self."

"What about Frank? He knew I could swim, but he also knows prostheses cost an arm and leg, pun intended. If they're not specifically designed for water sports they aren't supposed to be submerged."

Gayla shrugged. "He could have died. You, on the other hand, might simply have been out some money, which you probably could have made him pay."

"You don't know Frank if you think money could easily be pried from his Scotch-Irish pockets. He didn't die. And I did mess up a perfectly good leg anyhow, going in after him the minute I saw he wasn't coming up for air. Doesn't that buy me something?"

She couldn't help responding to that mischievous, little-boy grin that melted her heart. "Yeah, Doc, with that and five more good deeds you can have chopped liver."

"Chopped liver I can do without. I think I smell steak, though, and I'm famished. A certain little princess tired me out this morning."

Holding hands, they began ambling toward the delicious aroma. "You're not complaining, are you?" Gayla rubbed a finger over the back of his hand.

"Hardly. Just reminding you I need some fuel if I'm going to be expending energy like that again any time soon."

"Me, too."

"Yeah. You, too. Hey, Jim, is that cow about done?"

Jim speared a thick T-bone steak and waved it in the air. "This one's done enough for you, Newman. Charred outside, still cold inside. With a bit of luck you can still hear it bellow. How about you, Gayla?"

"I like my meat heated through." On closer inspection she noticed blood pouring from the spots where Jim had pierced the steak. "A little more cooked than that, please." She laughed when she noticed Dan's expression of mock horror.

"Okay. Here's yours." Jim waved the steak in Dan's direction again before plopping it onto a platter. "Enjoy."

Gayla couldn't recall when she'd had so much fun, but she had no doubt that Dan was the reason. He made her feel part of his circle of friends and cajoled her into joining a game of touch football that quickly evolved into playful tackling as well as some tricky moves she'd never seen the Cowboys try.

When Dan dropped her off at her place after the party because she had an adult swim group to coach at five a.m. and he'd scheduled an early surgery, Gayla could hardly wait until they could be together again. Before turning off the light, she picked up the album from the bedside table and traced its elegant cover with one finger. Soon, she promised herself, she'd be able to open it and recall the joys as well as the painful memories it evoked.

When she lay down she thought she heard her mother say good night from somewhere far away.

* * * * *

"Somebody should outlaw Mondays."

Dan glanced up from the third surgical microscope they'd brought to the OR this morning and nodded his agreement to the whining scrub nurse. It was only ten o'clock, and already this was shaping up to be the day from hell. Painstakingly he adjusted the eyepiece on the ten-year-old relic and stared at Zach Hamilton's mangled hand.

If the cop didn't lose the thumb and ring finger Dan had spent the better part of Saturday night struggling to save, it would be a goddamn miracle. Leaning over to get a better angle, he squinted through the lens of the scope and finally managed to identify the problem that had brought Hamilton back to the OR. An hour later, after accompanying his patient to the recovery room, he stood under a tepid stream of water in the shower, as drained as the hot water heater that supplied the surgeons' dressing room appeared to be.

Dan's day went downhill fast, but the memory of Gayla's sweet, sensual smile and the prospect of being with her again tonight kept his spirits high. In spite of having had to deal with an hysterical mother, a patient nearly frantic over losing part of the feeling in the foot he'd had surgery on just last week, and assorted crises of a lesser nature, he felt good when he leaned back in the leather chair at his desk and reviewed some charts.

"Hey, Dan. Got a minute?"

"Sure. Come on in." Frank hesitated, then stepped inside and sprawled on the sofa in the corner.

"Thought you might want to know before you get in too deep, my friend. Old Ironsides' pretty daughter has been into some heavy shit."

Dan clenched his fists so hard his nails dug into his hands. "Who told you that?"

"I heard some of the surgeons talking while you were finishing with Hamilton this morning. She could be poison if you two were to get serious."

"What the hell do you mean?"

"Gayla got hooked on prescription drugs before she graduated to street stuff. Had to spend months—"

"I know. Gayla told me. She's clean now."

Frank frowned. "For how long?"

"For good." Dan wasn't naive enough to be dead sure of that, but he'd do his damnedest to keep Gayla from getting hurt again. If she had no reason to escape from life the way she said she'd done four years earlier, he believed she'd be all right. "Besides, Frank, who died and made you God?"

"Take it easy. I only told you for your own good—had no idea you already knew."

"Well, I did. Can we drop this?" Dan's temples were beginning to throb.

"You may not want to hear this, but you've got more reason than most to be careful. You know how many amputees end up dependent on painkillers. If you prescribe them for her…"

"Can it. I'm not about to write 'scrips for her or me. And you know damn well I haven't used anything stronger than extra-strength Tylenol since a couple of weeks after you revised my stump. In case you've forgotten, that was more than eight years ago."

Frank shook his head. "It's not me you'll have to convince if you're wrong," he muttered. "Just remember, Gayla Harris could be as destructive as a goddamn land mine."

Apparently Frank had said his piece. The last comment reminded Dan of the sixteen-year-old girl who'd be arriving from Kuwait tomorrow for them to tidy up the mess one of the stinking land mines that still peppered half the battlegrounds of the world had made of her lower body.

"Speaking of land mines, did you get a chance to look over the Al-Youssef girl's X-rays that came this morning?" Somebody at *Medecins Sans Frontieres* apparently had been thinking their team was made up of gods instead of doctors when they chose this patient to send them.

"Yes. I scheduled an OR for her on Thursday."

"What do you think?"

Frank shook his head. "Left hip disarticulation for sure. Possibly a hemipelvectomy."

Exploding mines were anything but kind to human flesh, and repairing the damage they did presented a hell of a challenge. If it weren't that the leftovers of wars around the world had maimed more people than auto, farm, and industrial accidents combined, he and his partners wouldn't be taking on nearly the number of victims from war-torn countries of the world for secondary reconstructive surgery.

"That will depend a lot on how good a job the surgeon did with the initial treatment." This Arab teenager had been luckier than some. She'd been taken immediately to a modern hospital in Kuwait City rather than languishing for days at some desert outpost. "Jim and I will check her as soon as she arrives."

Dan watched Frank stand up and head for the door. "I'll be in surgery in the morning, but I'll examine the girl myself as soon as I finish my case. Ignore what I told you about Gayla Harris if you want, Dan, but don't forget it." With that the older surgeon walked out.

No one, not even the man who had been his champion, surgeon, and friend since he'd applied for his residency, could warn Dan off Gayla. Leaning back in his chair, he shoved Frank's warning from his mind, filling it instead with daydreams of steamy summer nights with the woman who had so quickly invaded his heart.

Chapter Eight

The Ghosts

೫

Ruth noticed Sylvia lurking behind her when she heard a gulp. The other ghost must have taken in all or most of the conversation between Danny and Frank, if the stricken look on her face was any indicator.

"Gayla wouldn't do anything to hurt your boy. She didn't forge prescriptions or steal drugs from Eli. The man she'd been about to marry gave them to her."

"For God's sake, why?"

The gentle ghost of Sylvia took on a fierce expression. *"Because it was easier for him to salve his conscience, telling himself he was easing her pain that way, than for him to act like a real man and give her the support she really needed."*

Ruth snorted. Sylvia herself must not have given her daughter much in the way of emotional comfort after Gayla had, as the other ghost had put it, *"lost everything that meant anything to her all in the space of less than a week."* If she had, Ruth couldn't imagine the child having fallen completely apart. Danny hadn't, even when faced with the possibility of dying.

"Ruth?"

Sylvia's speech pattern had reverted to an apologetic whine, and her diffident tone just about drove Ruth nuts. *"Where were you when your daughter was trying to cope with all this tragedy? Mothers are supposed to — "*

"Eli wouldn't let me see her. He threatened to divorce me if I gave Gayla any sympathy. Said she'd brought all her problems on herself."

"Well, I was always there for Danny. For months I hardly left his side. For years I worried that the cancer would come back and take him.

I still worry that he'll let his work — important as it is — keep him from being happy with a nice girl."

Sylvia's eyebrows lifted slightly. *"Gayla?"*

"From what I see, she makes him happy." The perpetual smile on Danny's face since he'd met Gayla, the spring in his step, had convinced Ruth she hadn't made a horrendous mistake after all — that Sylvia Harris's flawed little girl had whatever it took to make her son content.

"And that satisfies you?"

Ruth shrugged her ghostly shoulders. *"I'll worry the same as his partner does — more. After all, Danny is my boy — and a mother never stops worrying. But, yes, if Danny loves your Gayla, they will have my blessing."*

"Then they will have mine as well. All I have ever wanted is for Gayla to be happy. I haven't seen her smile the way she does at your son since..." Sylvia paused, as if trying to recall her baby ecstatically happy about someone or something. *"I've never seen her look so content,"* she finally concluded.

"You're through agonizing because Danny only has one leg?" Ruth asked, still steaming inside because this ghost had implied that Danny's loss made him less than worthy.

Sylvia shrugged. *"I'm afraid it would bother me, but it doesn't appear to concern Gayla. It doesn't look as though it slows Danny down much, either. I still think you should have told me first, before we decided to get them together."*

"And you should have told me about Gayla." Ruth couldn't resist one last dig. Her heart warmed, though, as she pictured Danny looking at Gayla as if she'd hung the moon, and she couldn't project her usual acidic venom into what came out sounding like a mild, Sylvia-like rebuke.

"Yes, I should have. Now what do we do next? I want to see my Gayla married to your son."

Laughing at Sylvia's eagerness, Ruth willed Danny's image to leave and prepared to float away. *"We watch. We wait. And if we must, we'll step in and give them a nudge to speed them along. Come on, let's find a bridge game to take our minds off the children."*

Chapter Nine

"You know, sometimes I think Mom is looking down on me from somewhere up there." Gayla sat cross-legged on the blanket Dan spread beneath an ancient oak tree near the bandstand. "A couple of times lately I've even thought I heard her voice."

He followed her gaze toward the star-studded evening sky. "You must miss her."

"Every day." She let out a sigh and leaned back against his warm, muscular chest, her fingers gently tapping out the rhythm of classical guitars and mariachi music that wafted on the breeze.

Dan missed his mother, too, but because of her unreasonable overprotectiveness Ruth Newman had sometimes made his adolescent years an exercise in evasion and subterfuge. For some reason he, too, had felt his domineering parent's presence these last few weeks. "Guess we never get too old to need them, do we, princess?"

"No. You were an only child, weren't you?"

"Unfortunately. There was just me. Mom wanted to stand over me like a grizzly bear protecting her cub—especially after my surgery and chemo. I was nearly thirty years old when she died, but I don't think she ever quit worrying that the cancer would come back—or that I'd kill myself by doing something stupid."

"Moms always worry. I'll never stop feeling guilty because she worked herself into the stroke that killed her, fretting about my addictive behavior."

Dan heard the pain in Gayla's voice and sensed her hurt from the way her back muscles tensed against his chest. "Worry doesn't kill mothers. It keeps 'em going. Anyhow, that's what my mom used to say. Like the music?" Maybe if he changed the subject her unhappiness would go away.

"Love it. There's something magical about being out here under the sky, listening and feeling what the composers must have had in mind."

"You like classics?" If she did, he could still get tickets for the symphony season this coming fall.

"Some. I really enjoy country-western. Stuff that makes you want to laugh and cry. Something about a Garth Brooks song gets to me, deep down inside."

Dan laughed. "Me, too. They tease me in the OR because I listen to country music during surgery. What's your favorite?"

After a long pause, Gayla replied, "Anything soft and sad and all about love. How about you?"

"Rodeo. Anything about rodeo cowboys so long as it's got a driving beat. Feeds a dream every Texas boy has— one I've never gotten a chance to experience firsthand."

"I'm sorry." Her hand stilled against his thigh, and she turned to face him.

"Don't be. I could have managed. Not doing it was my concession to Mom's fear. While I succeeded in keeping her from finding out most of the crazy things I did to prove I wasn't a wimp, I couldn't figure out how I'd explain coming home filthy from getting thrown—or smelling like a stable."

He loved the sound of Gayla's laugh. "We'll just have to go out to a dude ranch one of these days, then. Let you get ropin' and ridin' out of your system. Maybe I'll try my hand at it, too."

Dan had a hard time imagining any activity that wouldn't be fun if he was doing it with her. "I'm game if you are." He nipped her earlobe, worrying the tiny hoop earring with his tongue.

"Are you game for something else?" Her whisper was husky and full of promise.

"Just say the word." Suddenly he wanted to roll her over and make love right here under the stars, to hell with the thousand or so people who'd also come to hear the concert. Too bad following his instincts would probably land them both in jail. "Let's get out of here."

"Sir?"

When Dan looked up, he saw not the policeman he'd been envisioning but a long-haired young man with a high-tech camera. He shot the guy a questioning look.

"I got a really fantastic shot of the two of you. I'd like to use it in the *Star*," he said, his expression hopeful. "Would you mind signing a release?"

"I don't see why not. Gayla?"

Gayla turned toward the photographer and smiled. "Sure. If you can get us a copy or two."

Dan's heart beat faster. If Gayla wanted this memento, she must be feeling more for him than she'd put into words. "Can you?" he asked as he scribbled his name across the bottom of what looked like a standard release form.

"No problem. Just put down your address and I'll get them to you."

Dan printed his address, and handed the release to Gayla. "Here, princess, sign your life away."

He watched her give the form to the photographer and turn to gather up the remains of their picnic supper. "Let's go home," she whispered, her breath warm and damp against his neck.

Dan nodded. He couldn't trust himself to speak, not now when his heart felt as if it were in his throat.

* * * * *

"What do you want to do this weekend?" he asked later as he held her and stroked along the length of her back and buttocks after they'd made love in her narrow bed.

She'd like to stay like this forever, but she dared not say it. "I've got to take some kids to a swim meet in Austin. We'll drive down there Friday night and come back on Sunday."

"Want some company?" Dan asked.

Only dedicated parents actually enjoyed baking on deck, watching little kids show their stuff. Gayla didn't want to sentence him to a miserable two days when the only time they'd have alone together would be at night, in bed. "I wouldn't be able to think about anything but you, Doc. Better stay home and let me make my living."

"Okay. Sometime, though, I'd love to watch you coach. I might have gotten interested in competitive swimming when I was a kid if the coach had looked like you."

Moving one hand to her breast, he molded his palm around it and sent a new wave of sensation straight to her already wet, swollen pussy. "Flattery will get you anything you want." Needing more, she turned over to face him and began a sensual exploration of her own.

"Hey, stop that! I've got a ten-hour case scheduled first thing in the morning. I need my sleep." Dan sounded annoyed, but the way he crushed her to him made her doubt his words.

"Ten hours? That all? You held up pretty well after about that many hours of making love last Saturday." Gayla wrapped one leg around his hips and rubbed herself suggestively against his renewed erection.

"Woman, you're gonna kill me." He didn't sound as though he minded, though, as he rolled her to her back and reached for a fresh condom. "Satisfied now?" he asked as he flexed his hips and joined their bodies again.

She laughed. Sex with Dan was fun, not to mention intensely satisfying. "Not yet, but I imagine I will be soon."

They moved together in perfect rhythm. Gayla opened her eyes to meet his gaze, and in them she saw more than the need to bring this joining to its logical conclusion. She saw kindness and caring. And love.

Her hands came up to caress lean cheeks scratchy with dark stubble. More than she'd ever worshiped her unbending father, much more than she'd cared for his protégé Marc Solomon, Gayla adored Dan…loved him. She wanted him not just in her bed but in her heart. Tears of joy welled in her eyes as she strained to take his hot hard cock even deeper. The tension grew as they moved faster, strained harder. Sought nirvana. Sensations built deep in her belly from a small, pleasant twinge to a level of pure torture.

She concentrated on his hot, hard cock pulsing wildly, thrusting deep and then retreating, stroking and caressing her pussy and prolonging the sensation of falling free…to a place where there was no thinking, only feeling. She strained to take more of him, wanted this to last forever.

Then it happened. Her inner muscles convulsed around him as the wonder of it all spread like wildfire through her body. Vaguely she felt him plunge deeper still, as if he were invading her womb, before she heard his triumphant shout.

As he held her in the quiet aftermath of the storm, she knew she loved Dan. Really, really loved him.

* * * * *

"Newman, you look like hell. Long night?"

Dan glanced up from the shoe covers he was slipping over his Nikes to find Jim staring down at him. "Not particularly. I was in bed by ten o'clock." Actually he felt great.

"Now why don't I doubt that? You know, this is the first time I've ever seen you sporting a day's growth of beard."

"Maybe I'm taking after Frank. Where is he?" They had a miserable job awaiting them in the OR, and Dan was anxious to get on with it.

"He's already in the OR, driving Kelly nuts while she puts that poor kid to sleep." Jim flipped open his locker and grabbed some scrubs.

"Do you think her knee can be salvaged?" Dan asked as Jim undressed.

"Your call on that one. Whoever did the primary care did a good job on the skin grafts."

"Bone's shattered. Lots of hardware holding it together. There's bound to be extensive damage to the nerves, tendons, and ligaments. Guess we won't know until we take a look." Dan stood, leaving the bench for Jim.

"It's a crime, a kid getting blown more or less in half because some asshole invented the ultimate offensive ground weapon."

"Amen to that." Dan headed for the OR with Jim. "Speaking of crimes, do you know if I'm going to have to use that antique scope today?"

"Nah. You raised enough hell day before yesterday that they got the new one fixed. By the way, Hamilton's hand looked better this morning."

"Good." Picking up some soap, Dan began to scrub his hands and arms. "On this one, we'd better start praying for a miracle."

Jim nodded as he held up his hands for a nurse to slip on sterile gloves. "Put on that stack of CDs I brought you yet?" he asked when she turned to put on Dan's gloves.

"Uh-huh. Old Ironsides saw me do it. Stalked off, muttering about how he didn't see how anybody could listen to that redneck garbage and do surgery at the same time."

When they walked into the OR, the sound of Garth Brooks's voice greeted them. Nine hours later, after Dan had listened to all the team's eclectic mix of music CDs for what seemed like the hundredth time, he forced himself to ignore his aching body a few more minutes.

Somebody had to talk to their patient's anxious father, and he'd been elected. Pulling off his paper hat and mask and tossing them in the trash, he made for the waiting room—and the worried-looking robed man who was talking with a hulking, swarthy-looking guy in jeans and a western shirt. A guy that looked awfully familiar.

Bear el Rashid. One of the meanest linebackers Dan had ever watched tackle some unfortunate quarterback. The University of Texas legend he'd met at a holiday party hosted by Timmy Tanner's aunt nearly a year ago. Glad to have a personal connection, however tenuous, with the guy who'd be passing along the not too happy news, Dan approached them and held out his hand.

Bear frowned when Dan explained what they'd been able to do. "How in the name of Allah am I to tell her father this?" Bear clenched his meaty fists. "This happened in one of my oilfields."

Sighing, Dan explained as best he could that the girl eventually would be better off because of the surgery, but that she'd have to endure long, painful therapy before realizing the benefits, and Bear passed along his words to the girls father. Accepting the robed man's profuse thanks for the precious little they had been able to do for the child left Dan feeling sick as well as exhausted by the time he shook Bear's hand and headed back to the surgical suite to change.

Dan needed to talk to Gayla. No, he needed to see her, forget the horror of having witnessed firsthand, down and dirty, what an Iraqi land mine had done to a beautiful, innocent child. Picking up the phone, he dialed her at her office. When he heard her voice, some of his anger slid away.

"Thirty minutes?" she asked when he told her he'd pick her up.

"About that. See you then."

After a quick shower Dan headed for Gayla. On the way, he thought of how he'd have spent the coming night alone, brooding about things he couldn't do to make the world a safer place for people like his unfortunate patient, if Gayla Harris hadn't so magically come into his life.

* * * * *

"Sometimes life sucks."

Gayla nodded as Dan poured out his frustration. The story of how an exploding land mine had forever changed the life of a young Arab girl tore at her heart, as did his obvious concern for the child. "You did your best."

"She won't think so when she wakes up and finds less of herself than was there before we started."

"Dan, don't torture yourself. You didn't place those mines, and you didn't push her into one, either. You and your partners are doing everything you can by volunteering your skills to restore victims' functions as much as possible." Gayla couldn't imagine her father offering to do any surgery for free.

"I'm sorry. I'm not very good company tonight." He smiled, ruffling her hair with one hand, as if trying hard to force anger and regret from his mind. "Want to go get something to eat?"

Gayla sensed he needed solitude more than the company of a bunch of strangers. "I can fix something." She mentally reviewed the contents of her meager pantry. "How about soup and grilled cheese sandwiches?" That was all she had unless she went out for groceries.

"Sounds good. Can I help?"

She couldn't help smiling. The contrasts between Dan and her father never seemed to end. But he had to be exhausted. "I can manage. Why don't you close those gorgeous big brown eyes and get a few minutes' rest? You've got to be tired."

Like a big cat, Dan stretched and yawned. "Okay, princess. You've convinced me. I'll let you slave over the hot stove while I relax. But just this time, you understand. Next time I'll take a turn in the kitchen."

Gayla let herself dream of a forever with the man she loved while she set the little table in the corner of her kitchen and took out butter, cheese, and bread. When she opened the cupboard to get that can of tomato soup she was going to heat, though, the distinctive red label on a fifth of Smirnoff caught her eye.

She pictured the poor girl Dan thought he hadn't done enough to help, the horrors the child must have endured. How trivial her own losses seemed, compared with the tragedy that had befallen Dan's patient. That didn't help much. She needed a drink.

Trembling, Gayla reached for the bottle the way she'd done nearly every day since she moved in. She set it on the counter, and her fingers went to the cap. With the nail of her index finger she circled the unbroken seal the way she'd done a thousand times. The way she'd do until that day when her need exceeded her own will.

She set the bottle back in its place and took out the can of soup. As she heated it and grilled some sandwiches, though, her thoughts were not of forever but of the flaws within her that made her unworthy of forever with anyone—much less with a man she loved so much—a man she'd rather die than hurt.

Damn it, her mind focused on that bottle, too. That one and others like it, the ones that brought oblivion and temporary relief from sorrow that came back to pierce her. The booze and the insidious powdered stuff that bought a longer surcease of pain but at the price of her sanity.

Will I ever stop craving this poison?

"Not completely, baby. It will get easier, though, as time goes by."

Startled by that faraway but familiar voice, Gayla strained to see. "Mom?" she whispered, unsure whether her mind was playing tricks on her again.

"Yes. It's me."

"B—but you're dead."

"I'm still watching you, baby. You've made me proud. I like your young man, from what I've seen of him."

"Why can't I see you?" Gayla thought she heard her mother choke back tears.

"It's a miracle that you can hear me. I'm only supposed to be able to look at you, not talk with you. I'm glad, though. I always wanted to tell you I was sorry for letting you down when you needed me most."

It was Gayla's turn to cry. With the back of her hand she brushed tears from her cheeks. "I let you down, Mom. I needed to say I'm sorry, too."

"Oh, Gayla. If only..."

"I'm okay, Mom. Really." Gayla heard a sizzling sound from the stove. "Oh, no! I'm burning the soup."

"You'll never get Danny to propose if you feed him out of a can," her mother told her, scolding in the gentle way Gayla remembered so well. *"You should make him a brisket, the way I taught you. With potatoes and carrots. And cheesecake for dessert."*

Gayla laughed. "I will, Mom. I love you."

"And I love you, baby. This man's a jewel. Don't you let him go! By next summer I want you to make me a grandma again."

A cool breeze ruffled Gayla's hair, and she sensed that her mother was gone. Eerie, she thought—but hearing her mom's voice had gone a long way toward cheering her up.

By the time she called Dan in to eat, she realized her black mood had subsided.

Chapter Ten

The Ghosts

ဢ

Ruth couldn't believe it! Sylvia had actually talked to Gayla, and from what she could see, it seemed Gayla had heard her. *"How did you do that?"*

"I don't know. I just talked, and Gayla heard me."

"I've talked, but Danny has never heard me. I don't think. If he did, he paid me no mind." Suddenly Ruth burned with jealousy.

"Maybe it's because I want so much to make up for not being there when she needed me, back when I was alive."

Sylvia's explanation made Ruth feel better. Never had she turned her back on her son. *"I thought you said Gayla had gotten over depending on alcohol,"* she commented as she recalled the girl's apparent struggle against the lure of the bottle.

Sylvia shrugged. *"She hasn't used it or drugs for over a year. But they say you never get over wanting it. Gayla put that bottle in the cupboard when she first moved into that apartment. She hasn't opened it, and it's been there more than a year now."*

Her gaze fixed on Danny, who was getting ready for bed at his own apartment, Ruth considered the implication of Sylvia's words. *"What would happen, do you think, if Gayla had to face some serious tragedy? Could she set that bottle down?"*

"I don't know. Ruth, is there something wrong with Danny's leg?

"No. Nothing a night's rest won't cure." The stump was red and slightly swollen, which happened when her son overtaxed himself the way he had today in surgery. *"What about Gayla? You're her mother. You must know better than anyone what kind of strength she has."*

Sylvia's hands fluttered the way Ruth had noticed they tended to do when she faced unpleasant realities. *"I don't know. God help me, that's the truth. Before the trouble began, I'd always thought of Gayla as being able to face anything. She seemed so strong, so much like Eli. But I was wrong. I believe Gayla could handle most things without falling apart again. Something personal and devastating, though? I don't know."*

Ruth didn't know, either, but then she couldn't swear that Danny wouldn't go too far some day and tax his body beyond its endurance. She couldn't even guarantee, in spite of all the doctors who said his cancer had been cured, that the vicious killer that had taken his leg wouldn't ever come back for more of him.

"Let's not expect guarantees, my friend," she said as they looked in on Gayla, who had curled up around a pillow while apparently fighting her demons in her sleep. *"We can only hope our children get together from here on, on their own."*

Chapter Eleven

Friday night, no emergencies, and the prospect of downing a beer or two with the loaded pizza that should be delivered any minute should have made Dan content. Instead he paced restlessly through his empty condo, missing Gayla more than he'd have thought possible.

Mentally he replayed his partner's news. Frank and Michelle had casually announced that they were getting married, even before the date Jamie and Gary had set months ago for the big wedding Jamie was so set on having. Not to mention that Kelly was going to have a baby. Pretty soon, Dan realized, he'd be the only solo act in the group that had hung together now for five years.

Or would he?

If Frank could set aside his bitterness over losing Erica and their son and commit himself to making a new life with his good friend Michelle, why couldn't Dan get over the nagging feeling he wasn't meant for marriage and take the plunge with Gayla?

Methodically he made mental lists of why he should or shouldn't propose. The pizza came, and he ate it all without savoring so much as one spicy bite. He glanced at the empty box, and figured he could have eaten it as well and never have known the difference.

Dan almost let the answering machine pick up the call, but he didn't. Hearing Gayla's voice, imagining her alone in an Austin hotel room, and listening to her say she missed him, brought him to the decision he'd been fighting for hours.

"I love you," he said softly into the receiver.

He heard her breath catch. His chest tightened as the silence continued. Her whispered words, *"I love you, too,"* finally came through, sounding choked up with what he guessed must be tears. His tension dissipated, leaving a sense of jubilance that made him laugh out loud.

"I'll see you Sunday night," he told her after they had exhausted every topic except the one Dan wanted to save for a very special moment. "Take care, princess."

* * * * *

Dan loves me.

Standing on the deck, watching her twelve young swimmers warm up before the race, Gayla silently repeated those words. Dan Newman actually loved her—a washed-up swimmer with a monkey on her back, whose only marketable skill consisted of training others to succeed where she had failed.

She forced herself to observe the four boys and eight girls who'd qualified for this invitational meet. Between the ages of nine and twelve, the children had earned their trip to Austin with various combinations of talent and hard work.

An electronic beeper signaled the end of warm-ups, and Gayla's young charges converged on her. Forcing herself to concentrate on each swimmer's coming events, she handed out advice and encouragement over the din of a noisy crowd of parents and other competitors.

As the heats progressed from slow to fast, Gayla greeted each swimmer as he or she finished, finding something positive to say even when she had to point out how the swim could have been better. The hugs and smiles nearly made her forget that competitive swimming at this level should, in some of the parents' opinions, be taken as deadly serious.

Nine-year-old Todd Weldon, the most talented of the group in Gayla's estimation, won the fifty-meter freestyle, but failed to qualify for the upcoming Junior Olympics competition. When he came out of the pool, she rushed to congratulate him, but his mother had gotten there first and was tearing into him. The way the woman berated Todd reminded Gayla of how her father had reacted when she'd failed to reach some interim goal. The boy's tears tore at Gayla's heart. What his mother was doing to him wasn't right, or fair.

"Mrs. Weldon," she interjected as soon as she could get the woman's attention, "all Todd could do was his best. I thought he had a great swim."

"It wasn't good enough!"

"Mom, please." Todd looked as though he'd gladly sink into the concrete deck if only he could escape.

Gayla shuddered. Once she'd endured an immediate, in-person diatribe from her dad, and it had hurt worse than the chilly after-the-meet critiques that had been regular facts of her life when she was Todd's age. "Mrs. Weldon, could I talk to you somewhere private?"

"I gotta swim down." Todd must be dying to get away. He usually had to be prodded to get back in the water and cool down after an event.

"Go on. Do an easy hundred." The least Gayla could do was to give the boy an escape route.

"Todd, I'm not through with you," his mother yelled at his retreating back before turning to Gayla. "I don't appreciate your trying to excuse poor performance. The club director is going to hear about this."

"Fine. Do what you have to do. But don't expect me to stand by and watch you tear your child apart. He has trained as hard as any child I coach. He went out there and won a precision event with the fastest time he's ever clocked. I'm proud of him. You should be, too!"

"He was supposed to qualify for Junior Olympics." Mrs. Weldon's precisely painted lips clamped together, leaving her with a decidedly unattractive expression.

"He will. In his own time. Swimming, more than any other sport I can think of, is one whose results no one—not a coach and certainly not a parent—can dictate or even accurately predict at any particular meet. By badgering Todd, you're going to make him resent you and hate a sport he loves."

"I pay you to make him a winner."

"No, Mrs. Weldon. You pay me to teach your son competitive swimming and help him become as good a competitor as his talent and desire will allow. If you'll excuse me, I need to get back on deck. I have other swimmers to coach."

For how long, since her hold on this job was tenuous, Gayla didn't know. She had no doubt that Todd's pushy mother would complain to the club manager and that the complaint might put her out on the streets in search of employment. For the moment, though, Gayla didn't care. Watching Todd's expression turn from jubilant to morose had torn at her heart and made losing her job seem a small price to pay for taking up his defense.

Maybe she couldn't do anything except teach kids to do what had been the center of her identity before it became her ultimate failure. She'd found the courage to stand up for one of her young charges, though, and that made her feel good. When one after another of her swimmers came out of the water to greet her with smiles and hugs, Gayla felt her sense of self-worth inch further out of the gutter.

She was doing something worthwhile. Not anything as earthshaking as saving lives or changing the world, but she was making some small difference in these kids' lives. They cared, and so did Dan. She wasn't alone anymore, with only her sister Tess to offer halfhearted support. Somehow even her mother had managed to come back from her grave long enough to let Gayla know she still loved her.

When Gayla crawled into bed on Saturday night after talking with Dan on the phone, she felt better about herself than she had in years.

* * * * *

Gayla stayed gently on Dan's mind as he made rounds and while he worked out in the hospital gym. Being in love had its downside. It would be another twelve hours until he could hold his woman, and that made his balls ache. Catching a glimpse of Frank at the lat machine on the other side of the room, Dan wondered if Cupid's malady had struck his partner, too.

Somehow he doubted it. Easing the bar down on the leg press, Dan got up and headed Frank's way. "Want some breakfast?" he asked, hoping to heal the damage Frank's warning about Gayla had done to their friendship.

"Sure. Hospital cafeteria, half an hour?"

"How about Mel's?" The grill and coffee shop across the street appealed more than the antiseptic hospital dining room with its universally lousy food. "Unless you still have rounds," Dan added, not having seen Frank on the floors when he'd been there.

Frank grunted as he pulled against heavy resistance. "Mel's it is," he grated out between clenched teeth.

Over plates full of what had to be the worst example of what intelligent health professionals should choose to eat, Frank confirmed Dan's suspicion that love had little or nothing to do with his decision to marry their favorite physical therapist.

"Michelle wants a kid. I want a home and a warm woman to curl up with after a long hard day at work. Hell, I like kids, too. Seems like a fair trade to me," he concluded, turning his attention to the stack of syrup-drenched pancakes on his plate.

Frank's motives for getting married sounded pretty flimsy to Dan. "Sounds as if you're setting yourselves up to get hurt. Not to mention that you'll be hurting an innocent kid if that part of your plan works out."

"Why shouldn't it? Michelle's already pregnant."

"How?"

Frank chuckled. "The usual way. After I had to go over to her place a few weeks back to cajole her into doing the fundraising ordeal with me, she talked me into helping her become a mom."

"Just like that?"

"She said she wanted a kid. Things just fell into place from there. When she found out it took, she told me, and I decided we ought to get married."

Dan shrugged, unable to refute Frank's last statement. Having children out of wedlock didn't say a lot for a physician's sense of responsibility. Still, he felt for both his friends who would be beginning a life together without love. "So when's the big event going to take place?"

"Which one?"

"The wedding. I can figure out as well as you can, from what you've already said, approximately when I'm going to need to go buy some rattles and toys."

"We're going to do it next Tuesday at the hospital chapel. Nine o'clock or thereabouts. Figured we could fit in a quick ceremony between my total hip and the tendon transfer I'm set to assist for you. That way we can all be there, and it won't play hell with the schedule." With that, Frank began shoveling in food as if he were expecting to fast for the next few days. "Look, I've got to run. Told Michelle I'd meet her and I'm already an hour late. We've got to decide whether we're going to live in her house or buy something new."

After Frank left Dan sat there, shell-shocked. For the first time in his memory, he pictured himself growing old. The thought of doing it alone held no appeal. Forcing himself to finish his Belgian waffle, he washed it down with coffee and headed for his car.

Maybe I'll call Jim and see if he wants to play golf. The July sun beat down hard on Dan as he strode past the string of exclusive shops that preyed on hospital employees and visitors.

It's too damn hot to walk a golf course.

Dan glanced into the window of a store and had to blink. Something drew him inside, made him point out the stone that seemed more brilliant than the noonday sun. Before he knew it he'd become the proud owner of a diamond ring. The store owner had assured him that, though it was only a carat and a half, it was perfect in every way. Just the thing for Dan to give to Gayla.

When he got home several thousand dollars poorer, Dan took out the graceful band with its sparkly single stone. Pushing it as far as it would go onto his little finger, he held it to the light and imagined it where it belonged, shooting rays of rainbow colors when he admired it on Gayla's slender finger.

He was going to ask her to marry him. Dan still found that hard to believe. He couldn't imagine doing anything else, though. With Gayla he could celebrate life. Not just major milestones but the little joys like waking up to her soft, gentle smile…sharing things as simple as a Texas sunset or children playing in a park.

She said she loved him, and she'd made him a believer. Not just in her feelings. He believed in himself. Reaching down to release his prosthesis from the stump that was swollen from a long day encased in its socket, Dan smiled at the memory of how casually she'd accepted this missing part of him. If Gayla would have him, he was going to marry her. Damn her old man and the gossips who thought she'd drag him down. They were wrong. She'd make him whole, if only in his mind, and he'd do everything in his power to keep anyone from bringing her demons back to life.

Shoving his stump back into the socket, Dan got up and strode into the bedroom he hoped soon to be sharing with his bride. Stashing the ring in the top drawer of his dresser, he moved to the bed and stretched out across the coverlet. As he stared at the ceiling fan's lazy circular motion, he planned how he'd propose. He wanted to make the proposal special—an evening for them both to remember.

* * * * *

"You're awfully quiet tonight," Gayla observed as they drove toward her sister's house.

"I'm grousing because I'm not exactly where I wanted to be right now. Sorry, princess." Dan's hand snaked over her shoulder and gently squeezed her breast.

"And you call me insatiable! Well, love, it's all your fault. I couldn't resist telling Tess about you. When I did, she insisted that we come over tonight so she could give you the once-over." Gayla didn't see how her sister could do anything but fall in love with Dan. As far as she was concerned, the man was pure sex appeal. And lovable, too.

"You don't know what you're missing tonight," he said as he moved his hand up until his fingers cradled her cheek.

Gayla laughed. "What is this mysterious treat I'm going to miss out on because I roped you into meeting my sister?"

"I'll never tell. Not until Tuesday night, anyway. I want you to pick your favorite restaurant. I'll make reservations and do my best to arrange for the waiters there to fawn all over me. Isn't that the way you put it when you insisted our first date be at the pool?"

"I think so." She'd been so wrong when she tried to shove him into the doctor mold that her father fit so well. "What are we going to do?"

"Pig out on steak and lobster. Share a bottle of godawful expensive nonalcoholic champagne. Talk and laugh and see what comes up."

"Dan?" Did he mean to propose? If he did, would she have the courage to accept?

"Yes?" He drew the word out, as if he knew she was fishing for information he wasn't about to share.

"Why the fancy dinner out?" she asked point-blank.

"We might be celebrating Frank and Michelle's marriage. Or we might not." He pulled into Tess's street.

"Marriage? Frank and Michelle are getting married?"

"Tuesday morning at the hospital chapel, between two cases in the OR," Dan told her. "Which house is your sister's?"

"The one at the end of the block. It's the gray one with the red double doors." Gayla could hardly believe her ears. She'd seen Michelle with Dan's partner several times now, and they had struck her more as colleagues than as lovers. "How on earth did that come about so suddenly?" She tried to picture bubbly Michelle paired up with a man that struck her as just this side of surly.

Dan didn't answer until he parked and came around to open the car door. "She's pregnant."

"How?"

He shook his head and grinned. "I asked Frank that. He told me it happened the way it usually does. You know, a man and a woman, getting—"

"I don't need the details right now, Doc. You can show me later." With difficulty she tore her gaze from Dan's and glanced toward the house. "Here comes my nephew Jeff," she told him as they hurried up the curved brick walkway.

* * * * *

"Cute kid."

"What did you expect? He's my only nephew."

Dan watched the dark-haired, wiry boy practically leap into Gayla's outstretched arms. She had a way with kids, that was certain. "Hey there, aren't you getting a little too big to slam into your aunt that way? She's not a whole lot bigger than you." He was fairly sure that last comment would ruffle Gayla's feathers.

"You've got a way to go yet, don't you?" she asked the boy before turning back to Dan. "Meet Jeff. He's five going on twenty. Jeff, say 'hi' to Dr. Newman. He's a friend of mine." She set the boy down and clasped Dan's hand.

"Hello." The boy's gaze raked Dan from head to toe, leaving him with a quizzical expression.

"Hello, yourself." Dan had the strange feeling he'd been stretched out on a glass slide, stuck with pins, and set beneath a microscope.

Inside Gayla introduced him to her sister, brother-in-law, and eight-month-old Katie, whom she immediately picked up and cuddled in her lap. They struck Dan as comprising a caring, loving family, in spite of the boy's penchant for staring. Tess, particularly, appeared eager to learn more about him and his relationship with Gayla.

"Grandpa Harris said you were crippled, but you aren't," the boy blurted out just as Dan began to wonder if he'd forgotten to zip his pants or something.

"Jeffrey Aaron Wiener!"

"Well, Mommy, he isn't."

Dan took pity on the kid, whose indignant expression made him want to laugh. "No, I'm not crippled."

Jeff's gaze dropped pointedly to Dan's legs. "Then you don't have a wooden leg, either?"

"Jeff!" Bill Wiener sounded as if he'd like to cut his son's tongue out.

"It's okay. Kids don't mean any harm. Jeff, I do have an artificial leg." Dan tapped on the socket of his prosthesis to produce the hollow sound that always seemed to impress little kids. "It's made out of high-tech stuff instead of wood. Want to see?"

Dan watched Jeff's eyes widen. "Can I?" he asked.

"Sure." It always amazed Dan how the idea of artificial limbs fascinated kids, and how the subject invariably made their parents squirm the way he noticed Tess was doing, as if she wanted to sink into the plush carpeted floor but couldn't quite figure how to do it. At times like this, he wished he'd worn shorts so doing show and tell with the prosthesis wouldn't have become an issue. "How about taking a look when we take a swim after dinner?" he offered, taking pity on Gayla's embarrassed sister.

"You can swim?"

"Like a fish. I'm almost as fast as your Aunt Gayla."

Tess shot a nervous smile Dan's way before zeroing in on Jeff. "You go wash up and get ready to eat, young man. You've asked enough questions, don't you think?"

Still holding baby Katie, Gayla reached out and patted Jeff's plump cheek. "You won't learn if you don't ask questions, will you?" she whispered just loudly enough for Dan to hear.

"I'm sorry about the baby inquisitor," Gayla said later as they drove back toward her apartment. "He is cute, though, isn't he?"

"Seems smart, too. Don't worry about him asking questions. Kids always do." Dan pictured the easy way Gayla had dealt with her precocious nephew and his baby sister. "You're good with them."

"I love kids. They tend to accept people at face value."

"And adults don't?"

"Most of the time, no." Gayla sounded sad, and that cut at Dan's heart.

He took one hand off the wheel and stroked her shoulder. "I love you," he murmured, realizing as he said the words that this was the first time he'd declared his feelings for her face-to-face.

Her slender fingers meshed with his. "I know. I love you, Dan." She didn't sound as happy about that as he'd have hoped—more resigned, as though she doubted anything good would come from the emotional bond she'd just confirmed.

"We'll work it out, princess," he told her, wishing he had that ring in his pocket instead of in a drawer of his dresser at home. Why had he decided to ask her to marry him in the rarified atmosphere of some fancy restaurant?

Her only response was to grasp his hand tighter and sigh, and when he held her later in the small apartment she called home, he sensed her uncertainty. When she tossed and moaned in her sleep, Dan felt her demons as surely as if they were his own. The following morning as he drove to work, he wondered if his love would be enough to allay Gayla's fears.

Chapter Twelve

ഌ

Meeting Dan at a chapel, sitting beside him as they watched his friends murmur wedding vows...figuring that by having her come here to the hospital he was letting his world know they were more than casual bedmates...scared Gayla half to death.

She parked in the visitors' lot and hurried inside before the Texas sun could do its thing to the pale-pink linen dress she'd worn for what she assumed would be an informal wedding. Her spirits soared when she saw Dan waiting for her on the hospital's front steps.

She itched to run into his arms, but her mother's lessons in manners had paid off. Smiling up at him, she took both his hands. "I think I'm overdressed," she quipped, letting her gaze rake down that dynamite body garbed in OR greens.

He chuckled. "Gotta match the groom. I've got a white coat, though." He slipped on the starched lab coat he'd apparently been holding behind his back, and Gayla's breath caught as she noted the sharp contrast between his tanned, olive skin and the stark white jacket. "Come on. Frank should be coming downstairs any minute."

Arm in arm they strolled toward the chapel Gayla remembered from having been there years ago to see her father receive some kind of award. Dan held the door, and she went inside, pausing to admire the subtle tones of blue and green that flowed through small stained-glass windows near the ceiling.

"Where *is* Frank?" Gayla saw Michelle standing at the front of the chapel beside Jamie and a man she didn't recognize, and wondered what the bride might be thinking about her bridegroom's absence.

"He ran into some trouble with the total hip replacement he started at seven o'clock," Dan whispered. "He'll be here."

The damp heat of his breath on her earlobe made her wish they were at his condo—her apartment—anywhere except in the hospital that symbolized her father and the pain that still made her shudder inside and long for even the most temporary of releases.

Gayla noticed how Michelle's expression changed, and when she turned she saw Frank standing in the doorway. Attired like Dan in surgical scrubs, he strode down the single aisle and took his place at Michelle's side.

In less than five minutes Frank and Michelle made all the traditional promises to love, honor, and cherish each other in the least traditional manner Gayla had ever witnessed. "Was this the kind of wedding Michelle wanted?" she asked Dan as they followed the bride and groom out of the chapel, thinking of her own thwarted dream of walking slowly between both her parents to her future husband...standing with him under a huppah draped with fragrant flowers...confirming the promises they'd made earlier for a lifetime full of love.

"I guess so, princess. They wanted quick, not fancy. Thanks for coming." He paused at the hospital entrance, as if trying to decide whether he had time to walk her to her car. Then he kissed her briefly and brought butterflies to her midsection the way he did so well. "See you at seven?"

"Yes." If she hadn't read Dan wrong, tonight would bring her the chance to realize at least part of her dream. She wanted nothing more than to marry him, except to bring him the happiness he so deserved. If only she could persuade herself that by becoming his wife, she'd give him joy, not despair.

As she drove back to the club, Gayla indulged her fantasies.

Dan was wearing a silly smile on his face and a boutonniere on his tux lapel. Her gown, pristine white as it swirled against his legs, made her feel like his princess, and the aroma of roses and gardenias in her bouquet surrounded her like a fragrant cloud. Traditional words and admonitions repeated for thousands of years rang in Gayla's ears until finally the smashing sound of crystal against a marble floor and the good wishes from the crowd made her look into her beloved's eyes. They turned together in slow motion, to greet their families.

There would be Tess and Bill. His father...and hers. His friends and hers, standing with them to wish them well.

Oh, who was she kidding? Gayla punched the brakes harder than was necessary to stop the car. If and when she dredged up the nerve to saddle Dan with more hassles than he deserved, it was certain she'd be walking down the aisle alone. As her father had told her five years earlier, hell would freeze over before he'd acknowledge his screw-up of a daughter. And her mother was gone.

* * * * *

So Gayla was going to want more than a quick visit to a judge when they got married. It amused Dan that she felt so bad about Michelle and Frank having such a sterile ceremony. As he watched her walk toward the parking lot, Dan wished to hell he didn't have surgeries scheduled clear up to five o'clock. He could hardly wait to give her the ring he now had in his locker upstairs. The idea of being a major player in the blowout wedding celebration he imagined she had in mind didn't bother him at all.

He concentrated on his patients, half listening to the country songs and keeping Gayla comfortably in a corner of his mind. He'd have finished early if the ER hadn't sent up this last add-on case. As he backed away from the surgical field so Jim could do his thing on soft tissue and skin over the bones, tendons, and nerves Dan had just reattached on fingers that had met earlier in the day with a circular saw, though, Gayla became the focus of his thoughts.

He could hardly wait to propose. Dreams, long dormant until Gayla had come bounding into his life, surfaced. *Damn, our kids could all be playmates if Gayla wouldn't mind getting pregnant right away.* "Goddamn it to hell!"

Jim looked up from the tedious job of sewing the skin of the last finger. "What's wrong?"

"Chemo. Fucking chemo."

"What the hell?"

Judging from the look on the visible part of Jim's face, Dan guessed his partner must think he was flat-out nuts. He didn't feel like explaining, though. This was too close, too damn personal to share with every gossipy nurse and technician in the OR.

"Nothing. I was just thinking about another patient."

Jim shrugged, then turned his attention back to his precision stitchery. When it became evident that his partner wouldn't be needing extra hands to complete the job, Dan left the OR and went into the lounge, his med school oncology professor's warning ringing in his ears.

"Hair loss. Nausea. Cramping pains. Those side effects are always temporary. On the other hand, sterility, while it isn't inevitable, is permanent."

Dan sank onto a lounge chair, in no mood now to shower and get ready to pick Gayla up. He pictured her laughing with her nephew and niece, enjoying the time she spent with her young swimmers. As the knot in his throat grew bigger, making breathing difficult, he tortured himself by picturing her with their baby at her breast.

Jim came in, stripping off his mask as he ambled across the room. Glancing around to be sure they were alone, Dan called him aside.

"What do you remember about chemotherapy and sterility?" he asked after learning that Kelly would be busy for a while, monitoring their patient in the recovery room.

"Not much. It's not a red-hot issue in plastic surgery any more than it is in ortho/neuro. Why?"

"I'm afraid I may be sterile."

Jim sat down and met Dan's gaze. "So? Have a sperm count done and find out."

Dan felt like an idiot. Even he, who had stayed as far away from the study of OB/GYN and urology as he could manage while in med school, knew enough to have thought of that. "Yeah. I will. Who should I go see? Taylor?" He assumed a urologist could do the job.

"See Greg Halpern."

"He's a gynecologist."

Jim laughed. "He's the god of fertility. Tests wanna-be daddies as well as moms. I warn you, though, be prepared to pay. Our health insurance policy doesn't cover fertility studies."

The cost was the last thing on Dan's mind. He was trying not to squirm at the idea of being tested, and hurting because he wouldn't propose now, not until he knew the outcome of those tests. "Do you have any idea how long the tests take?"

"At least as long as it takes you to jerk off in a specimen cup."

"It's not funny." Dan couldn't see anything humorous, and it annoyed him to watch his partner smirk.

"Yeah, it is funny. Real funny. Your timing couldn't be better. Think about it, Newman. Kel's pregnant. Michelle's pregnant. Now all of a sudden you're losing sleep over whether some treatment you had a quarter century ago may have fucked up your ability to reproduce."

"It's not that." Or maybe it was. All Dan could think of at the moment was that he couldn't offer Gayla marriage with a family — or without one either. Not until he knew.

"Are you and Gayla talking about getting married?" Jim asked, suddenly serious.

"I want to ask her."

Jim reached out and patted Dan's shoulder. "Go ahead and ask. Whether you can give her kids — whether *she's* able to have them, for that matter—isn't something you need to know up front. It's a crapshoot. It was with Kelly and me, anyhow."

"Neither of you knew there was a damn good chance one of you was sterile."

"We didn't know we weren't, either. Did you know we kept having unprotected sex for eight years before we figured there might be something wrong with one of us?"

Dan met Jim's gaze. "No. I didn't know. I just assumed you were purposely waiting to start a family. It's still not the same. If I remember correctly, a fairly high percentage of people who undergo chemo become sterile. I had a round right after they amputated my leg. I can't ask Gayla to marry me until I know."

"Call Halpern, then. He's the one who's been treating Kel since we decided we needed some help. When our baby or babies are finally born, I'm going to send him a whole damn box of cigars—because he had more to do with us having them than I did."

"Kelly had artificial insemination?"

"Nope. My baby-making equipment all works fine. Halpern just kept prescribing fertility drugs until Kelly finally dropped an egg. As far as I'm concerned, he's a miracle worker."

Jim's admission shook Dan. "Aren't you worried about Kelly having twins—or worse, a litter?" He grinned at the thought of fastidious, put-together Kelly trying to cope with a house full of screaming infants.

"I'm so happy because she's going to have the baby we've been wanting for so long, I don't care if we have quints."

"Keep telling yourself that, my friend. Do you have Halpern's number?"

"Yeah." Jim reached in his locker for his wallet and fished out a tattered card. "Good luck," he said quietly as he headed for the shower.

* * * * *

Gayla toweled herself dry, enjoying the damp, sweet smell of steam, scented soap, and talcum that filled her small bathroom. Wiping the fog off the mirror so she could see herself, she began to brush out her hair.

The more she thought about tonight, the more she knew she'd accept Dan's proposal. She had to. If she didn't, she'd regret it for the rest of her life.

That decision made, Gayla let herself dream of weddings, babies, and the man she loved more than life. Wanting to look her best, she searched through her closet for a dress she sensed he'd love.

It was the color of moonlight, soft and swirly, sexy without being blatant. To Gayla the dress symbolized love and happiness. She recalled the day she'd bought it nearly six years ago, not long before the trouble that nearly killed her had begun. She'd never worn it before — until tonight.

The fabric caressed her as she skimmed it over her body, the way she expected Dan to do after asking her to be his wife. Slipping on high-heeled sandals and draping a sheer shawl around her shoulders, she sat on the edge of the bed and opened up the photo album.

She'd always wished she could have known her grandparents, whose images stared up at her from the first two pages of the book. Her father's parents appeared reserved and stern, but Grandma and Grandpa Cohen looked as if they'd found fun in even the simplest pleasures.

They'd all died long before she was born, but Gayla remembered how her mother used to tell her and Tess that they looked down on them from heaven. When she closed the album and looked at her mom and dad's wedding picture on the cover, she felt her mother's presence.

"Mom?"

"I'm here, baby."

"I think Dan is going to propose. Should I marry him?" Gayla paused, searching the gentle face in the photograph. "I could hurt him so…"

"I think you'd hurt your young man more if you told him no. I've been watching you together. I'd say you've found something rare and wonderful."

Was this really her mother talking to her from somewhere in the spirit world? Or was Gayla only hearing what she wanted to hear? She didn't know. "Are you really here — there?"

"I'm here — well, sort of. I can see you. Talk with you, which I understand is not that common. I haven't figured out how to let you see me, though."

"Where are you? How…"

"I don't know how, honey. I'm in heaven. For a long time now, I've been able to see you, feel your joy and pain. I guess when I want to talk with you badly enough, I just…can."

Suddenly Gayla felt her mother leave, as though something had jerked her back into the spirit world. Paging through the album while she waited for Dan, she recalled the good times Mom had recorded there. For the first time, the memories didn't trigger the ripping, painful knowledge that she'd thrown all this away.

When Dan arrived, he looked good enough to eat. His pale blue shirt and paisley tie set off a tropical-weight gray suit with faint pinstripes of a dark grayish blue. He also looked tired, Gayla noticed when he stepped back after greeting her with a kiss. Tired — and troubled.

The faint lines around eyes that didn't sparkle as brightly as usual, the tight set of his jaw, and the distinct lack of passion in his kiss told Gayla something was wrong. But then he smiled and hugged her, and she told herself her first impression had not been on target.

They went to the restaurant she'd chosen, chatting about everything except what was foremost on Gayla's mind while they waited for their meal and as they ate. Her excitement built when a waiter brought her one perfect rose, and her heart started beating in double time when Dan sent a request for some special song to the piano bar.

She'd felt something small and square in his inside jacket pocket when he hugged her earlier, and she longed for him to bring it out and make this the happiest day of her life. Mesmerized by the sound of a slow lovers' melody and the seductive timbre of Dan's voice, she met his gaze.

She saw love. Instead of the joy she expected, though, she saw pain in his sober expression. "What's wrong?" she asked, but she thought she knew. His love had to be warring with fear that she was not as she appeared, but as she'd been before she began her long journey back from hell.

"Nothing. I was just thinking how much I love you." Hesitating so briefly Gayla barely noticed it, he moved his hand inside his jacket, then withdrew it, empty.

What was he thinking when he took her hand and brought it to his lips? Was he suffering as much as she, wanting them to commit to each other yet afraid of a future full of uncertainty?

"I love you, too." She wondered if he wanted to hear those words right now, since he obviously must be having second thoughts about his sanity because he'd fallen in love with her.

For the first time, Gayla felt awkward with Dan—so uncomfortable that she welcomed the strident beeping of his cell phone. He dropped her off to wait alone at his condo while he rushed to the hospital, and there she felt as if the walls were closing in on her.

She had to get away. She'd promised Dan she'd stay, though, so she paced the floor, circling the conversation pit where she'd sobbed out her sad tale. Her gaze wandered to the bar in the corner.

Rows of bottles stood in front of the mirrored wall, their reflections taunting. She could almost hear that Texas fifth of Jack Daniel's inviting her to sample it as she inched closer to temptation. A blue-label Smirnoff bottle called out, taunting her with its graceful, slender lines and memories of forgetful times they'd shared. She paused when she saw the fat bottle of Chambord in its metal filigreed jacket, recalling how it gave a deceptively fruit-juice-like taste to vodka and added its distinctive flavor to the concoction someone had named Sex on the Beach.

The voices coming from the bottles sounded strangely like Gayla's own. She stepped up to the bar and reached for a crystal tumbler. Her conscience stinging now, she set the glass down and took another look at the bottles that promised oblivion.

Most of them still had intact seals. That didn't surprise Gayla. She imagined Dan kept the booze for guests, not for himself, since she'd only seen him take one drink. That, she recalled, had been at the hospital's benefit party before he brought her here. Before she told him about her addictions.

Tears flowed in rivulets down her cheeks when she recalled her father's harsh expression that awful night. Her eyes stung from the salty fluid when she brushed a hand across them. Feeling utterly defeated, Gayla reached into the small ice machine built into the bar and fished out a handful of cubes.

They tinkled when they hit a crystal glass. What to drink? There were all those bottles, their various colors reflecting off the mirrors and tantalizing her with the power of forgetfulness they held. Jack Daniel's taunted her with his possibilities, practically shouting out in the silence that he was already open. Available.

She picked him up, noting that someone had already sampled his wares. In slow motion one hand wrapped around the cool, narrow neck while the other grasped the cap and twisted it counterclockwise until it came off, releasing the distinctive aroma of cask-aged corn whiskey.

Not Gayla's first choice but so much more civilized than the rotgut she used to toss down by the bottle as she neared bottom, the whiskey settled slowly over the ice cubes when she tilted the bottle. Half a glass. That's all she'd pour, she told herself as she watched the amber liquid slowly fill the glass.

As if she were outside herself looking on, Gayla capped the bottle and replaced it on the shelf. Then she turned and lifted the tumbler, her nostrils flaring at the familiar smell of the liquor. She brought it to her lips, then set it down.

Frantic to get away before she destroyed all she'd worked for, Gayla scrambled around to locate a pen and paper. Settling uneasily at the bar, oblivion within easy reach, she began to scribble a note.

When she finished she propped it against the untouched drink and hurried outside, pausing only to ask the doorman to order her a cab. On the long ride home she wondered if she'd run away from Dan — or herself.

She needed a friend. No — she needed her mom.

* * * * *

Dan's head pounded as if someone had taken a hammer to it. His mouth felt fuzzy, and he was certain his eyes must have looked like road maps. He couldn't help limping because his swollen stump felt as though it were in a vise, and his stomach ached for food. Still, he could hardly wait to strip down and crawl in bed with Gayla.

Being as quiet as he could to keep from waking her, he made his way through halls that weren't really dark since it was already morning. He sank onto his bed, noticing only after getting his second wind that Gayla wasn't there. Groaning, he retraced his steps to the living room. No Gayla there either.

Dan rubbed his gritty eyes. There on top of the bar, propped against a sweating glass full of what he guessed was whiskey, was a folded note.

When he left the hospital after working all night over a teenage girl who had died from internal hemorrhaging that the general surgeon hadn't been able to control, he'd thought his day had nowhere to go but up. After all, it had hardly been an auspicious beginning to perform successful surgery only to have the patient die.

Apparently he'd been wrong. Taking the note, Dan limped back to his bedroom, setting it on the bed before starting to undress. He shed the scrubs he hadn't bothered to change out of, then released his prosthesis and eased it off. Gingerly he rolled down the stump sock and silicone sleeve, wincing at the sting from blisters inevitable after wearing his prosthesis for twenty-six hours straight.

Grabbing Gayla's note, Dan hopped to the bathroom and turned on the Jacuzzi jets in the hot tub that he'd filled and heated earlier with lascivious thoughts of sharing it with her. Easing himself onto one of the built-in seats, he let the swirling water work its magic on his tortured flesh.

Tears came to his eyes as he read what Gayla had written:

Dan,

I'm leaving now. No, not now, but in a few minutes. I'm starting to want so much of you and from you, and it's tearing me up inside.

You have no idea how hard I'm trying not to pick up this drink and toss it down my throat, or what it's like never to know when I'm going to start tumbling back into hell. If I'm going to survive, I can't let myself feel too much or want too much, and I find that's exactly what I do when I'm with you.

We both knew from the start that our relationship couldn't be more than temporary — that the fantasy couldn't become anything lasting or real. Not because of you, but because of me, love. It's gone too far, and if we don't stop it now it's going to tear me apart again, because we both know our love can't survive.

You want me, yet I see in your eyes that you're afraid. You couldn't not be, as much as you stand to lose when your colleagues start questioning your good sense because you love a woman who has been places, done things that will make her forever suspect in their minds.

I'm afraid, too, Dan. Afraid that if we don't stop this flirting with disaster now, I'll be right back where I started all those years ago, living for the next drink — the next snort of coke.

Please stay away and let me try to heal. Fall in love again with someone who won't wreck the life you've made for yourself, and be happy. Part of me will always love you, more than I've ever loved before.

Gayla

Dan wadded the letter into a ball and hurled it against the bathroom wall. By setting her up for a proposal, then backing off because he was too proud to tell her if he didn't have to that the fucking cancer might have taken more than his leg, he'd made her think he changed his mind because of *her*.

Climbing out of the tub, he grabbed a towel and dried off, leaning against the wall in deference to his exhaustion. He made his way to the bed and sat on the edge, glancing at the clock as he picked up the phone. "Hell."

It was already seven o'clock, and he had office appointments beginning at eight. Instead of punching in Gayla's number, he called the office and told the sleepy receptionist to reschedule his patients. Damn! Why had he agreed to take calls for Frank?

He knew why. He'd thought his partner deserved a wedding night—and he'd hoped there would be no calls to keep him from spending *his* night with Gayla. Now Dan had made one hell of a mess, and he couldn't reach Gayla to try to make it right.

Too physically exhausted to stay up yet too emotionally charged to sleep, Dan stretched out on the bed and forced his eyes to close.

Chapter Thirteen

The Ghosts

A none-too-gentle hand clamped tightly over Sylvia's mouth, and another hand encircled her wrist to drag her away from Gayla.

"Sylvia, you ninny! You were on the verge of letting your daughter know we got together and arranged for her and Danny to fall in love. You'd have ruined all we've been planning."

"I was?" She paused, recalling the conversation that Ruth had so rudely interrupted. *"I guess I was. Thanks for keeping me from spoiling everything."*

Ruth shrugged. *"Let's leave them alone for a while. Give him a chance to give her the ring. Come on. My sister wants us to play bridge with her tonight."*

Several hours later, after Ruth's sister and mother-in-law had floated off to bed, Sylvia and Ruth looked in on Danny's condo.

"What has Gayla done? I've never seen Danny so distraught." Ruth's voice rose, as if she were about to scream.

"I don't know." They'd seen Dan pick up a note he'd found propped up against an untouched drink. Whatever it said had brought tears to his eyes, made him crumple the paper and heave it across the room. Sylvia wouldn't have thought him capable of such fury if she hadn't seen it with her own eyes.

"Well, do something. We can't let her hurt Danny like this."

"What can we do?"

Sylvia thought she might get a better idea of what was going on, if only Ruth would calm down so they could check on

Gayla. The other ghost, though, flatly refused to leave her son alone.

"Ruth, please. Let me try to talk to Gayla."

The other ghost stared at Danny, almost as if she were in a trance. Only when he'd stripped down to his underwear did Ruth finally let them leave him. When Ruth turned to Sylvia, her expression was bleak. *"I can't reach Danny. I can't make him hear me, no matter what I do. I wish—"*

"Let's look in on Gayla." She wasn't at her apartment. Concentrating, Sylvia located her sitting in her office by the pool deck, staring out a window and looking as if she'd lost her only friend.

"There she is. Looks as though your daughter fought a battle with the bottle and lost," Ruth observed when she looked at Gayla's tear-ravaged face.

Sylvia couldn't prevent her tears from falling. Her baby looked more devastated than Dan had, if that were possible. Gayla's expression mirrored pure, hopeless sorrow. *"Gayla hasn't been drinking. Alcohol always made her laugh. That's why she used it, I guess—to take away hurt too deep to bear."*

Ruth stared at Gayla for a long time. *"You're right,"* she finally said. *"Whatever it was that Gayla wrote to Danny, it left her as miserable as he is."*

"What could it have been?"

Ruth settled onto a chair. *"Let's try to figure this out. I think we can safely assume that Gayla broke off their affair. Could she be holding out for marriage?"*

"That's ridiculous. They've been sleeping together since the night of that silly banquet—the one you arranged them to go to. The one where Eli made my Gayla feel like dirt again, I might remind you."

Ruth snorted. *"Danny wouldn't—"*

"Your Danny would. And did. Ruth, your son is thirty-four years old. Do you seriously believe he spends the night with a woman he's attracted to and doesn't have sex with her?" Sylvia paused,

amazed at the look on the other ghost's pale face. *"You do, don't you? You believe your son is still a virgin."*

"Y-yes. I taught him to respect women." Ruth's expression softened, and she smiled. *"I guess I'm the kind of mother who likes to bury her head in the sand. I don't like to think of Danny having sex without the benefit of marriage, any more than I enjoyed knowing when he was a boy that he played baseball and several other sports I'd forbidden him to try."*

"What?"

"If I didn't know he was taking risks, I wouldn't worry about his getting hurt — so I pretended not to know."

Ruth's explanation smacked of self-deception on a level not even Sylvia had practiced when she was alive. But she'd let it pass for now. *"All right. So we know Danny and Gayla have been having sex, and that Gayla has apparently backed off from the relationship. What can we do?"*

"We could wish they'd get back together. I say we wait. See what happens. Maybe they'll work whatever the problem is out all by themselves."

Sylvia nodded. *"Let's give them two weeks. If they haven't worked it out by then, we'll have to give them another nudge. I'm going to see if I can reach my baby again, though. I can't bear to see her hurt like this."*

Chapter Fourteen

ಸಿ

Dan felt as if someone had punched him when he opened his eyes and realized it was nearly noon. Rolling over, he checked his messages. Nothing. Gayla hadn't returned his call.

He could go to her, explain that his fear had everything to do with himself and nothing to do with her. By doing so, though, he'd be asking her to commit to him without knowing if he couldn't give her a baby. He had to know for sure before he could face Gayla again. Better that she think he was the world's biggest jerk than that she condemn herself to a life without kids of her own.

Grabbing his wallet off the nightstand, Dan rifled through it, finally finding the card Jim had given him the night before. His fingers trembling, he dialed Greg Halpern's number.

"He's *where*?" Damn it, what was Halpern doing, taking off for two weeks at the time Dan needed him most?

The bubbly feminine voice on the other end of the line explained that Dr. Halpern's wife was in labor and that he, Dan, might locate the doctor at the hospital if it were truly an emergency. Turning down her friendly offer of an appointment some two months in the future, Dan hung up and shook his head.

He knew Halpern from somewhere. Suddenly, as he was getting dressed, Dan remembered. The "fertility god," as Jim had good-naturedly called him, was the uncle-by-marriage of one of Dan's favorite patients.

Settling on the edge of the bed again, Dan flipped through an address book. Moments later, after a call to his patient's helpful mom, and another to Halpern who invited him to come on over to labor and delivery so they could talk, Dan was on his way to meet with the other doctor. If he were lucky, he'd get to congratulate a new father — and find a few answers to his questions.

* * * * *

Hardly limping now after a few hours' rest, Dan strode into unfamiliar territory. Moans and occasional outright screams greeted him as he went farther into the labor and delivery suites someone had decorated in pink and blue. Quickly he approached the nurses' station and asked for Dr. Halpern.

"Dan. Good to see you again!"

Pink scrubs didn't make Greg Halpern appear any less formidable, Dan thought as he shook hands and exchanged pleasantries with the man he'd only known before as Timmy Tanner's concerned uncle. "They making you wear pink now?" he asked, pretending an interest in something other than the question that had made him seek Greg out.

"These are for expectant fathers. The docs wear blue. Sandy's labor is going pretty slowly now. Actually my partner Josh Levine kicked me out of the labor room. He says I make him nervous."

"Your first?"

"Second. First for Sandy, though. No matter how many times you do it, it's always a miracle. Terrifying, too, if it's your own kid." Greg grinned, as if poking fun at himself. "What's your problem?" He settled into a chair in the corner of the doctors' lounge and motioned for Dan to join him.

Dan sat down. He felt like examining his hands in minute detail, but instead he met Greg's curious gaze. "I want to know if I'm sterile."

"What makes you think you might be? Other than a blessed absence of paternity suits, of course."

Dan took a deep breath. "I had a round of chemotherapy when I was nine years old."

The grin on Greg's face disappeared, replaced by a half-frown. "What for?"

"Osteosarcoma. Left ankle. No evidence of metastasis before or after the amputation."

Greg shook his head. "Do you know what drugs they used?"

"No. Neither of my parents had a medical background. I doubt they ever asked. If they did, they didn't share that knowledge with me. The records might be available from the hospital — Parkland."

"That's okay. Just thought you might know. Whatever they used could have caused some damage. Besides, I can get results back from the slow but oh-so-thorough lab I use, a hell of a lot quicker than I can extract twenty-five-year-old information from Parkland's medical records department. Why don't you just meet me at my office about six tomorrow? Assuming Sandy and our boy are doing well."

"Okay. Just what does this testing entail, and how long will it take before you know?"

"Depends on how fast my tasteful collection of porn flicks and skin magazines gets you ready to produce a sample — unless, of course, you'd like to bring your significant other to take care of the foreplay. I make a quick slide and put it under my electron microscope, and I can tell you then and there if you're shooting blanks. If I see possibilities of a future fat OB fee, I send the rest of the sample to the genetics lab. The full battery of tests takes about ten days for the lab to run."

"Why? You said you could tell right away if the sample's got sperm." That was all Dan needed to know, before he got on his knees and begged Gayla to forgive him.

Greg leaned back as though his wife's labor had taken a lot out of him. "Might as well know the whole story…"

"Dr. Halpern!"

"Wait here, I've got to see what's going on." With that Greg charged out of the room.

Dan leaned back and propped his legs on the cluttered cocktail table in front of him. Two weeks, more or less. Eleven days before he could ask Gayla to marry him, if by some miracle the results of Greg's tests assured him he could give her the children he knew she'd want.

He reached for the phone, anxious to hear her voice. For the fourth time he got no answer at her apartment and nothing but the damn message machine at her office. "Damn it, pick up the phone," he said irritably, pausing a moment before asking, "Please call me, Gayla."

When his cell phone vibrated in his pocket a few minutes later, Dan snatched it up, certain Gayla would be on the line—if only to chastise him for the rude comment he'd just made. Instead, the message sent him sprinting for the ER.

* * * * *

"Dan, do something. They won't let me in there or tell me anything." Michelle clutched his shoulders, as if she had to have something solid to hang onto.

"What happened?"

"The damn fool tripped over a garden hose and fell into the pool. God only knows how long he was under before the housekeeper found him. Dan, Frank may be dead."

Dan nudged Michelle into a chair in the waiting room. "Calm down, sweetheart. Remember your baby. Frank will be all right." He had no idea whether that was true, but if she didn't calm down, he was afraid she'd need the ER's services as much as Frank apparently did.

"Go in there. You're a doctor. They can't keep you out."

Dan got up. "Okay. You sit right here and try to stay calm. You don't want to make yourself sick. Frank's going to need you."

Seeing his friend lying still as death, his chest moving in time to the rasping sound of a mechanical respirator, hit Dan hard. "You damn fool!"

"Hey, Dan. Grogan's a lucky man. Rescue squad got to him in time. Just barely from the look of him." Al Walters, the chief of the ER physicians' group, didn't sound overly concerned.

"Will he be all right?" Frank didn't look anywhere near all right to Dan, but then treating drowning victims hadn't been part of his training. He guessed Al saw cases like this nearly every day.

Al looked up and met Dan's gaze. "He's taken in a lot of water."

"Can he breathe on his own?"

"Yeah. This is just a precaution. I'll take him off the ventilator in a few minutes, after his lungs get a bit of rest. He has aspiration pneumonia. Pretty much inevitable after a near drowning."

"You're admitting him?"

"Yeah. He's going to be seeing the hospital from the other side for a few days. What the hell was he doing, anyhow? I thought he was on his honeymoon."

"He was. Michelle's outside, practically hysterical. What shall I tell her?"

"That somebody had better make this old boy learn to swim or keep him the hell away from any body of water bigger than a bathtub. This is the second time I've had him here, damn near drowned. Luck only goes so far, you know."

"Yeah." Dan hadn't been aware of Frank having a previous trip to the ER because of his personal war with water, but he couldn't help recalling the near-miss at Jim and Kelly's housewarming party. "I'll talk to Michelle."

He found her exactly as he'd left her, sobbing quietly on a chair in the corner of the waiting room. "Frank's going to be okay, honey," he told her as he pulled another straight chair next to hers.

"Thank God."

"Exactly. He won't be so lucky every time. As it is, he's going to be fighting pneumonia from this episode. Someone needs to make Frank learn how to swim. At the very least, he has to overcome the fear of water that makes him freeze up so he can't even help save himself. Maybe a shrink?"

Michelle dried her eyes and met Dan's gaze. "No. I'm not going to live in constant dread that he's going to fall in water somewhere or run his car into a lake or river, just because of his stupid phobia. He's going to learn to swim if I have to kill him to make him do it!"

"Spoken like a truly loving wife," Dan observed, chuckling.

"Well, I do love him! Not that I harbor any illusions that he feels that way about me."

"He married you. And he's looking forward to being a father again."

Michelle choked back a sob. "He sent me out to work this morning, said he'd spend the day working in my yard. You call that a sign of love, the first full day we've been married?"

This whole conversation was making Dan uncomfortable. *He* certainly couldn't imagine spending his first day as Gayla's husband anywhere except in bed. "Everybody shows their feelings differently."

"I'm going to arrange for him to have some swim lessons. Do you think Gayla—?"

"You'll have to ask her. I don't think Gayla and I are communicating at the moment."

"I will." Michelle paused a minute, as if digesting what Dan had said. "Can I help?"

"No. Thanks anyhow, but we'll have to work things out in our own way."

"Because of Frank's stupidity, you won't be having a lot of time to work things out right away, will you? Dan, I'm so sorry!"

"Don't worry about it." Until Michelle reminded him, Dan hadn't thought of the increased workload he'd be shouldering while Frank recuperated. "We'll reschedule his cases that aren't emergencies. It won't be all that bad." *Maybe.*

"How long is he going to be out of commission?"

"A week. Maybe two. My guess is Al will keep him in the hospital two or three days, if all goes well." Dan felt his cell phone vibrate, so he pulled it out. Maybe this would be Gayla returning one of his calls. "Newman here."

It wasn't Gayla, but it was a call he'd been expecting, just not so soon. Last night's surgery had not only been futile, but it had set in motion the bureaucratic process required when a patient died in the OR.

"I can be there in ten minutes," he told Old Ironsides' secretary before hanging up. Apparently Ironsides wanted to rake him and the other participants over the coals privately before convening what staff members not so jokingly called the Death Committee.

Considering how Eli Harris had hurt Gayla, Dan didn't want to see him at all, much less have him second-guess what could have been done differently to keep the unfortunate patient alive. Stalling the man, however, tended to make him more obnoxious than usual, so Dan chose not to delay.

"I've got to go see Dr. Harris," he told Michelle. "Al should be calling you in to see Frank soon."

"All right. Take care. I'm going to make that big lug get waterproofed." She stood, giving Dan a hug. "Thanks for coming."

"Any time."

Walking to Harris's office reminded Dan that he'd shown Gayla the way there the day they met. He forced thoughts of everything except last night's surgery from his mind when he opened the door and stepped into Ironsides' outer office.

* * * * *

"So, why did Allison Robbins die?"

Dan stared at the chart opened in front of Harris. Ironsides knew damn well why the teenager had died. Not daring to point that out, he said, "Massive internal hemorrhaging."

"From where?"

"The belly. A major artery."

Harris met Dan's gaze for the first time since he'd walked in and sat down. "The autopsy report indicates the renal artery was cut, not torn."

Taking the report, Dan scanned it quickly. "I'm surprised this is finished so soon."

"The girl's father is livid, to put it mildly, as well as crazed with grief. Bob Robbins is also a big contributor to the hospital. I thought it best to settle the cause of death expeditiously."

You would. Dan read the report again, more carefully this time. "Why am I here? This barely addresses my part in the surgery."

"You are here because I want to know what went on in that OR last night, and you were there. You—or rather your honeymooning partner Grogan—and Hap Randall were called in on the specific request of Mr. Robbins."

"What do you want to know?"

"Everything that isn't in your consult and operative reports." Handing Dan copies of reports that normally wouldn't have been transcribed for weeks, Harris demanded, "Do you usually dictate reports immediately? Even on an emergency case?"

You're not going to nail me on that. "I dictate during surgery. Always have. When my patient's unconscious, I do the same on a preliminary exam."

"All right. Let's go over this. See if you recall anything that isn't down in black and white. And, Newman, start at the beginning, before you even saw Allison Robbins."

Trying hard to hide his exhaustion, Dan scanned the report, then leaned back in the chair and looked at the chief.

"I got a call from the orthopedic resident around nine o'clock. He gave me her symptoms and advised that Ms. Robbins was losing blood at a fairly rapid rate from an incomplete crush amputation of her right thigh."

"What did you do?"

Damn it, the man was looking straight at the orders he gave Evan Cohen. "I told Cohen to have five units of whole blood typed and crossmatched. I also ordered surgical prep and pre-op medications."

"How much do you normally use in this type of case?"

"Blood? Normally around two units. I thought it best to order too much rather than too little."

"Did Cohen address the belly injuries with you?" Harris asked.

"Only to mention that there were some, that a general surgeon was being called, and that the ER resident had ordered x-rays."

"How long after you got this call did you arrive at the hospital?"

"Forty-five minutes."

Harris frowned. "Where the hell were you?"

"As I said, I was having dinner with a friend." *Gayla. I didn't know it at the time, but I was breaking her heart.* "I was not on call for the ER. The restaurant was out in Plano."

"So you strolled into surgery and went directly to work on Ms. Robbins' leg?"

Dan nodded. "I believe the operative report describes the procedure in adequate detail."

"It does." Harris sounded pained, as if he found this whole process distasteful. "Elaborate a bit more about how you came to end up being Randall's first assist when Ms. Robbins started bleeding out."

"There's no more to say than what I dictated. Randall asked for help. When I first observed the opened abdomen all I could see was blood. I held retractors and soaked up blood with sponges while Randall tried to locate the bleeder."

"Why was there no general surgery resident there?"

Dan pitied whoever had screwed up on that score. "I don't know."

Harris's fist came down on his desk hard, making papers shift around as if trying to evade his wrath. "Damn it, Newman, don't try to protect Hap Randall. You know as well as I that he refused the services of a resident."

"I'm not trying to protect anyone. I didn't arrive until after Randall had opened Ms. Robbins's belly. My primary concern was her crushed leg."

"You didn't think it odd that no general surgery resident had scrubbed in?"

Dan sighed. "From what I've heard, Randall doesn't like to work with residents."

"I don't imagine he cares to work on trauma victims, either, especially after last night. Pity Bob Robbins didn't know the big-shot surgeon he asked for by name specializes in overcharging rich patients for laser gallbladders and appendectomies."

Dan wasn't about to respond to *that*. "What do you want from me?"

"It was unnecessary for Allison Robbins to die. I want you to help me see that Hap Randall never gets the chance to do to someone else what he did to her."

"I don't know, sir." Harris was trying to put him squarely on the hot seat. "Randall must have cut an artery when he excised the damaged spleen, but I didn't see him do it."

"What did you see when you entered the OR?"

Dan met the older man's penetrating gaze, understanding that what he said now, he'd have to repeat to the Death Committee. "A patient who had suffered critical blood loss, apparently from the right femoral artery which had been severed approximately at the midpoint of the femur."

"What did you do?"

"Read my operative report."

Ironsides leaned back in his chair. "What was her condition when you closed your operative site?"

"She was stable."

"What were you doing when Randall called for help?"

"Preparing to do an open reduction of the patient's fractured left femur."

"You went to his aid immediately?" Harris asked.

"Yes. All I could see in the surgical field was blood. I asked Randall what to do."

Harris shifted in his chair. "Why?"

"Because the only time I ever performed surgery inside the abdominal cavity, I was in medical school and the patient was a cadaver." Dan thought he saw a hint of a smile on the chief's round face. When he realized Ironsides wasn't going to respond, he continued. "Randall said he needed more retraction, so I retracted. For a few minutes I did that and used sponges to soak up blood. It was pumping out so fast the suction machine couldn't make a dent in it. The anesthesiologist called for more blood, stat. Then the bleeding slowed down when the patient coded. The team tried everything, but we couldn't bring her back."

"What went wrong?"

Dan looked Harris in the eye. "All I know about general surgery came straight out of textbooks."

"You know enough to know patients don't stay stable and then suddenly hemorrhage to death from a cut artery that happened in an accident almost six hours earlier, don't you?"

"Yes, sir."

"Then that's what I expect you to say when we convene the Board of Inquiry—the Death Committee as most of you irreverent youngsters like to call it. Any questions?"

Dan stood up. "No questions. It surprises me that you want to see Dr. Randall disciplined."

"Sit back down. You and all the other young surgeons may hate my guts, but don't you ever believe I'll tolerate anything except top-quality surgery from anyone on this staff. That includes my own contemporaries. Randall screwed up; therefore he will pay."

Somehow Dan doubted Dr. Harris would have been as vehement had the unfortunate patient not been the daughter of one of the hospital's major contributors.

"Newman, I don't understand you," Harris said, punctuating his remark with a shrug of his rounded shoulders. "I still think you should have chosen a specialty less physically demanding than trauma surgery, but you've shown tremendous fortitude and succeeded beyond anyone's expectations. You're meticulous. Thoughtful. It appears that you're unflinching in your principles when it comes to medicine. Yet you choose to consort with a woman who has no values, no strength of character. One whose addictions could drag you into the gutter. Why? Does your being disfigured turn decent women away?"

Dan itched to climb across the desk and punch Ironsides out. "My personal business is none of your concern," he snapped, standing and turning to walk out.

"It is when you're sleeping with my daughter."

Ignoring his exhaustion, Dan whirled to face Harris. "According to you and Gayla, you disowned her. Turned your back on her when she needed you most. You forfeited any right you may have had to butt into—"

"So you are sleeping with her. I thought so."

"As I said before, Dr. Harris, you have no right—"

"You young idiot, I am trying to save you from sure disaster. I'm shaming myself to keep you from making a monumental mistake. Gayla is no good. She threw away every opportunity she was given—let herself and everyone who trusted her down."

"No. She let you down. Failed to get the Olympic berth *you* wanted her to have to feed *your* monumental ego. Proved she was human and not a puppet for you to manipulate."

"You're treading on dangerous ground." Harris's cheeks became mottled, and Dan noticed a vein beginning to throb at his right temple.

"Go ahead and spout your poison. There's no way you can persuade me Gayla's the monster you portray. She's beautiful, talented, and more fun to be with than anyone I've ever known. By tossing her out of your life, you've lost a whole lot more than she has."

"Damn it, boy, you've actually gone and fallen in love with her, haven't you?"

"Yes." Dan met Harris's incredulous gaze without flinching.

"How can somebody who graduated third in his class at Stanford Med be so goddamn stupid?"

Dan's tenuous hold on his temper snapped. "Same way the chief of surgery at a major teaching hospital can be so dumb and heartless as to kick his own kid when she's down because she doesn't quite reach the level of success he expected, I guess."

Harris slammed a fist on the desk again. "You know, I could ruin your career, myself, before I let you get so hung up with my loser of a daughter that *you* do it," he said through clenched teeth.

"Have at me. There are other places I can go, places where I won't have to deal with bastards like you. Places where Gayla won't be so close to memories that tear her up inside." Again Dan stood and made for the door. Ironsides wasn't going to corner him again.

"If you marry Gayla, you're asking for nothing but trouble." Whatever Ironsides said after that blurred into a muted bellow as Dan strode through his outer office into the hallway.

Chapter Fifteen

The Ghosts

☙

"Did you hear what he told Eli? Ruth, Danny loves Gayla."

"I heard. I also heard your miserable ass of a husband insult my Danny. The idea—suggesting that he can't find a proper woman because of his leg. Why, I'll have you know Danny had to chase girls away when he was in school. Sylvia, how did you put up with Eli Harris all those years?"

Sylvia shrugged. *"He was my husband. I never argued with him."*

"You spineless worm! If my Bernie had ever tried ordering me around the way Eli did with you, I'd have taken a rolling pin to him—if I'd been stupid enough to marry a man who thought he was God in the first place, which I certainly wouldn't have. What on earth made you want to marry Eli?"

"I thought he'd take good care of me," Sylvia replied in that sniveling tone that made Ruth cringe. *"Actually he did."*

"What? You call setting you up in a fancy house and buying you trinkets taking care of you?" Ruth couldn't believe that Sylvia, after all she'd seen of Eli Harris's brand of caring and what it had done to Gayla, still would defend the man.

"I loved him. And he loved me. I know he did."

"Did he love Gayla? I think not. If he had he'd have helped her when she was down instead of throwing her to the wolves. As a matter of fact, when he disowned your daughter, you should have left him and taken him for every cent he had. Maybe you'd still be alive, enjoying your girls, if you'd had even a hint of backbone."

Sniffling, Sylvia moved closer to the window. Ruth wondered uncharitably what her ghostly friend had ever seen in Eli. He reminded her of Humpty-Dumpty the way he sat perched on the edge of his desk, apparently reading some kind of papers. The way he'd attacked her son had her in a fine rage!

"Eli's worried."

"Too bad. That didn't give him any excuse to insult Danny. If I were you, I'd skin the rat alive for talking about Gayla as though she were worse than poison. I'd wish — "

"Ruth, don't!"

"Well, I would!" Frowning at Eli's rotund image, Ruth pondered just what form of torture she might inflict on him that might adequately repay him for maligning her precious son, and Gayla, she added a bit grudgingly. *"You should, too."*

"We can't use wishes to cause people harm," Sylvia reminded her.

"Don't try to save your precious husband. Why you'd want to is beyond me, anyway." When he shifted positions, Eli tottered on the edge of his desk as if he were about to roll off. Ruth didn't even try to suppress an impolite chuckle. *"Look! He's wobbling. God, but the man reminds me of an enormous egg with arms and legs. Humpty-Dumpty. I wish he'd fall off that desk and shatter, the way Humpty the egg did in that nursery rhyme Danny used to love! Remember? 'All the king's horses and all the king's men, couldn't put Humpty together again.'"* Ruth nearly doubled over laughing at the thought of that pompous ass getting his comeuppance.

"Oh, no. Ruth, now you've done it. With your vicious tongue you've wished harm on Eli. You know you didn't mean to do that."

Ruth managed to curb her laughing so she could calm her unwilling partner in crime. *"Old Eli may have brainwashed you, but he can't fool me. He needs a comeuppance."*

"We're not allowed to use wishes to harm people," Sylvia repeated as Ruth silently pondered how many people would be relieved if Eli Harris was out of commission for a while.

Chapter Sixteen

"You think just because I married you I put you in charge of my life?"

Michelle felt like screaming, but she resisted the urge. After all, other patients might have been trying to sleep. "You are going to learn to swim. Gayla's going to give you lessons as soon as you get home. It's arranged. A done deal. I'm not about to agonize over the likelihood that you'll eventually kill yourself, and I'm not taking out the pool."

"I didn't ask you to." Frank's voice still sounded raspy from having had a tube down his throat for nearly twenty-four hours. Apparently his near-death experience hadn't affected his perpetual scowl.

"So, are you going to give me trouble over this?"

"Will it make you back off and leave me the hell alone?"

"No. I've got a vested interest in you now. You persuaded me this baby's going to need a father. You talked me into marrying you. No matter why you did it, you're stuck. I'm your wife and I have no desire to become a widow any time soon."

A slow grin transformed Frank's face. "You're cute when you get mad."

Michelle sat on the edge of the bed and brushed her fingers through his hair. "Am I going to have to drag you, kicking and screaming, to your sessions with Gayla?" She liked the way Frank absently rubbed her thigh, as if confirming that they were progressing toward real intimacy from merely being friends and sometimes lovers. Smiling, she met his gaze.

"I'll give Gayla a shot. She won't be the first to fail, you know."

"You've tried before to get over being afraid of water?"

"More than once. Even tried a shrink for a couple of visits a few years back. He said my obsessive fear stemmed from having nearly drowned when I was little, which I had already figured out for myself. He tried to hook me for God only knows how many weekly sessions to cure me. I didn't think that would work. I hate being afraid, and if anybody could cure me of it, it would be me."

"But you're going to let Gayla try?"

"Yeah. Since she's so tight with Dan, I want to get to know her better anyhow. I just hope I don't drown her along with me. She's too damn tiny to be able to save me if I muster up the nerve to get into a pool on purpose." Frank gave Michelle's thigh a squeeze.

Needing more, she bent and gave him a quick kiss. "I worried about that, too. Gayla assured me she'd pulled out drowning guys as big as three hundred pounds. You've got a ways to go before you get there." She ran her hand suggestively down his rangy body.

"Stop that. You're getting me horny, and I'm under doctor's orders to rest."

"Really?"

Frank laughed out loud. "Yeah, really. It's amazing how fast you've gotten me used to having regular sex again. I can hardly wait for Al to spring me so we can crawl into that big bed in your room and get it on."

"Our room." Michelle said that lightly, but she wondered when if ever Frank would think of that room as theirs. She'd gambled when she accepted the proposal he made on account of their unborn baby. How long would it be before she knew whether she'd won?

"Your room, Shel. All that pink and all those ruffles definitely make me feel like a visitor." He paused as if he sensed his words had hurt her. "A very welcome visitor, honey. Don't get all honked off at me now. Not after you've badgered me into what I'm certain will be another humiliating experience, trying to overcome the terror I should have outgrown long ago."

What could she say? Michelle didn't know, so she simply smiled and kept on stroking the arm that Frank made no effort to move away from its resting place against her hip.

* * * * *

Gayla picked up the phone and dialed Dan's number, then put it down. He was never far from her mind, even when she slept. Especially then, when visions of his hard, fit body invaded her dreams. Just thinking about him had her wet and swollen, wanting him.

Wondering how he'd fared at the meeting with her father that Michelle had mentioned, and hurting for how she sensed he must feel after losing that patient, Gayla wished she hadn't agreed to give Frank those swimming lessons. Being with Dan's friends would make her task of forgetting him impossible—as if it weren't already.

Gathering her swim bag and keys and driving to Michelle's house, she made and discarded plans for helping Frank get over his fear. When he met her at the door, his skin clammy and his fingers trembling, she realized she'd set herself up for a daunting task.

"Michelle's out by the pool," he said as he led her toward the back of the house. If Gayla hadn't known better, she'd have thought Frank was on death row, on his final march to an appointment with whoever it was that gave the lethal injections.

After exchanging a few pleasantries with Michelle, Gayla turned to Frank. "Ready to get started?"

He looked as if he were going to have a heart attack. "Look, are you sure you can pull me out of the water by yourself? Maybe we should wait until Dan or Jim can come over—just to be safe."

Standing and setting her hands at her hips, Michelle stared Frank down. "No excuses. Gayla's perfectly capable of fishing your inept body out of the water if you should panic. If she needs help, I'm here. Go on. Get in the water. It's only three feet deep at this end." She stood up, as if she was prepared to shove her husband into the pool if he couldn't be coaxed to take the plunge on his own.

Gayla unfastened the wrap skirt she'd put on over her swimsuit and waded down the steps. "Come on, Frank." She practically smelled his panic when the water lapped across his feet. "Trust me. I will not let you drown."

His eyes dilated despite the brightness of the sun at noon, he took another step toward Gayla.

"Be calm," she told him again, meeting his terror with an illusion of confidence. Had she made a mistake, agreeing to do this? She couldn't recall ever having seen anyone so obviously terrified of water.

"Go on, Frank," Michelle urged from the deck, distracting Gayla just long enough for Frank to stumble into her, nearly knocking her down. Desperate to prove she wouldn't let him sink, she wrapped both arms around him until she felt his feet touch bottom.

"Okay. You're in the water now and you're still alive," she told him, trying for a casual tone. "Now stretch out on your back. I'll hold you up on my arms."

Frank's disbelieving expression told Gayla as much as the words he seemed unable to form.

"Come on. Trust me."

He kept staring at her, his features frozen.

"Trust me, Frank. More important, trust yourself. You'll float on top of the water if you'll just relax. Look." Praying Frank wouldn't decide at that moment that it was time for him to slip and go under, Gayla lay back and showed him a body indeed would float while still alive.

"How do you do that?"

So he'd finally decided to talk "By doing nothing. The water's doing all the work." She got back on her feet and walked in his direction. "You try it."

"No."

Damn it, this forty-something-year-old man was behaving like a recalcitrant child. So, she'd treat him like one. "Yes." She met his gaze with what she hoped was a show of her own stubborn will.

As if testing her, Frank backed toward the steps, only to slip and go down on his knees. Gayla stared at the mask of terror on the face that now rested only inches above the water.

"Take a deep breath and put your face in the water. When you need to breathe in again, bring your face back up."

Miraculously Frank did as she asked, coming up sputtering and coughing but very much alive. "There. That doesn't mean I'll be able to swim the English Channel next week, no matter what you may think. You, either," he added, twisting his head around to address Michelle.

"I'm trying for something simpler. And you will do it. By next week you'll be able to paddle across this pool." Gayla wondered again if she'd be able to help Frank achieve even this ridiculously simple goal.

For the next few days she spent two hours each afternoon, coaxing and cajoling, threatening and browbeating Frank into trusting himself enough to let the water's buoyancy support him. She felt as though she'd won the U.S. Open the first time he actually tried to move his hands and feet. The sixth day, when Frank managed to cross the pool doing an awkward elementary backstroke, Gayla was as proud as if she'd made the Olympic squad that had once been her primary goal.

That night when she got home, she nearly broke down and returned Dan's latest call.

* * * * *

With Frank back at work half days and his own schedule nearly back to normal, Dan had no more excuses to postpone the testing. If he didn't go on into Greg's office and get it over with, he'd have to admit he was too afraid of the results to go through with the tests. Dan refused to let fear rule him. Slowly he got out of his car, pausing to admire the lush foliage outside Halpern's impressive office building.

"How's the baby?" he asked Greg after saying hello.

"Perfect. Sleeps all day and screams all night." The grin on Greg's face erased the bite of his complaint. Dan guessed this man who made his living delivering other people's babies had to be thrilled with his own. "Come on, we'll get this show on the road." He led the way to an examining room and left Dan there.

An hour later Dan waited for the verdict in Greg's office, silently telling himself it didn't matter all that much. He'd survive without the ability to make a woman pregnant. After all, it's not as though he were impotent. Dan kept repeating that like a mantra, but it didn't stem the other voice that said he shouldn't ask a woman he loved to be his wife if he couldn't give her a child.

"Dan?"

Greg wore a guarded expression. Still Dan managed a greeting of sorts, and even a chuckle or two at the jokes Greg cracked.

"Want some coffee?"

At least Greg wasn't offering him hard liquor. Maybe there was hope yet. "No, thanks." He'd take his news straight up.

Greg sprawled on the chair opposite the sofa where Dan had sat down. "I'm sending the sample to the lab."

"Then there's something there?" Dan let out the breath he just realized he'd been holding.

"I see live sperm. The reports from the lab will give us an accurate count and motility analysis. Roll up your sleeve and I'll draw some blood. They'll do some more tests to see if they can find any nasty genetic markers."

As the needle pricked his skin, then jabbed a vein in his right wrist, Dan noticed Greg's sober expression. "You're not giving it to me straight, are you?"

"You aren't sterile. The lab's not going to report a very high sperm count, though. Unless I'm mistaken."

Dan met Greg's gaze. "What does that mean?"

"If the count's too low, it won't be easy for you to get a woman pregnant. It's not impossible, mind you, so don't come suing me if you suddenly find your significant other in the family way. It may be the lab's count will be well within normal range. I have no idea whether the slide I made is representative of the sample as a whole."

"What do you mean, it won't be easy?" Dan thought he knew, and the prospect didn't make him any too happy. Still, if he could give Gayla what she wanted he'd go through hell.

"Artificial insemination with fresh sperm. If that doesn't work after a few tries, you give me several samples over several weeks. I freeze them, then thaw them out, combine them, and spin the semen down to concentrate the sperm—and use that for the next insemination. If that doesn't work I can try direct injection of sperm into a fallopian tube—or in vitro fertilization."

"That's what I thought." While the prospect of providing multiple semen samples the way he had a few minutes earlier was singularly unappealing, it would beat never being able to father children.

"Doesn't sound like fun?"

"Not particularly."

Greg laughed. "Don't feel bad. Most of my male patients feel the same way you do."

"That's good to know."

"Well, we're through for now. Come on, I'll go out with you. I don't like leaving Sandy home alone with just the housekeeper and Tyler."

"That's your new son's name?"

Greg grinned like a fool as he dug in his wallet and produced a snapshot. "Meet Tyler Andrew Halpern. Most perfect kid I ever saw. Looks like me, don't you think?"

"Hmmm. He's dark like you. I think he's better looking, though."

"Gets that from his mom." Greg unlocked the back door, and they went out into the parking lot.

Dan pictured Timmy's young, blond aunt. "I've often wondered what she saw in you." Dan took another look at the photo. "Tyler does take after his mom, except for his hair and eyes."

Greg paused by Dan's car. "Come over and see him in person. Any time. Any friend of Timmy Tanner is a friend of mine. Give me a call in ten days or so, and we'll go over your lab results. Meanwhile don't take my word about your sperm count being low. And for God's sake take precautions if you crawl into bed with somebody unless you don't mind if she gets pregnant. Mother Nature sometimes does peculiar things. I'm just a damn good doctor, not God."

"Warning registered. Twice now. Don't worry, I won't sue you if I end up hearing I'm a prospective father this time next month." Sliding into the car, Dan adjusted the seat and started the engine. "Thanks for coming in today."

He was halfway home before it registered in his mind that he wasn't sterile. Whatever humiliating processes he might have to endure to give Gayla a baby, he'd do gladly to make her happy. He could go to her now, beg her to forgive him. Tell her his doubts were about himself, not her. He'd take that ring and put it on her finger.

Punching the accelerator to get around a line of slow traffic, Dan headed straight for the club. Gayla should be nearly finished with her last group of swimmers by the time he got there.

* * * * *

When he walked onto the deck, she was standing there alone, staring at the water.

"Hello, Gayla."

When she turned to face him, her arms went out, and she smiled — the most beautiful smile Dan had ever seen. Then her gaze met his and her smile disappeared. "Why did you come here?" Her voice was a voice of despair.

Once he'd waited for just the right moment, only to hesitate. This time he was determined to let her know without a doubt just what was on his mind. "Because I love you. I want you in my life. Damn it, Gayla, I want you to marry me."

He hadn't expected her to fall into his arms, not after he'd let her believe he hadn't proposed because of flaws she perceived in herself. Still, it tore at his conscience when she burst into tears.

"Princess, if the idea of marrying me is that ludicrous, you're should be laughing, not crying."

Instead she sank onto a cushioned chaise lounge and buried her face in her hands. Dan sat beside her, tentatively wrapping an arm around her quaking shoulders. "Hold me," she choked out between heart-wrenching sobs.

He held her, and she cried. Tears flowed until Dan felt their dampness through the soaked material of his shirt. The few minutes before she regained her composure seemed like hours.

Damn, he hated not knowing what to do. "I'm sorry. So sorry. Give me a shot at explaining my rotten self."

"You — you aren't rotten. You're the most wonderful man in the world, and I love you. That's why I can't screw up your life by marrying you. I want you, though, something fierce. My place?"

"Mine." That diamond ring was sitting in the dresser drawer, and Dan wanted to put it on her finger where it belonged. Maybe, just maybe, he could help her over her ridiculous notion that if she married him she'd ruin his life.

"Ready?" he asked, standing and holding out a hand, trying as he did not to think of the numerous other people who shared her fears. Her father, Frank, and a few others. They could take their opinions straight to hell. After all, he wasn't in love with any of them.

Chapter Seventeen

ೞ

"So tell me, how are my partner's swim lessons going?" Dan asked while he drove.

Frank's progress the last day or two had amazed Gayla. "He's coming along. Still doesn't like getting his head under, though. By the time he conquers that particular phobia, he may be a world-class backstroker." She loved the deep, rumbly way Dan laughed.

"Wow! You've actually got him swimming? I'd have thought you'd done a fantastic job if he could just paddle to the edge of the pool."

Gayla didn't kid herself into believing all Frank's success was entirely due to her expertise as a teacher. "Michelle and I have him badgered into taking lessons. Frank's the one who deserves the credit. You have no idea how hard it is to set aside real, overwhelming fear until you've done it."

Dan shot her a quizzical look, then turned his attention back to the road. "Yeah, princess, I've overcome that kind of fear. I came to you today after you said to stay away, and I was damn well terrified that you'd tell me to go to hell."

"Are you serious?"

"Yeah."

"I've missed you." How could she not have, when he'd visited her every night in her dreams? She feasted her eyes on him now, loved the way the setting sun backlit his handsome profile.

Gayla's heart beat faster as Dan turned the key in his front door, the door she'd slammed behind her when she'd felt the walls closing in around her. She was still afraid, but now she wanted more than she feared.

"You must not have planned this," she said when she went inside and glanced at the bottles still lined up behind the bar.

He squeezed her hand. "I didn't. Sorry the place is such a mess." Apparently his gaze followed hers to the bar because he suddenly turned serious. "I wouldn't have done anything with those even if I had made plans. You proved the other night that you don't need a keeper."

He had a lot more confidence in that than she did. But she *had* managed to resist temptation. "Thanks."

He sat on one of the sofas and pulled her onto his lap, stroking her back as though to calm her fears. His touch had her wet and needy. "Want to know why I got scared and backed off from proposing to you that night?"

"Not now." All she wanted at the moment was for Dan to stop this sensual torture and take her to bed. Twisting around to face him, she cupped his face between her hands. "I just want you."

"All in good time, love. Do you know how bad it made me feel to know you believed I'd had second thoughts about your past?"

Gayla nodded. "I think so. I've had plenty of experience at disappointing people by my mistakes." What she hadn't experienced before was anyone backing away from her because he believed himself somehow less than worthy.

"I can't imagine you thinking that I'd be losing out on anything because I love you," she murmured, but then she thought about his leg. If being an amputee pricked at his ego, he didn't show it. But then Gayla didn't go around advertising her insecurities for public consumption, either.

"Trust me. If what I thought had been true, you'd have lost out on plenty by saddling yourself with me."

Confused, Gayla met Dan's gaze. "I guess you'd better tell me, then. Let me tell you something first, though. I'd love you if you'd lost both legs. Both arms. So you'd best think up another story fast if you're planning to say you decided to save me from loving you because of this." She reached down and tapped the socket of his prosthesis the way he'd done for curious little Jeff when she took him to meet her sister's family.

"No. At least not specifically. I thought I might be sterile because of the chemotherapy I had after they amputated my leg."

"What?"

"It's a fairly common side effect of some of the drugs they use. They're controlled poisons, the idea being to kill the cancer cells without killing the patient."

"I know that. Are you telling me that all of a sudden you realized this and decided that instead of finding out how I felt about it, you'd just back off? I don't believe you."

"I guess I'd known the possibility for years, but it never registered in my mind. The day Michelle and Frank got married, I was thinking about us getting married, too. I stood there in the OR waiting for Jim to finish up our last case, picturing our kid playing with the ones he and Frank are expecting. That's when it hit me that there was a good chance I couldn't father a child." He paused, as if putting that fear into words had been harder for him than running a marathon. "I couldn't ask you until I knew for sure."

"Why not? Did you think it would matter to me? That I wouldn't love you if you couldn't give me babies?" Gayla felt tears forming again, and she fought to keep them from falling. She'd cried enough for one day.

Dan picked up her hand and stroked it. "The way you obviously love kids, I knew I wouldn't love myself if I condemned you to not having any."

"If I believed in myself enough to marry you, Dan, I'd do it in a minute. There are plenty of children I can love without them having to be my own."

"They can be, though. I'm not sterile."

Dan's smile drew Gayla in and made her want to put her arms around him and hug him, hard. "How do you know?"

"Because I got up the nerve to get tested."

"When?"

"Today."

So he'd taken the test and come directly to her. This man loved her so much he'd have given her up if staying meant he'd risk denying her what he thought she wanted. If she were as strong as he, she'd send him far, far away before she could fall off the wagon and destroy him. "Dan, you didn't have to."

Cupping a hand around her chin, he gave her a quick, hard kiss. "Yeah, princess, I did. I tell you, getting the sample was impossible until I concentrated on you. On remembering your gorgeous body and how I feel when you touch me. You're my addiction. I've got to have you to feel whole."

Gayla needed him, too, but unfortunately she couldn't afford another addiction. "I have enough addictions now, Dan. I can't afford to drag you into my life and risk hurting you when I can't resist them any longer."

"You hurt me when you refuse to let me in."

She knew what he couldn't possibly comprehend — that the demons within her could overpower her own fragile will at any time, with any trigger. Just as he could overpower her with the sweetest love she'd ever known. "Dan, I want to let you in. I'm so afraid — afraid I'll drag you down. Afraid people's disgust with me will rub off on you. Damn it, I'm scared stiff that I'll fall off the wagon again and destroy us both."

"So you want us to say good-bye?"

Gayla traced the hard line of his jaw with her fingers. "I'm not that strong. I want to be with you for as long as you want me."

"That will be forever." Pulling her close, Dan sealed that promise with a hard, deep kiss. "So why won't you marry me?"

"Because I don't trust myself enough to risk hurting you. Can't we be together without strings—without lifelong promises I'm not certain I can keep?"

"I want you any way I can have you, princess. If you insist, I'm willing to live with you in sin for a while. I'm not willing to spend another night without you in my bed—or me in yours. Without you I feel as though I'm missing part of myself."

He'd give her space, and she'd give him time to realize she was no good for him—not the woman he needed by his side, and certainly not the woman who deserved to bear and raise his babies. Gayla laughed. "Come on, Doc. Let's go to bed. I'm anxious to examine certain parts of you in minute detail."

* * * * *

He set her down beside the bed and shrugged off the shirt she'd unbuttoned while he held her in his arms. The hungry look in her eyes got his cock hard and throbbing, and when she released the snap and zipper on his pants he scrapped his original plan to drive her slowly nuts before giving it her the fucking she'd asked for.

He stepped out of the pants and kicked them away before lifting the hem of the long, loose dress she was wearing and pulling it off over her head. God, but she was beautiful, more so even than in his memories. The black competition swimsuit she wore gave him a moment's pause. Skin-tight and none too giving, it resisted his gentle attempts to get it off her.

"Like this," she told him, crossing her hands and grabbing the straps on each shoulder. He watched her tug the suit down inch by inch, revealing her satiny breasts, her flat belly, and finally the dark curls that shielded her pussy from his searching gaze. His balls aching and heart pounding as she bent and worked the tight material down her gorgeous legs, he shed his briefs.

She went down on her knees while he stood there, naked except for shoes, socks, and his prosthesis. At first he thought she meant to take it off.

Her touch on his inner thighs sent a fresh rush of blood to his cock, and when she cupped his scrotum gently in both hands he damn near came. Her damp warm breath tickled him, and he got harder yet. The touch of her tongue on his swollen flesh almost made him explode, and when she took his cock and began sucking it, he felt like crying for mercy.

Closing his eyes and concentrating on the incredible wet warmth of her mouth, the softness of her hands as she squeezed the base of his cock, Dan laced his fingers through her hair. He trembled at each damp puff of her breath that tickled his belly when she exhaled. Her hair felt soft as silk against his fingers. No one had ever loved him quite like this, with such care, such abandon. Her swallowing motions had him ready…but he wanted the pleasure to go on forever.

Damn it, he wanted to taste her, too. But she had him so hot, he'd come like a shot the minute he touched his tongue to her hot, slippery cunt and then it would all be over. Sinking his fingers into her hair, he lifted her off his cock. "Enough, princess."

Dan sat on the edge of the bed and pulled her onto his lap. He bent his head and sucked her nipples after she sank onto his cock and began to move.

Every contraction of her inner muscles dragged him closer to the edge. Needing more, he strained upward, as though he could propel his entire being into the comfort of her womb. God but she felt good, so tight and hot. Pressure built in his balls with every thrust, each greedy squeeze of her inner muscles on his cock as he pulled out. Gayla's pants and whimpers fed his need, and when she wrapped her legs and arms even tighter around him, he could barely hold back.

Then her pussy clamped down hard, spasming wildly against his cock. She let out a little scream, dug her nails into his shoulders and back. Dan drew back and thrust one last time, collapsing against her chest as he came long and hard and deep. The swirling sensation of his semen squirting against the wet, hot tip of her cervix was like nothing he'd ever felt before. Spent, he groaned and fell back onto the bed.

When he recovered enough to think, Dan discovered Gayla resting against his chest, her pussy still cradling his cock inside its warm, wet walls. Rolling her over with him, he withdrew and sat for a long time on his knees, just looking at this woman who turned him inside out and made him forget everything but loving her.

"Hi." Her eyelids fluttered and opened, and when she met his gaze she smiled. "You forgot something."

"What?"

"Your leg. You forgot to take it off."

Dan grinned. "I did, didn't I? You have a delightful way of making me forget everything except getting inside you, princess. Thank you."

"My pleasure. Believe me." Gayla stretched out across the bed like a contented kitten and patted the spot beside her. "C'mon. Hold me. Let me go to sleep feeling your heart beat close to mine."

Dan grinned. "Just a minute. If I don't take this prosthesis off, I'd likely kick you with it in my sleep. Don't want to put bruises all over your gorgeous legs. Not to mention that I'd be limping for a couple of days if I left it on all night." He scooted to the edge of the bed and methodically removed the prosthesis, sock, and sleeve—but when he reached to slip off the condom, his penis was bare.

He hadn't put one on. At first he panicked before recalling Greg's prediction that it might take unnatural means for him to get Gayla pregnant. "Princess," he admitted as he lay back and gathered her in his arms, "I forgot to protect you."

"I know." She didn't sound upset.

"You don't mind?" He didn't—not at all. But he couldn't dredge up the words to reassure her the chance of his getting her pregnant by fucking with him was probably slim.

She snuggled tight against his chest. "No. I should, but I don't mind. I love the feel of you inside me with nothing between us."

"Me, too. But I won't forget again. I'd rather our kids be born at least nine months after I marry their mother."

* * * * *

"All I do is sleep," Michelle complained, yawning as she let Gayla in. "Frank just got home. He's changing clothes."

Gayla smiled. She didn't envy Michelle her pregnancy as much today as she had before spending the night in Dan's arms again. Being with him again had left her with a warm glow that wouldn't go away, no matter how often she told herself she was soon going to have to walk away.

"He's back to work already?" Gayla had thought that after his brush with death, Frank would give himself more time to recuperate.

"Half days. Next week he'll resume his regular schedule. That ought to give you more time with Dan. Poor guy, he's been doing his work and Frank's while Frank has been lazing around and taking swim lessons." Michelle grinned. "I thought so. You two are back together, aren't you? I can see it in your eyes."

Gayla shrugged, but she felt the corners of her mouth turn up in a silly grin. "For the time being. Nothing permanent." It hurt when she said it, but she wasn't into fooling her friends any more than she believed in deceiving herself.

"I can't believe you're not jumping at the chance to be with Dan. He's one of the nicest guys I've ever met—good-looking, too. Gayla, he loves you. I've never seen him so crazy over a woman before."

Just then Frank came in. "What was that you said about good-looking guys?"

"We were talking about Dan." Michelle got up and gave him a hug, making Gayla ache for Dan's touch.

"So, Gayla, are you ready to put my partner out of his misery?"

She forced a laugh. "Nothing as permanent as that. We're just enjoying each other's company for as long as it lasts."

"If you say so. If I read Dan right, he's looking for more than that with you. Come on, let's get this ordeal over with," Frank said, heading for the patio door.

The lesson went much better than Gayla had expected. Frank finally seemed to be coming to grips with his fear of going underwater. By the time they climbed up the pool steps, she felt confident that after a few more lessons it would be safe to leave him alone in the vicinity of water.

"Could we talk for a minute?" Frank asked as Gayla was slipping a terry cover-up over her swimsuit.

She nodded and sat down, hoping it wasn't her relationship with Dan that Frank wanted to discuss. She didn't feel up to that, not when her conscience was fighting so hard against her emotions. Frank pulled another chair up to the umbrella table and sat down, stretching his long legs out and crossing them at the ankles. He didn't say anything right away, which added to Gayla's discomfort.

"Have you ever thought about setting up an aquatic rehab program?" he finally asked.

Gayla couldn't have been more surprised if he'd asked if she ever thought about becoming a surgeon. "College dropouts don't get very far dealing with medical professionals," she replied before she could stifle the words.

"You dropped out?"

"My senior year at SMU. I thought Daddy had made sure the entire Dallas community knew that. To be precise about it, I'm sixteen credits short of having a bachelor's in kinesiology. Not that the bachelor's would have made me much more marketable than I am now. I'd planned to get a master's in physical therapy before…"

"Before everything came tumbling down around your pretty shoulders, as Dan once put it so eloquently?"

Apparently Frank wasn't interested in the details of her downfall. Gayla wasn't anxious to relate them to him anyhow. "You might say that."

"Well, you've got a hell of an ability to teach psychos like me to swim. I thought you might be interested in setting up a program to work with kids and adults who have real physical problems. Michelle and I have been talking about adding an aquatic program to our rehab facility for a long time, and we were getting ready to implement it the beginning of next year. Now with the baby coming, she isn't going to have time to set the program up."

Gayla couldn't believe her ears. Frank Grogan, who she'd have sworn considered her a menace to society before she started these lessons with him, apparently trusted her to establish a swimming regimen for his patients. "What does Dan think about my doing this?"

"He doesn't know yet." Frank's solemn gaze held Gayla's. "At least he doesn't know yet that I'm asking you to get the program going. Michelle and I have talked it over with Jim and Kelly. We have no doubt that Dan will be happy to have you on board."

Gayla loved coaching the children and teenagers at the club, but if she did as Frank was asking, she could really help heal people—almost as if she'd gone on to become a physical therapist as she'd once planned. "What about my coaching job?" she asked, hating the idea of giving it up.

"This job should only require about twenty hours a week of your time, at least for the first few years. You'll hire swim instructors to do most of the actual teaching. I see no reason that you couldn't keep on coaching the club team. Your boss there, by the way, can't say enough nice things about you."

Gayla wished the pompous manager would say some of those nice things to her occasionally, instead of constantly whining that she was alienating the parents of some of the swimmers. She also wished someone would pinch her so she'd wake up. "You're sure you want me to do this?"

"Positive. Since Michelle's certified in aquatic physical therapy, she will be nominally in charge. You'll have free rein, though, to set up the group classes. Dan or I, and occasionally Jim, will prescribe specific water exercises for patients, and you will make sure our orders are carried out."

"I don't know. I'll have to talk with Dan. He may not like the idea of me working for him." That was the first excuse that came into her mind, but not the only reservation she had about taking on what would be a very real challenge.

Frank laughed. "Newman will be thrilled. Our group is rife with nepotism. Always has been, even before Michelle and I got married. Think of it this way, Gayla. For at least four hours every day, he'll know exactly where you are and what you're doing."

Gayla laughed out loud, but that last remark disturbed her. Did Frank think she needed watching twenty-four, seven? No. She was being paranoid. Just because Frank hinted that Dan would enjoy knowing her whereabouts was no reason to assume he was thinking that during those four hours each day he could feel pretty certain she wasn't somewhere falling off the wagon.

"I see I've taken your breath away. Think about it. I believe you'll find it rewarding to help people overcome their handicaps by doing what you do so well. And we need you. This is no made-up job, Gayla. Remember that. You're not getting this offer because of Dan. You've got it because I believe that since you've done miracles with me and my phobia, you can do just as much for my patients."

Gayla didn't know what to say. She could do this. She knew she could. Something inside her wanted to shout, "Yes!" while that doubt born of past failures and weaknesses made her want to run as fast as she could away from this latest opportunity to prove herself a loser.

"I'll think about it, and talk with Dan. I appreciate your asking me, and I'll let you know. Soon." With that Gayla got up and left.

* * * * *

"Take the job, Gayla. You want it. You can barely wait to see how you can help people regain part of what they've lost."

She'd told Dan when he came to pick her up about Frank's offer, and he'd barely been able to conceal his surprise. He guessed she'd wound his partner around her finger almost the same way she'd taken over his thoughts and dreams.

"I'm going to. As long as you're sure you don't mind." She rubbed her cheek against his arm, like a kitten wanting to be petted. "I like being here with you." Kicking off her sandals, she tucked her feet underneath her on the sofa.

"Why not see how you like it all the time?" He grasped at the opening she'd given him to talk her into moving in. "No ring. No promises. Just us, seeing if we can make it, sharing more than a few nights a week."

"Hmmm." She paused and shifted around, half sitting and half lying across his lap. "I've never lived with a man. It might be fun."

"Fun I can guarantee you, princess." Bending his head, he kissed her, lapping at the seam of her lips until she opened them for his eager tongue. By the time he came up for air his swollen cock was pulsing against the zipper of his pants. "How about starting this togetherness off with a long weekend at a dude ranch Jim told me about?"

"This weekend?"

"Yeah." Should he have asked her before making the reservations? "Can you get someone else to coach your kids on Friday and Saturday?"

"Tess will. She coached at Bluebonnet before she persuaded them to hire me. I'm sure she'll do it." When Dan handed her a portable phone, she punched in some numbers.

He listened as she asked her sister to fill in for her and returned her thumbs-up signal when Tess apparently said she would. After a few minutes' animated conversation in which it seemed he was the main topic under discussion, Gayla hung up and set the phone back on the table.

"What was that all about?"

"My sister thinks I've caught myself a keeper fish." It looked to him as though she could barely keep from laughing out loud, and seeing her so happy gave him a hopeful feeling about their future together.

"Better pay attention to her and hold onto me real, real tight," he teased. "Prizes like me don't come along every day."

"That's what Tess told me. I think you're both crazy." She snuggled up in his arms and kissed him, though, as if to let him know she was only kidding.

The next morning as Dan made rounds at the hospital, he found himself thinking of ways to keep that radiant smile on Gayla's face.

Chapter Eighteen

The wind tossed Gayla's hair and stung her cheeks. She glanced at Dan, who maneuvered his convertible expertly over the hills and around curves on the secondary road he'd taken off I-20 two hours out of Dallas. There was something wonderful about being out in the country—especially with the man she loved.

Exhilarated by his company, the fresh, clean air, and the wide-open spaces, Gayla vowed that this weekend she'd look only to the present. She wouldn't let demons from her past or the uncertainty of the future spoil their fun.

"Princess?" Dan had pulled off the road and stopped the car.

Gayla turned and met his gaze. "I love this! I love you."

"Me, too. Want to walk around a bit?"

"Sure." Not waiting for him to come around and open her door, she got out of the car and met him halfway. Standing on tiptoe, she brushed her lips across his. "Getting stiff?"

"Just trying not to. There's a bronc down at the Circle Bar B, just waiting to get a shot at me."

"Dan!"

He laughed. "Don't worry, I'm not about to do anything to get laid up and keep me from getting in plenty of my favorite exercise," he told her with a playful leer.

"And what might that be?"

"Guess."

"Line dancing?" Gayla couldn't resist teasing him.

"Hardly. If you want to try it, though, we will."

The way his whole face lit up when he grinned nearly took her breath away. "Maybe." Feeling herself clumsy at the few activities that she'd tried on land instead of water, Gayla would just as soon skip the spirited line dances. If she said so, though, Dan might think she was trying to baby him the way he said his mom always had. That was the last thing she wanted to do.

For a half hour they wandered around the small rest area, being careful to stay clear of the sticky mesquite bushes with their colorful flowers. Dan took out his camera and shot some photos, reminding Gayla of their date at the outdoor concert. When they climbed back in the car and headed toward the dude ranch, she asked him if that photographer had ever sent him copies of the picture he took.

"Not yet. If he had, I'd have gotten it framed and hung it in the bedroom so I could look at your pretty face when you wouldn't talk to me."

"I'm sorry."

Dan squeezed her hand. "Don't be. Just stay as content as you looked when I took that last picture. If it comes out the way I hope it will, I'm going to frame it for my office. Look. There's the Circle Bar B." Slowing the car, he drove under the ranch's brand on an arch over a paved driveway, past a grassy field to a wide circular clearing.

A big house built of native sandstone dominated the scene, dwarfing all the outbuildings except for a barn set a good distance away. Gayla counted five cozy-looking log cabins half hidden among cottonwood and live oak trees, and her heart beat faster at the prospect of spending three days alone with Dan in one of them.

* * * * *

"Ready to go ride a bucking bronc?"

Dan glanced up from the duffel bag he'd been unpacking and met Gayla's teasing gaze. "Sure. How about you?"

"I think not. I've never even been on the back of a broken-down nag. I'm ready to watch you, though. Need some help, cowboy?"

"I'm finished." Dumping the last of his stuff into a drawer, Dan set the duffel bag next to an overstuffed chair before going to Gayla and pulling her into his arms. "I could be persuaded to put off the bronc riding until tomorrow," he whispered as he nibbled at her ear.

"No. We came almost two hundred miles so you could learn some rodeo tricks. Now you're going to do it."

This woman was priceless. While most women he'd known, from his mother to the women he'd dated over the years, had done all they could to coddle him and make him feel like a cripple, Gayla treated him as if he had a whole, fit body as well as a brain. He hugged her fiercely, then let her go, sat down, and kicked the shoe he was wearing off his right foot.

"Dan, I told you to go ride that horse."

She looked so damn sexy he'd gladly skip his appointment with the bronc in favor of tumbling into bed with her. He'd told her he wanted to try some rodeo tricks, though, and he doubted that she'd rest until he fulfilled that particular youthful dream.

"Hold on and let me get on my boots." Reaching into the duffel bag, he pulled out a pair of boots, one already attached to an old prosthesis he'd wrestled it onto at home. The other boot he tugged onto his foot before rolling up the left leg of his jeans and popping off his prosthesis.

As used to his appearance as he'd become over the years, Dan had never felt so comfortable baring his stump as he did with Gayla. From the first she'd accepted it, paying no more but no less attention to it than she did to the rest of him. Casually he slipped his stump into the socket of the prosthesis with the boot.

"Just in case," he told Gayla with a grin when he noticed her puzzled expression. "I don't want that bronc to tear up my new one. If I break bones I get professional courtesy. I break these, I pay."

"Insurance doesn't cover them?"

"Not very well. Not at all if they break because of what the company considers abuse. Bronc riding, I think, would fit into that loophole."

Gayla frowned as she appeared to study the limb Dan had laid down next to his bag. "Dan, what do amputees who can't afford these do?"

"In many parts of the world, they do without. Here, most insurance companies cover the first prosthesis, and some will pay for repairs and replacements. There are organizations—the Barr Foundation is one—that help get prostheses for amputees with no resources."

"Ones like this?"

"No, my socially conscious darling, I don't know of any health insurance companies that will spring for thirteen thousand for a below-knee prosthesis, which is what Jamie assured me was the bare-bones, actual cost of this one. A lot of amputees have to settle for less." He smoothed the top of the suspension liner over his thigh and then rolled his jeans leg back down. "Ready?" he asked as he got up.

She held out her hand. "Sure. Hey, you're suddenly taller," she teased, pretending that she couldn't stretch enough to plant a kiss on his lips.

Playing along, Dan bent his head and nuzzled at her neck. "Six feet of hungry cowboy, princess," he growled, pretending to drag her toward the big bed with its wagon-wheel headboard.

"Six feet in those boots, maybe. Come on, let's go let you rope some dogies or whatever it is that big bad cowboys do. We'll feed our other appetites later," Gayla promised as she picked up his Stetson and adjusted it on his head.

* * * * *

She certainly was no expert on anything having to do with ranch work, but she thought Dan looked pretty good twirling that rope. Squinting into the sun, Gayla watched him chase calves around the paddock, trying to lasso them. She got up and squealed when he finally managed to drop a loop around one poor creature's neck.

"That your man, honey?"

"Uh-huh." Gayla didn't look over because she couldn't tear her gaze away from Dan, who had gotten off the gray horse he'd been riding and was moving toward a bunch of chutes on the opposite side of the grassy enclosure from these bleachers.

"He's absolutely gorgeous." The words were drawn out, each syllable emphasized.

Tearing her gaze away from Dan, Gayla glanced at the blonde with the pronounced southern drawl. "He is, isn't he?" she replied. "I'm Gayla."

"Suellen. I just love rodeo, don't you?"

Gayla nodded, her attention focused again on the small ring—and Dan, who had just burst out of the chute on a big spotted horse that didn't appear at all happy to have a rider on its back. For what felt like hours but Gayla knew were only a few seconds, Dan held on while the horse twisted and bucked. When a worker came up beside the crazed animal and grabbed Dan, she let out her breath. "Wow," she said as he landed safely on the ground.

"He do this often?"

Gayla thought the other woman looked as though she'd like to consume Dan alive. "No."

"Well, here's my man. Won't see him on any bucking horses, that's for sure." Suellen moved toward a portly guy who was headed their way. "We'll see you two tonight at the chuck wagon."

"Who was that?" Even dusty and smelling of leather and horse, Dan looked none the worse for wear.

"Suellen. I'm sure she'll make certain she meets you later. You're gorgeous. Absolutely gorgeous," Gayla told him, mimicking the woman's slow, flat speech pattern.

"Jealous?"

"Yeah. You do look good on a horse, Doc. Sure you haven't done this before?"

He grinned. "I've ridden horses, but never one that was trying so hard to get me off his back. That SOB jarred every bone in my body."

"And you loved it."

"Put it this way, princess. Riding a saddle bronc is something I only thought I'd like to do. From now on I'll stick to riding tame horses."

"And wild women?" Wrapping an arm around his waist, Gayla gave him a playful squeeze.

"As long as all of them are you."

Arms around each other's waists, they wandered over to the stable. Gayla almost bolted when she saw the size of the sleek chestnut-colored horse that Dan apparently expected her to ride. Standing as close as they were to the animal, she couldn't see over its massive back. "Don't they have something smaller?" she asked, imagining which of her bones would get broken when she fell off this creature.

"Yeah, but we're going to ride double. Climb aboard."

"How?" As short as she was, she'd have to be a professional contortionist to get onto that horse.

She'd never noticed before, but Dan definitely had a sadistic streak. His grin developed into a rumbling belly laugh as he swung into the saddle and held out a hand. "Come on, tenderfoot, I'll pull you up. Put your right foot in the stirrup."

Putting her hand in his took trust of monumental proportions. Once she'd settled in front of him and gripped the saddle horn until her knuckles turned white, though, Gayla began to enjoy the ride.

The bridle path wove through a grove of cottonwoods, up and down sloping hills and past a meandering stream. Gayla leaned back against Dan. The slow, rocking motion of the horse and the gentle friction of the saddle between her legs heightened her awareness of his cock pressing firmly against her bottom.

"You're hard."

"Uh-huh. And it's a damn long ride back to our cabin, unless you want to let me try letting the horse have his head."

She laughed at his forlorn tone. "I read once about a couple who made love on horseback. Think we could do it?"

Moving the hand that had been stroking her thigh and cupping her breast, Dan rubbed his thumb over her nipple, making her squirm with anticipation as he made the horse turn back toward the stable. "I can't imagine how. Quit rubbing your tush against me like that. I'm about to explode already."

She did it again, and he kept tweaking her nipple. "As I remember, they did it sort of like we did the other night—face-to-face, sitting up."

"And just how, pray tell, did she get her jeans off? Or were they both riding around naked?"

It was Gayla's turn to laugh. "Oh, it was an historical romance. She was wearing a long dress."

"Well, princess, you've got on skintight jeans, and there's no way in hell they're going anywhere while you're sitting on this horse. Besides, I can just imagine us having so much fun that we lose our balance and go tumbling off into a heap. Broken bones, concussions, bruises…"

"Spoken like a surgeon…"

"A horny one whose balls are just about to explode. Hold on tight. We're going to find out how fast this horse can run."

* * * * *

"We both smell like the barnyard," Gayla said, wrinkling her pretty nose when she snuggled up to Dan's naked chest.

"Shower time?"

"No, let's try the hot tub." Gayla's tongue darted out and licked his nipple, and the sensation slammed straight into his already-throbbing groin.

"It's now or never, princess. At least it's now or not until after we try out that bed."

"Okay." With that she sauntered into the bathroom, leaving him to salivate at the sight of her rounded bottom.

By the time he got undressed he could barely see the small hot tub through a wall of steam that smelled like the fresh mint he'd noticed earlier in a pot by the window. It might as well have been some aphrodisiac, the way it turned him on.

Easing into the whirling water, he groped for Gayla. When she reached out and tugged him onto the bench beside her, desire slammed into him again. "I've waited too long, princess. Come sit on my lap."

Silently she did as he asked, wrapping her legs around his hips when he slid forward to give her room. Her breasts bobbed in the swirling foam, and he dipped his head to sample their sweetness. Sputtering when the water filled his nostrils, he raised his head and laughed.

"Trying to drown me, are you?" he asked, using his hands to skim over every luscious inch of her compact body.

She leaned closer and nipped his earlobe. "I wouldn't do that," she whispered. Raising her hips, she found his cock and let herself slowly down to take him in. "You're magnificent." Apparently not content to wait, she began a slow-motion dance, taking him deeper with each slick hot stroke of her cunt on his aching flesh.

Warm water sluiced over them, sliding over their skin, settling in the hollow between her breasts, the creases where thighs met hips. Between his fingers that caressed her firm outer thighs.

He'd never loved a woman so much until now. Gayla was laughter and tears, fun and sadness—everything he'd ever dreamed of. And the sex exceeded his wildest fantasies. It had begun like nothing he'd experienced before, and it got better every time. Steam surrounded them, enveloped them as fully as her pussy sheathed his throbbing cock. Pulsating bursts of water pounded their heads and shoulders, staccato, rhythmic, erotic in their intensity.

His hips beat out an increasing cadence in time with hers. His heart pounded, and hot blood coursed through his veins. She squeezed his cock with her strong vaginal muscles, murmured that she wanted him to come. He couldn't wait any longer when her whimpers and the spasming of her pussy announced her climax, so he leaned against the wall of the tub and let go. The pulsing jets of his semen sent her over the edge again, made her flood his spasming cock with more of her sweet honey.

Gayla was his other half — the half that made him whole.

"Dan?"

"Yeah, princess?"

He sounded sleepy, grumpy, and thoroughly satisfied. "If you want to eat tonight, we'd better get up. It's nearly six thirty." Frankly Gayla couldn't care less if she missed the chuck wagon-prepared dinner and barn dance. Her time alone with Dan was so precious, she hated to give any of it up.

"We've got to get some nourishment." He rolled to the edge of the bed and sat up in slow motion before beginning to get dressed. "Come on, sleepyhead."

Gayla stretched. By the time she dragged herself out of bed and found the outfit she wanted to wear, Dan had pulled on dark jeans and was rummaging through the closet, she guessed, to find a clean shirt.

"Hey. Anyone there?" A knock at the door accompanied the slow, feminine drawl.

"Just a minute. Can you get that, Dan?" Gayla asked as she grabbed her clothes and hurried into the bathroom.

She heard muffled conversation followed by a high-pitched scream. Quickly she jerked her dress over her head and opened the door. "What's wrong?"

The door to the cabin swung back and forth in the breeze, but there was no sign of their visitor. Gayla stared at Dan, who was practically doubled over, he was laughing so hard. "Dan!" she prompted.

"Suellen. She came to ask us to join her and Bill tonight. When she saw that, she yelled like a banshee and took off running."

For a minute Gayla couldn't figure out what Dan was pointing toward. Then she realized. The prosthesis with the boot. Seeing it propped against a chair while Dan walked around must have unnerved the woman. "It shocked her to see you up walking around when she saw the prosthesis over there?"

"I guess so. She looked, screamed, and took off like a bat out of hell. Never saw anything funnier. Come on, let's finish dressing and go eat."

After they ate listened to the music for a while, Gayla was ready to leave, and she sensed that Dan was, too. She reached up and brushed a hand across his cheek. "Let's go, Doc. I want to spend this time without your cell phone and beeper, just being with you."

As they strolled through the cottonwoods to the cabin, Gayla realized that for the first time in her recent memory, she'd faced an evening watching everybody else drinking without yearning once for the temporary oblivion of booze. Feeling good about that small triumph, she held out her arms to Dan when they stepped inside the cabin door.

"Marry Danny, honey. Don't worry about the past. You're going to be just fine now."

Her mother's sweet, soft voice filled Gayla's mind in the moment before Dan scooped her into his arms. "How about having some down and dirty fun with your favorite cowboy?"

"Oh, yeah." She loved his grin, his deep sexy voice. She loved the way his hard muscles flexed against her legs and back when he held her. Most of all she loved the way he made her pussy throb with the slightest touch, even a look from his gorgeous dark brown eyes. "Put me down so we can both get naked."

"Gotcha." When he set her feet down he made sure as much of her as possible slid against his aching cock. Once she was standing and had kicked off her sandals, he started inching down her zipper, stroking the sensitive skin along her spine as he bared it. "Do you mind?"

"You know I love it. Keep going, cowboy." Her nipples tingled once freed from the pressure of the tightly fitted bodice with its built-in bra.

He slid his hands under her loosened dress, sent it sliding down her arms and onto the floor. Then he cupped her mound through her lacy bikini panties. "Take these off and sit on the edge of the bed."

Her honey gushed from her pussy as she dragged off the damp panties and did as he'd asked. "What now?"

"Spread your legs and play with your pretty pussy while you watch me undress." He unsnapped all the buttons of his western-style shirt with one fierce tug and shrugged out of it, baring his muscular chest and arms while focusing his heated gaze on her wet, swollen slit.

Gayla longed to sift through the light dusting of soft, dark chest hair, play with the coppery flat nipples that had already beaded with sexual excitement. Her juices flowed over her fingers when he looked at her like that, as though he couldn't wait to taste her. The sound of his zipper opening, the straining teeth slowly giving way, made her focus there, eager for his big, satiny cock to spring free. To fill her.

When he freed himself, her mouth watered at the sight of his long, thick cock jutting from the nest of dark brown curls she itched to touch, run her fingers through. Would he let her kiss his cock, suck it now the way she suddenly longed to do?

Apparently not, because he shot her an evil grin as he fished out a length of soft rope she thought when she'd watched him pack it was too flimsy for lassoing cows and horses. Before she could even think of protesting, he had her spread-eagled, her ankles neatly tied onto opposite bedposts. Very securely tied, she found when she tentatively tried to pull herself free.

"Knew learning to tie knots would come in handy for something other than suturing. You're not goin' anywhere, cowgirl. Give me your hands now. I want you even more helpless than I am when I've got my leg off." His hot, wet kiss took the edge off the delicious fear of being totally vulnerable to his desires.

Dan stood back and admired his handiwork. Apparently seeing her tied up like this turned him on, because his hard-on grew, made her mouth water.

Once he shoved his pants off, he went to his knees and stroked her inner thighs with long, languid motions that made her nipples harden and her clit throb against his fingers. He spread her legs wider apart, then lowered his dark head. "Lie back and relax, princess. I'm about to make you feel real, real good."

His warm damp breath made her clit tighten, her pussy gush its honey. Laughing softly, he blew on the distended nub. Hot, delicious ringing sensations started there, spread and built before disseminating, making her whimper for more. When he leaned in and caught her clit between his teeth, she thought she'd faint from the pleasure.

He stroked her slit, delving into her pussy with one finger, then two before moving back, tracing the puckered opening to her rear passage and gently pressing his finger as though he planned to invade there.

"Oh, yesss." When he sucked her clit, the tingling grew, spilled over, made her see rainbow colors, feel incredible pleasure…pleasure she'd never experienced quite this vividly before. She wanted to touch him, too. Give back some of the erotic pleasure that threatened to take away her senses. She tugged again at the rope he'd twisted around her wrists, desperate to thread her fingers through his hair, hold his face to her pussy. Wave after wave of undulating sensation spread through her body like wildfire. So good. So right.

Gayla whimpered and moaned. Then Dan cut away her bonds and joined her on the bed, fucked her long and hard and deep until she came again and triggered his own shout of triumph with the wild spasms that overtook her.

Too bad this couldn't last forever.

Chapter Nineteen

༄

"How often can you take a weekend off like this?" Gayla asked as she and Dan hauled their gear into his apartment from the car.

"Have fun, did you?" Juggling the packages in his arms, Dan unlocked the door.

"I loved it. You know, I can't recall ever having taken a trip when I was a kid, unless it had something to do with my swimming."

She sounded so wistful, Dan wanted to hug her. Unfortunately his arms were otherwise occupied with gear. "I can usually take off every other weekend or so. Frank and I switch off."

He dumped his bags on the bedroom floor and took the ones Gayla had been carrying. "Come here, princess. It's been almost three hours since I gave you a hug."

"I've got to put my clothes away," she murmured against his shoulder.

He glanced at the two small bags, then remembered the boxes they had brought here from Gayla's apartment on Friday morning before they left for the ranch. "Need some help?"

"Sure."

"Then let's get you moved in."

Her dresses in the closet and the sweet-smelling feminine things they dumped into drawers made a statement. Gayla was here — without a ring, at least for the moment — but she'd taken that first step toward commitment. When he woke in the morning, he'd be holding her in his arms.

"Dan?"

Her soft voice brought him back to the here and now. "Do you need more drawer space?" he asked when he noticed her staring at the dresser.

"No, I've put everything away. Dan, hold me. Make me believe this is real, that I'm here with you and that I'm not going to wake up at my place alone."

Gayla rested her head against his shoulder, letting the circular motion of his hands against her back and the heat that radiated from his body reassure her she wasn't dreaming. Needing to touch him, too, she ran her hands down the length of his back, exerting gentle pressure to nudge him closer. "I love you," she murmured, the words coming out muffled against the hard wall of his chest.

"Any time you need reminding this is real, princess, I'll be thrilled to put the ring that's in my top drawer on your finger. Are you ready?" he asked when she met his gaze.

Oh, how Gayla wished for the strength to set aside her fears and say yes.

"Do it, baby. Reach out and grab your happiness. Don't let it slip away."

Each time her mother spoke, Gayla heard the words more clearly. Tonight she could almost picture Sylvia's face, her expression soft and dreamy, as if she expected kindness and goodness in everyone she encountered.

"I'll stand by you now, like I should have done when I was alive," the voice murmured. Then Gayla felt her mother's presence gently slip away.

"Gayla? Are you all right?"

"I'm fine." She toyed with telling Dan about hearing her mom's voice as clearly as if she were across the room, but the encouragement her mom had just given was so precious, so personal, she wanted to savor it quietly, let the warmth spread through her. Maybe she'd share it with him later.

"Then how about it? Are you ready to wear my ring?"

"Maybe soon. But not yet."

"It's your call, princess. I'm ready anytime." Cupping her chin in one hand, he moved to take her mouth.

Gayla let the sensual promise of Dan's hot kiss flow through her body, ignite a warm glow in her heart and a fierce fire in her belly.

"Let me love you," he whispered when he broke the kiss.

When she nodded, he began undressing her. With each button he opened, every brush of his hands against skin already attuned to the pleasures of his touch, he made the simple act a sensuous journey. If it weren't for the flames inside her begging for him to squelch them, she could have stayed like this all night. She wanted to savor the feel of his hands on her body, but with every touch he ignited a desire so fierce that her body screamed for immediate release.

She reached to unbutton his shirt, but he stilled her hands. "This one's for you, princess," he said, his voice raspy, as though he were fighting to maintain control.

Vaguely she realized they were moving to the bed, and that when they got there Dan had her sit on the edge. He cupped her breasts in his hands, his thumbs fanning lightly across her nipples. Then he went down on his knees.

"Lie back and spread your legs, love." When she did, he moved between them. His fingers worked their magic, making her writhe and moan, and when he touched her clit with his warm, wet tongue, her exhilaration mounted. Unable to stay still she lifted her hips, offering herself fully for his pleasure and her own.

He made her soar as though she had wings, though she lay passive, feeling nothing but his gentle fingers holding her open, his soft lips and agile tongue playing an incredibly erotic dance on her most sensitive flesh. Fists clutching at the coverlet, she tried to maintain her balance, but what he was doing to her had her in a tailspin. Falling...tumbling in a spiral to some unfamiliar place, a place where she'd never gone before...a place where there was only her sopping pussy, her swollen clit where he kept focusing all his seductive attention. Closing her eyes, she gave in and followed where he led, to a maelstrom of light and color and crescendos of sound. The colors converged behind her eyelids into a kaleidoscope of blue, red, and gold as silence replaced the pounding rhythm. Her muscles tensed, then went slack as her climax faded to a soft, warm glow. A languid peace flowed over her, like a warm shower after an exhilarating swim — yet so much more.

"You like that, don't you?"

She nodded, couldn't talk for the sensations still slamming through her body.

"Want more?" Dan bent his head again and blew lightly on the little knot of nerves that was still sending arousing messages through to the rest of her body. "Princess?"

"I want you inside me," she said, reaching down to touch the silky hair at the crown of his head. "Dan?"

He kissed her clit again, then raised his head, slowly getting up and sitting beside her to undress. Naked now, he came to her, stoking fires he'd set to simmering beneath the surface of her consciousness.

"God but you feel good." As though he wanted to prolong the pleasure, he slid his cock in her pussy slowly — so slowly she wanted to scream with frustration, waiting for his pulsing flesh to fill her completely. Unlike other nights when he'd eagerly sought release, tonight it seemed Dan wanted to prolong and savor the heat, the friction...the love she felt flowing between them.

The tension built by inches, spreading cell by cell until she was whimpering, begging him for more, praying for release. She dug her nails into his shoulders, tightened her pussy muscles. Clutched his waist with her legs. "Oh, yesss. Fuck me. Fuck me hard."

When he thrust in her hard and deep, over and over, sinking in her until his thick cockhead nudged her womb, she came in long waves that never seemed to end. Her pussy clamped down on his hard, hot cock, spasmed around him. His shout of satisfaction came as his scalding semen jetted into her womb, enhancing her pleasure and leaving her with a warm, comfortable glow. Threading her fingers through Dan's dark, thick hair as he rested his head against her shoulder, Gayla felt a part of him—no longer separate.

The next morning when she fixed his breakfast before sending him off to work, she hummed a slow country tune. When he came in, kissed her briefly, and poured a cup of coffee, she let herself imagine being with him like this forever. Only after he left did she force herself to remember the unpleasant truth that she was only one drink—one snort—away from sinking back into the muck and mire of addiction.

* * * * *

Later, as she toured the new facility where she'd be working with Michelle on rehabilitating the patients Dan, Frank, and Jim had done surgery on, Gayla's self-confidence began to return. She realized she had a skill that could make a difference in people's lives.

The building still needed work before it would be ready for the doctors to move into their offices, but Michelle assured Gayla that the three-lane lap pool would be finished by the time they needed to begin scheduling patients. Michelle's land-based therapy section, with gym equipment, massage tables, and whirlpool tubs, needed only the mats and other small pieces before it opened in another week.

"This is going to be wonderful. When will Dan and the other doctors be moving in?" Stepping over rolls of carpet padding and assorted boxes, Gayla guessed it would be a while yet.

Michelle frowned. "They may be camping out in here at first, from the look of things. Their lease with the hospital will be up in three weeks, so they'll be coming here, ready or not."

"Where will Jamie be working?" Gayla liked the prosthetist, despite Dan's good-natured comments about her inherent greed.

"She's already set up and in business as of this morning. Shall we go bother her for some tea?"

Actually Gayla preferred coffee, but she guessed Michelle wouldn't be drinking it because of her pregnancy, which was now just beginning to show. "I'd like that," she said as they made their way toward the rear of the large building.

When they stepped into the prosthetics lab, Jamie glanced up from what Gayla guessed must be components for artificial limbs. "Taking the grand tour? By the way, welcome to our little madhouse."

"Thanks."

"No need to thank me. If you managed to teach Frank Grogan to swim, you can teach anybody. How was your weekend?" Jamie picked up what looked like a very small stump socket and fit it onto a plaster cast. "Did you and Dan have fun?"

Michelle laughed. "What Jamie really wants to know is whether Dan managed to tear up another leg so she can sock it to him for fixing it."

It was Gayla's turn to smile. "We had a ball. Dan's legs—real and prosthetic—are all doing fine."

"All?"

"He used an old one to ride the bronc. Said he could get his bones fixed for free, but that you'd charge him a fortune to fix his prosthesis." Gayla glanced at the pieces Jamie was putting together. "That's for an arm, isn't it?"

"Yes. You'll be seeing some when you start the aquatic therapy program."

"Really?" Gayla hadn't thought about developing a program for upper-limb amputees—although during the thirty minute tour Michelle had given her of the rehabilitation facility where they would be working, she'd seen photos of a few patients with missing arms. "Will they be using prostheses?" She envisioned some kind of modified hand-paddles that could be attached to residual limbs.

Jamie grinned. "They certainly will. Leg amputees should, too. They could move a lot more efficiently. I've given up trying to persuade Dan of that, though. He learned to swim without one and he insists he doesn't need one now. Maybe you can talk him into trying a swimming leg. You know, I could convert his old everyday prosthesis. That FlexFoot should be okay in water so long as the cover's waterproof."

"I'll leave that up to Dan. He swims very well without one."

"You'll get no help from Gayla. You know how women in love can be," Michelle told Jamie. "Come on, Gayla, I need to talk with you about a very special patient."

Back in Michelle's office they finally got their tea. As they sat and drank it, Michelle handed Gayla a chart. "I need to know if this child can do competitive swimming."

Gayla hesitated. She wasn't a doctor, and the importance of keeping patient information confidential had been ground into her head since she was a child. Then she remembered. She was going to work with these patients and she'd have to look at their medical information. Reading quickly, she noted that the child had a below-knee amputation as well as significant loss of function in the other leg.

"Well, can he?" Michelle asked.

"He can be taught to do the competitive strokes, except possibly breaststroke. That's questionable because of the kick. I don't know if he could dive in, but the rules allow for swimmers with disabilities to begin in the water. Does he swim with a prosthesis?"

"He hasn't. Timmy wants to swim for the team at the club where he goes with his mom and dad." Michelle named what Gayla knew to be one of the most prestigious country clubs in the Dallas area. "Can he?"

"That would be up to the coach." Knowing Briarwood's head coach, Ray Yancy, she doubted he'd take the time to do much coaching of a kid who wasn't destined to bring him more fame and prestige, but she hated to tell Michelle that.

Michelle got up and stared at the pool through the glass window in her office. "Put it this way. Can Timmy swim in regular, non-handicapped competition?"

"Without a prosthesis, I'm sure he can. I don't know if the rules would allow him to compete if he was wearing one. He won't be winning often, though, if that's what he expects."

Michelle smiled. "I think it's just the idea of doing something 'normal' that appeals to Timmy. He's a great kid — and he darn near worships Dan."

"Dan was his surgeon?"

"Dan, Frank, and Jim. Plus half-a-dozen residents. Timmy had six surgeries in the first four years after the accident."

No wonder Michelle wanted so much to give this little boy something special. He must have gone through hell. Gayla glanced through the chart again and shuddered. "I could talk to the coach at Briarwood."

"Would you?"

Gayla nodded. She didn't particularly relish dredging up old times with Yancy, who had been her teammate when they were teenagers, but she'd do it.

It proved to be surprisingly easy. Instead of bringing up her inauspicious swan song as a competitor and the downward plunge to the gutter that had followed, Ray chatted easily about their earlier years. Surprisingly, he seemed to be almost eager to work with Timmy Tanner and promised to keep Gayla apprised of the boy's progress.

"That was easy enough," Gayla told Michelle after setting the phone in its cradle. "I'd never thought Ray had that much compassion."

Michelle laughed. "I doubt he'd refuse, even if he wasn't eager to take Timmy on. Don't you know who this boy's father is?"

"No."

"Blake Tanner. Big, big money. Oil, I think, although Blake himself is a lawyer. I do Timmy's physical therapy at their house. Their house, mind you. Blake outfitted his gym with every piece of equipment imaginable the minute he moved Tim and the boy's mother in. The place is sort of art-nouveau, but as big as Southfork."

"That sounds like an interesting story," Gayla murmured, understanding better now why Ray had been so very accommodating. "You'll have to tell it to me sometime."

"Ask Dan. Timmy's one of his favorite people."

Suddenly Gayla recalled the conversation she had with Dan on their first date. "Is Timmy the boy he showed his prosthesis to?"

"Yes. He is. Dan must already have told you about him."

"Not really, except to tell me I was the second person he'd shown his stump to without telling them about it first—and that the first person was a little boy who had just had a leg amputated."

Michelle laughed out loud. "He just rolled up his pants leg and showed you? Without saying anything? That must have been a shock."

"I had challenged him to a race. I realized he was an amputee when he popped off his prosthesis and slid into the pool."

"What did you do?"

Gayla shrugged. "I dived in and raced him for five hundred yards. Beat him by less than thirty seconds, and I'm damn good. Of course I did this after my mouth fell open and I stared longer than was polite."

"Priceless. That had to have been absolutely priceless! Just wait till I tell Frank. This will make his day."

After reading some orders Frank and Dan had written for aquatic therapy, Gayla mentally planned the exercises that would work best. The instructions were very, very general.

"Michelle, isn't this the police officer whose car was bombed the night of that hospital fund-raiser?" The night she confessed what and who she was to Dan. Gayla handed the chart to Michelle.

"Zach Hamilton?"

"Yes."

"He's the one. He'd be up on crutches now, except for the fact that his right hand is all but gone. The longer he doesn't get to exercise, the more his muscles will atrophy. We'll use aquatic therapy to let him move without having to bear weight on either the leg or the hand."

The more charts she reviewed, the more a sense of purpose began to surface within her. More than she had for years, she felt good about herself and what she'd be doing.

On the way home to Dan's condo after coaching her team, Gayla made a decision. She was going to agree to marry Dan as soon as she faced her father and made peace with him. Surely he'd come around when she showed him how well she was doing.

* * * * *

Disappointed at first when she listened to Dan's voice on the recorder telling her he'd be tied up in surgery for several hours, Gayla quickly recovered the good humor that had marked her day. It took her only a few minutes to tidy up the condo and heat some soup.

Taking it to the kitchen table, she tried working up the nerve to call her father. Failing that, she tried to conjure up her mother. She needed moral support almost as much as she craved her father's forgiveness. Sylvia didn't respond to her silent entreaty, though, so Gayla dialed her sister's number and flipped on the speakerphone. That way she could talk while she ate.

"You're going to do what?" Tess asked, her tone incredulous.

"I'm going to ask Daddy to forgive me."

There was a long pause, and Gayla thought she heard Tess sigh. "Why, Gayla?" she finally asked.

Slowly, weighing reasons as she spoke, Gayla explained how her father could destroy Dan's career—perhaps even the careers of his partners, if he chose to. "I let Daddy down. I can't get on with my life until I prove to him that I'm worth forgiving," That was it. The key to her self-respect lay in persuading her father she'd become something, someone, worthwhile.

"Daddy will hurt you. He hardened his heart toward you, and he'll never admit he might have been wrong. Take my advice. Forget it. Forget him. He isn't worth your tears."

Gayla fought back an urge to pour a shot of Jack Daniel's as she struggled to maintain a facade of confidence. "You're probably right. Daddy may not be worth it to me, but Dan is. For his sake I have to try."

"You love him, don't you?"

Resolutely she averted her gaze from the bar. She didn't need a drink. "Yes."

"Then marry the man already. Don't screw up your head by trying to talk sense to Dad. We've both known that was impossible to do almost since we learned to talk. Just wheedle a proposal out of your good-looking doctor and live happily ever after, for God's sake."

"If only it were that simple. Thanks for listening, Tess. I've got to go."

Removing herself from the temptation of the bottles on the bar, Gayla put her spoon and soup bowl in the dishwasher. Then she went in the bedroom. The shadowy image plopped on her side of Dan's king-size bed looked suspiciously like...

Gayla ran across the room and sank to her knees. "Mom! You came." When she reached out to hug her, though, her arms encountered only air.

"You can see me?"

"Yes. But I can't feel you."

Sylvia smiled, that half-smile Gayla remembered as her usual expression when she was alive. "Mom, don't get me wrong. I need you tonight. I'm so glad you've come. Why weren't you here for me when I needed you most, though?" She sat on the leather lounge chair in the corner.

"Because I saw it as my duty to support your dad's decision."

"Even when he was wrong?"

"Yes. I'm sorry, baby. I know now I should have stood up to him. Am I forgiven?"

Gayla couldn't help smiling. Her mom looked so earnest, sitting there on Dan's bed, her hands fluttering as if she weren't quite certain of her welcome. "Yes. Am I?"

"For what? Not being able to cope when your whole world collapsed around you? For being human? Forgiveness you don't need. What you do need is this young man who has put the glow back in your pretty eyes."

"I love Dan. More than anything, I want to marry him. But Mom, I'm so afraid."

"Afraid? Of your daddy?" Sylvia frowned, as if disturbed at the reminder of Gayla's estrangement from her father. *"He loves you, baby. I know he does. He's a hard man. Demanding. No more on others, though, than he is on himself."*

"I'm going to ask him to forgive me and wish Dan and me well. I can't get married knowing Daddy may try to destroy Dan because of me. Mom, what will he do?"

As her throat constricted at the thought of her father hurting Dan because of her mistakes, she watched her mother move toward the open photo album on the table. Glancing at a rare candid shot of herself and Tess taken shortly before Tess's high school graduation, Gayla made a conscious effort to relax.

"I wish you were still ten years old and that I could tell you everything was going to be all right, but I'm finished with glossing over your father's faults. I don't know what he will do, Gayla, other than vent the anger he has nursed since — "

"Since I disgraced him and you, not to mention myself?"

Gayla watched Sylvia get up and float across the room, graceful in spite of her apparent agitation. *"Not that. Never that. He just wanted so much for you. He hurt for you, baby. Eli just didn't know how to help you. He lashed out because anger was the only way he knew to react when things didn't go his way."*

Searching her memory, Gayla recalled her dad's fury long ago when she'd broken a crystal wineglass, one of a set his great grandmother had brought all the way from Germany. "He forgave me when I broke that antique glass," she murmured, trying not to remember that it had taken months and her breaking two long-standing state records before Eli relented.

"Yes, he did. And he may forgive you now. But, baby, I'm afraid. If he doesn't…"

"I'll live."

"And you'll marry Danny?"

"I believe I will. Mom, I love him so."

"Your young man can hold his own with Eli. I'm certain of it. And if you fall, Danny will be there to help you get back up. He's a good boy. Handsome as sin, too. You'll make beautiful babies together."

Sylvia sounded almost as if she knew Dan. "Mom, did you know Dan?" From the way her mom talked about him, it sounded as though they might have met, maybe at some hospital function or other.

"No. But I've been watching the two of you."

Gayla's cheeks suddenly burned when she recalled some times with Dan she hoped her mom hadn't witnessed. "You — you have?"

"Yes, baby. From the time you collided with him in the hall at the hospital. Don't worry. I'm not so nosy and meddlesome that I'd stick my nose into your very private times together." Sylvia chuckled, the way Gayla remembered her doing when she or Tess had done something only slightly naughty when they were small.

"I'm glad. Glad Dan meets with your approval, that is. Mom, tell me what to say when I go to Daddy. You never made him angry."

Sylvia stopped floating, settling again on the side of the bed, her gaze fixed on a photo of Gayla with her father. *"That's because I made it a point never to cross him, to my eternal shame."* Tears flowed down her pale, translucent cheeks.

Then her expression changed, as though she'd drawn strength from somewhere deep inside herself. *"Here's how I would approach him now — if I were still alive."*

They talked for hours, it seemed, and when Sylvia finally faded away, Gayla wished they'd taken time for this conversation long ago. Instead of resenting her mother for never having stood up for her or Tess, Gayla admired her uncompromising love for her husband.

She was glad that at least one person agreed with her that the slim chance of her father's forgiving her justified the risk she'd take of having him hurt her again.

Stretching out on the bed where her mom's very real spirit had sat not long ago, Gayla told herself she could withstand whatever Eli Harris might dish out. God, did she wish Dan would get home. She needed him tonight. So much.

* * * * *

Pulling off his cap and mask and tossing them in the trash, Dan glanced up at the clock in the surgeons' lounge. Eleven o'clock.

"Long night," Jim commented as he began stripping off bloody scrubs.

"Yeah."

"Nasty case." Frank came in and sat down, as if he was too exhausted to stand for another minute. "Want to get a drink before we head home?"

Ordinarily Dan would. He'd always liked to wind down after a marathon surgery like the one they just finished. Tonight, though, he wanted only to get home. "Count me out. I need to get home."

Frank shot him a tired grin. "Gayla waiting up for you?"

"I don't know if she'll be waiting up or not, but she's there." Dan pulled his clothes out of his locker and started to change.

"Do you think having her move in with you is a good idea?" Jim asked, his expression suddenly serious.

"What do you mean?"

"That it doesn't look good for you to be shacking up with the chief of surgery's daughter, without even a hint of a wedding in the works."

"Jim's right," Frank said as he pulled the top of his scrubs over his head.

His partners' admonitions smacked of rank hypocrisy. "Didn't you live with Kelly for almost three years before making it legal, Jim? And, Frank, I seem to recall you got your wife pregnant before deciding to marry her. Both of you need to remember the saying about glass houses and stones."

Jim had the decency to look sheepish. "We weren't in the position you're in now, Dan. At the very least, couldn't you give her a ring? You wouldn't actually have to marry her."

"I'd marry her tomorrow. And I've already bought a ring. Gayla won't agree to marriage or an engagement because she has some idea that if she does, Ironsides will destroy my career. I think she's coming around, though." He hoped to hell that was true.

"Get her pregnant," Frank suggested. "She'd marry you then."

"I'm not so sure she would."

"You all decent?" asked Kelly through the closed door.

Dan welcomed the interruption. This conversation was beginning to make him mad. "Come on in, Kel."

"How's our patient doing?" Jim asked as he gave his wife a hug.

"He's stable. Strong as a horse, apparently. If he weren't, he'd be going to ICU on a respirator—but he's breathing just fine. I left orders for him to go straight to the orthopedic surgery floor."

Dan smiled. The patient, a swarthy guy with long hair, multiple tattoos, and several rings that the ER staff had gotten a kick out of removing from various parts of his anatomy, had gotten in the way of an armored truck while riding his Harley chopper. Dan figured the guy would probably scream as much about the loss of the naked woman tattoo that had decorated his lower right leg as he would about the loss of the limb itself.

"He'll probably be riding that bike again in a month or two," Jim predicted with a chuckle.

Frank laughed. "Not that particular bike. But you're probably right. He'll get back on and ride until he either kills himself or loses at least one more limb."

"Why do they do that?" Kelly asked, her expression thoughtful.

"It's a macho thing. Sort of like our friend Dan here, going out and climbing on the back of a bucking bronc."

"Hey. What am I? Tonight's punching bag?"

"You guys leave Dan alone."

"Yeah. Leave me alone. I'm out of here to go defy conventions and be with the woman I'm not engaged or married to. If it weren't too late, I might stop by the rodeo grounds and ask to take a quick spin on a bull." Grinning, Dan stood up and left his partners to their own devices.

* * * * *

Finding Gayla curled up in his bed banished the aches and pains Dan felt after a fifteen-hour day, better than any whirlpool treatment or high-powered liniment. He rolled into bed beside her, reacting instantly when she awakened and snuggled up close. Suddenly he wasn't tired anymore.

At least he wasn't too tired to get a massive hard-on, slip it into her hot, wet cunt when she wrapped one leg around his waist, and fuck her slow and easy. He loved the way she stroked him, raking her nails very gently along his spine, cupping his butt cheeks as if she were afraid he might let her go. Fat chance of that. His cock throbbed inside her warm, tight sheath, and his balls tightened with every little shift of her hips, each slow thrust of his own.

Damn, he was coming. Too fast. Wanting her to join him, he cupped her breasts and tugged gently on the hard little nipples. "Come on, princess. I don't want to take this trip alone."

"You won't. Oh God." Her little moans and the contractions of her sopping flesh around his cock triggered the jets of come that spurted from him moments later, before he clutched her rounded ass cheeks and drifted off to sleep.

The next morning when he sat at the breakfast table and poured their coffee, he noted that she seemed a little on edge. "Something wrong, princess?"

"No. Something's very right. I've never felt better."

He got the feeling Gayla was telling him the truth, just not all of it. "But?"

"But nothing." With apparent enthusiasm, she told him about her day with Michelle and that she was eager to begin working with rehab patients in the new facility where he'd soon be moving to his new offices. "I feel as if I'll be doing something useful."

"Are you ready yet to wear that ring?" he asked, unable to hold back the words. More than anything he wanted to stake his claim for everyone to see.

She let him pull her onto his lap. "Not yet, love. But soon, I think."

No matter how he coaxed, Dan couldn't get her to open up and tell him what was on her mind. That bothered him, but he forced himself to focus on the hope she'd given him that soon she'd be willing to shove aside her fears and give him that lifetime commitment.

* * * * *

Gayla had wanted nothing more than to tell Dan she'd marry him and let him put the ring she'd refused even to let him show her onto her finger. Tonight, if she could corner her father today and make him understand how sorry she was for having let him down, she'd reach out for the future Dan kept offering.

Between driving out to the club to coach two groups at different times of day and working to set up aquatic therapy programs that would meet the needs of patients with various disabilities, she had a full day. By seven o'clock, when she arrived at the hospital to find her father, she was pleasantly exhausted.

"Gayla?"

Turning, she saw Dan in the same hallway where they had run into each other that first time. "Dan." Remembering where she was, she managed to restrain herself from running into his arms.

"What are you doing here?"

"I thought I'd try to see Dad. He isn't here, though."

Dan frowned. "Why?"

Damn it, he'd try to talk her out of this. That's why she hadn't shared her plan this morning, why she'd hoped not to run into him here until after she'd seen her father. Gayla looked Dan in the eye, trying hard to sound a lot more casual than she felt. "If I'm going to get on with living, I need to make my peace with him."

He took her hand, rubbing his thumb gently over her palm. "Princess, do you think that's possible?"

"I don't know, but I've got to try. Do you have any idea where he might be?"

"Thirty minutes ago he was presiding over the Death Committee. Raked me over the coals along with the others who were there when that girl died. Where he might be now, I have no idea. Possibly at home, enjoying dinner?"

If that were true, it would be a change for her father, who never had come home before nine or ten o'clock for as long as Gayla could remember. "I guess I could try going there."

"Want me to go with you?"

She stood on tiptoe so she could brush a kiss across Dan's lips. "You don't know how much I appreciate that offer, Doc, but this is something I have to do on my own."

"No, you don't."

Placing a hand across his mouth to cut off his protest, she met his warm, loving gaze. "Yes. I have to do this myself. I can't explain why, Dan, but there's no way I can put the past behind me until I face Daddy and tell him I'm sorry."

"Damn it, he's the one who should be down on his knees, begging for your forgiveness. He let you down. It wasn't the other way around."

"Hush. Whatever happened, he's still my father. I have to try to make him understand that even though I lost control and did things no one should forgive, I've come back. I'm worth another shot."

"I don't want him to hurt you, princess." Dan stroked her cheek, as if afraid her father would harm her physically.

"He never laid a hand on me."

"There are other ways than beatings to tear a kid apart. Please, let me go with you. At least let me drive you there. I'll wait in the car while you talk to him."

"No. Go home. I'll be there as soon as I can." Before he could persuade her not to go, Gayla kissed him quickly and walked away.

* * * * *

Memories assailed her as she wound her way through the upscale residential area where she and Tess had grown up. When she lifted the brass knocker on the front door of her childhood home, Gayla's bravado nearly disappeared in a fog of anxiety and fear.

She knocked once…twice…three times. Finally the door swung open, and Gayla met her father's disbelieving gaze.

Chapter Twenty

The Ghosts

ಐ

"Ruth, come quickly. Gayla is talking with Eli."

"What?" Tossing down cards that would shortly have produced her a grand slam, Ruth hurried to see what was going on.

"Where are they?" The tastefully decorated living room wasn't familiar to Ruth.

"At home. Listen."

Settling onto a chair, Ruth listened as Gayla tearfully tried to make Eli understand how she'd felt before going off the deep end into a world of temporary fixes. The exasperating man was refusing to listen. When he came back at Gayla, spouting venom from those thin, tight lips, Sylvia slammed her fist into the arm of the couch. It was the first time since they met that the ninny had shown even a sign of having a temper.

"See what he's doing to her?" Sylvia ground out, her eyes glued to the screen. *"I wish — "*

"Sylvia! Don't."

"You did."

Ruth could hardly believe her ears. What Eli Harris had said to Danny hardly held a candle to the garbage he was dumping on Gayla's small shoulders. *"Where is Danny, anyway? He should be there, lending Gayla his support. No one should have to face the monster you were stupid enough to marry and live with for God only knows how long. Not alone."*

"She wouldn't let Danny come with her," Sylvia said, her tone flat and defeated. *"She said she had to make peace with her father by herself. My God, Eli is going to send her right back to the bottle, if not*

the drugs. I should have done something when all the trouble started..."

"Now's not the time for whining about what you should have done when you were alive. What can we do?" Chafing at the restraints that being a ghost imposed, Ruth searched the room for something appropriate to throw.

"Maybe you were right to wish Eli harm," Sylvia ground out through clenched teeth as they watched Eli pace across the room, getting redder in the face as he repeated every wrongdoing Gayla had ever done and some she probably hadn't. Ruth had never felt more malice toward anyone except the fates who had let her nine-year-old son get cancer.

"If only I'd found the courage to stop him, maybe Gayla wouldn't have needed to go through all she did."

Why must Sylvia keep dwelling on the past? What Gayla needed now was love, and Ruth knew for certain Danny could provide that. *"I wish Gayla would leave now and go home to Danny so he can comfort her."*

"You used a wish for Gayla," Sylvia said, her voice tinged with wonder. *"Look, she's leaving now, and Eli's stomping up the stairs. I wonder..."*

Suddenly all Sylvia and Ruth could hear was a series of deep-pitched thumps. Afterwards they saw Eli lying sprawled on the landing, breathing but otherwise as still as death.

"If I were you I'd divorce him if he ends up here with us," Ruth told Sylvia as they concentrated on their loved ones on earth to see what would happen next. She couldn't help but feel a twinge of conscience, though, when she recalled having rashly wished injury to Eli Harris—a wish she'd hate to think might just have come true.

Chapter Twenty-One

ත

"Princess, it's all right. No one cares what your father thinks. Here, dry your eyes and give me a smile." For the past hour Dan had held Gayla, getting little out of her except for an impression that her meeting with Ironsides had gone worse than she'd expected.

At least she'd come to him instead of trying to take whatever pain her old man dished out alone. "What say we take off and spend the weekend on the beach down in Galveston?"

"Dan, could we?"

When Gayla sounded like that, as eager as a child, he couldn't deny her. "Sure. Pack a bag, and we'll take off. Frank's covering for me, since I took three straight weeks of call for him. Want to drive or fly?"

"Fly." Dan guessed she'd picked the method that would get her away from Ironsides as quickly as possible. "Do you have a plane?"

"No. We'll have to go commercial."

She sniffled, then managed a tiny smile. "That's good. I don't like small planes."

An hour later they were waiting at the gate at the airport, and within two hours they were putting on swimsuits in preparation for walking on the rugged beach outside their hotel. Only then did Dan feel Gayla had settled down enough to ask her about what he feared must have been a trauma as devastating as the goriest accident.

* * * * *

"What? Wait a minute, Dr. Wills, I'll get him." Setting down the phone, Michelle stepped onto the patio and called for Frank.

"You okay, honey?"

"I'm fine. You've got an emergency call. Dr. Wills."

Frank gave her backside a casual pat as he passed by on the way to the kitchen. The weekend had been quiet until now, and they had been working in the yard. When she followed him in, she noticed the frown on his face.

"Eli Harris took a fall down his steps at home last night. Apparently he couldn't get up or to a phone, so he lay there until his housekeeper arrived a little while ago. George says his right hand's got some serious problems."

"Shouldn't you call Dan?" While Frank was good at repairing upper extremities, he made no bones about the fact that Dan was better.

"For Harris? I doubt he'd let Dan touch him. If it's a fairly simple repair I can do it—if not, then I'll try to persuade him he needs Dan. He's already gone a good while without treatment—anything that would get worse from waiting has gotten worse already."

Michelle lifted her head for a kiss as Frank picked up the keys to his car. "Have somebody call me if you're going to be tied up all day. Otherwise, you've still got some weeds to take care of here."

"Slave driver." Frank grinned—then his expression sobered. "Don't you strain yourself, little mommy. The weeds can wait."

* * * * *

"Surgery can wait."

George Wills, the chief of orthopedic surgery, was obviously trying to placate Ironsides when Frank strolled into the tiny ER cubicle. "George. Dr. Harris," he murmured, picking up the chart to see what was going on.

"Grogan. Where were you? It's been over a half-hour since I had George call you."

Frank grimaced. "I was home. As George told me when we spoke on the phone, if you need surgery, it can wait." Privately he figured Ironsides must have done a number on the hand for George to want it foisted off on someone else.

"It has already waited over twelve hours. I want it done and done now." Ironsides riddled him with a malicious stare.

For Dan's sake, Frank hoped Gayla never made up with her demanding old man. "I don't operate on demand. Give me a few minutes to review your chart, and I'll give you my recommendation."

George tried to placate his recalcitrant patient while Frank sat down and studied the images. "Ouch." Then he looked at the MRI and saw immediately why the older surgeon had passed on doing the repair. Somehow Ironsides had managed to screw up half the nerves, tendons, and ligaments in his primary operating hand, as well as fracturing his wrist and eight small bones in his hand and fingers.

"Can you fix it?" Ironsides' voice boomed out, startling Frank into glancing up from the scan.

"Sure." Frank set the chart down and strolled over to the bed. "I can fix it. Of course I don't guarantee you'll ever be able to use that hand again for anything more complex than holding a fork or spoon."

"What do you mean?"

"What I mean, Dr. Harris, is that you did a number on your hand. You not only need an orthopedic-slash-neuro trauma surgeon, you need one who can piece together a bunch of severed nerves and tendons, and do it right. You need Newman."

Ironsides snorted. "Over my dead body."

Frank laughed. "I wouldn't go quite that far. I'm not likely to kill you."

"This is not funny."

"No, and I'm not kidding when I say you'd be better off with Dan. He's a genius when it comes to piecing arms and hands back together. My preference is for legs."

"There's no one else?"

"No one as good. Not in this state. There might be a couple of others as good somewhere in the country."

"I've got to be able to keep on doing surgery." Harris looked to George as if expecting the older man to deny Frank's prognosis. "Well?"

George pushed off from the wall he'd been leaning against, and ambled to the bed. "Eli, Frank is saying the same thing I told you. Your hand is a mess. Right now it's more realistic to assume that with the best surgeon—and I agree with Frank, Dan Newman is the best when it comes to repairing hands—you will almost certainly regain use of it for tasks that don't require precise fine motor skills."

"Will I be able to operate?"

"I don't know. No one can know until the surgery is done and your rehabilitation is well underway."

Harris shook his head. "All right. Get Newman in here and schedule an OR." Frank thought Ironsides was going to choke on those words, they came out so haltingly. Sorry to be intruding on Dan's weekend, he picked up a phone and punched in his partner's number.

"George, you'd better wait to schedule that OR. Dan's not home."

"Did you try my daughter's apartment?"

Frank couldn't believe the man would ask that in front of their colleague. "No." He didn't think it necessary to let Harris know Gayla had moved in with Dan.

"For God's sake, get him here."

"I'm trying his cell phone now. He isn't on call, though, so he may not have it with him." After hearing the canned voice telling him his party was unavailable, Frank left a message for Dan to call him as soon as possible.

"What kind of surgeon goes off without letting people know where to find him?" Harris bellowed, his face flushing so beet-red that Frank ordered the nurse to get a blood pressure reading.

He met the man's angry gaze. "He's off duty. I can try to reach him or I can patch you up the best I can. If I were you, I'd calm down and wait. Another hour—even another day—isn't going to cause any more damage than you already did to yourself."

"Are you telling me you may not be able to find Newman for twenty-four hours? He was here yesterday at the preliminary hearing into the Randall girl's unfortunate death."

Frank hung up the phone after leaving a message with Dan's beeper service. "Dan is off this weekend. As I told you, I'm covering for him—and if you insist, I'll perform your surgery."

"I'll wait. Get me out of this closet and into a decent room upstairs. Have someone go to the medical library and find me some videos of the kind of surgery I'm going to have. I intend to know what that young fool is doing, every step of the way."

By the time the orderlies had transferred Ironsides to a gurney and hauled him away, Frank felt the need to hit someone.

* * * * *

The peaceful atmosphere of this quiet beach apparently had helped take Gayla's mind off the painful meeting with her father. She still hadn't told Dan much about it, but there would be time for that later, when he could hold her in his arms and persuade her she didn't need Ironsides' forgiveness.

Opening the door to their room, he stepped back so she could go inside.

"Dan, what's that noise?"

For a minute the source of the insistent beeping eluded Dan's mind. Then he remembered. He'd left his beeper in the pocket of the shirt he'd been wearing when they left Dallas. "My beeper. I'll get it and shut it off."

"Somebody must need you," she said as he found the small device and pressed a button to quiet the annoying noise.

Out of habit he glanced at the number on the tiny screen, immediately recognizing Frank's code number. "It's just Frank," he told Gayla, wondering what his partner needed, since Frank rarely used their service to get in touch with him. "I'll give him a call."

As he dialed Frank's number, he noticed the worried look on Gayla's face. "It's probably nothing important, princess," he told her. Then Frank came on the phone and Dan realized his worst nightmare.

Not only had Eli Harris managed to tear up his dominant hand, he'd done it soon after the confrontation with Gayla that had so nearly decimated her. Now the man apparently expected Dan to work miracles and put him back together as good as new.

Dan's first uncharitable thought was to refuse. Ironsides didn't deserve his services, not after he'd cruelly rejected Gayla. His conscience kicked in, though, and he told Frank he'd get back to Dallas as fast as he could.

Hanging up, Dan turned and took Gayla in his arms. "We're going to have to cut this short, love. Your father has had an accident."

Damn it, the old bastard didn't deserve the kind of shock and worry Dan saw in Gayla's tear-filled eyes. "He's not..." She swallowed, hard, as if she dared not voice her fear.

"No, love. He's okay except for a bashed-up hand that Frank and his own choice of surgeons have persuaded him I'm the one who should fix. I need to call and get us on the first flight home."

"Daddy will die if he can't work," Gayla said, obviously aware of the importance of working hands to a surgeon. "How did it happen?"

While he waited for the reservationist to find them the earliest possible flight to Dallas, Dan repeated the few details of the accident that Frank had told him. "All right," he said when the woman came on the line and told him they could depart in less than two hours. Hanging up, he stuffed the few items he'd unpacked into a duffel bag while Gayla changed out of her swimsuit.

His shorts and T-shirt would have to do. Last night when he and Gayla had strolled along the beach, he'd gotten sand and salt water on the only long pants he'd brought with him, and he'd be damned if he'd itch all the way home. Stomping sand off his shoes, Dan gathered up their bags while Gayla held the door.

During the flight to Dallas, he tried to talk Gayla into going home, but she remained determined to be there for her father even if the man wouldn't acknowledge her. When they arrived at the hospital, he managed to persuade her to wait outside her father's room while he examined him.

"Dr. Harris. Sorry to hear about your accident."

"Well, I see Grogan finally found you. What have you been doing? Baking out by your pool?"

"We were in Galveston, enjoying the Gulf beaches." Picking up the chart that Ironsides obviously had been reading, Dan flipped through it for the MRIs Frank had mentioned. "We flew back as soon as I got Frank's message. Your daughter's outside. Would you like to see her?"

"Tess is out there?"

"No. Gayla is." It gave Dan a certain perverse pleasure to see Harris squirm. "Shall I call her in?"

"No. Damn it, just take a look at those pictures and tell me whether you can make this hand as good as new." He punctuated his demand by holding up his heavily-bandaged right hand.

"Keep that arm still if you don't want to risk further damage," Dan ordered. "I'm surprised Frank didn't order that it be completely immobilized."

"He did. I countermanded his order."

"Well, Dr. Harris, if you want me to try to repair that hand, you'd best be prepared to follow my orders."

Ironsides shot Dan a dirty look. "Can you fix it or can't you?"

Dan put the chart down and met the older surgeon's gaze. "I can fix it. Whether or not I can fix it well enough for you to do open heart surgery is a crapshoot. I'll tell you this, though. I'm good. Damn good. If I can't put you back together pretty much as good as new, no one around here can."

"Cocky bastard, aren't you?"

"Yeah. I wouldn't be a good surgeon if I weren't."

"Get to it, then. Mind you, I know every step you're going to take and I intend to let you know if you're doing something wrong. Let's get this show on the road. Grogan's standing by to assist, and your pretty anesthesiologist has already put a block in my arm."

Within the hour Dan strolled into the OR, where Ironsides was ordering the entire team around from his place on the operating table. Dan stepped up, adjusted the operative microscope, and prepared to make the first incision.

Harris barked out terse instructions as to where to make the cut. Laughing from behind his mask, Dan recognized the words as coming from a video he and Frank had made a while back for the orthopedic residents. If Ironsides didn't shut up, Dan figured he'd get so distracted he might well slice off a finger or two.

"Did you hear me, Newman?" Harris bellowed.

Raising his head, Dan looked to the head of the table. "Knock him out, Kelly," he said. "I don't need instructions."

When Kelly nodded, Dan settled on a stool and pulled the surgical microscope into position. "Give me some Garth, and we'll get this show on the road." At the first beat of "Rodeo" he asked for a scalpel.

Chapter Twenty-Two

๛

Michelle couldn't have arrived at a better time. Pushing the guilt and worry from her mind, Gayla followed her friend into a room on the same floor where her father had been before Dan had taken him down to surgery.

"Gayla Harris, Zach Hamilton. Zach, meet the lady who's going to get you on your feet ."

The man on the bed greeted Gayla with a lopsided grin. "So you're the one who's going to be teaching me to walk on water." His eyes twinkled with apparent amusement.

Gayla smiled. "In it, not on it."

"Whatever." Zach turned his attention to Michelle. "So when is your husband going to get around to taking this traction off my leg?"

Michelle shrugged. "You'll have to ask him."

"And where is Dr. Grogan today? Or is it Dr. Newman who's supposed to come see me this weekend?"

"Dr. Grogan. He's in the OR now, though, assisting Dr. Newman on an emergency case."

"Okay. Just as well if he doesn't come here today. Every time he does, he gets the tech to tighten up this torture rack some more."

Gayla liked the cop. She guessed his injuries must prey on his mind, but he appeared to have faced what had to have been an initial shock and cultivated a healthy attitude about the degree of recovery he should expect. "I've worked out a program I hope you'll enjoy."

"Honey, if I can watch you wearing one of those tight swimsuits with the legs cut up high on your pretty hips, you can bet I'll be enjoying my sessions in the pool."

"Zach! You're talking to Dr. Newman's girl."

Not his wife. Not even his fiancée. What she was, was Dan's lover, but Gayla guessed Michelle hadn't said that because it sounded...sordid. Gayla felt as though she'd slipped back in time to her high school days, when she'd liked the sound of being "someone's girl."

Zach grinned, showing straight white teeth Gayla bet were natural, unlike hers and most of her friends' whose perfect smiles had come only after years of orthodontia. "Too bad. I was thinking how much fun it would be to see if I could interest Ms. Gayla in giving me some after-hours therapy of a different kind."

"Thanks. I think."

"Any time, pretty lady. Don't suppose I could interest you two in a few hands of poker?"

Michelle laughed. "How about it, Gayla?"

"Sure." There was nothing Gayla could do for her father by waiting alone downstairs. She might as well hang out up here and help alleviate Zach's boredom. "Where are the cards?"

The cop certainly knew how to bluff. It took him only a few minutes to win all the change she and Michelle had been able to dig out of their purses.

"Enough already," Michelle said, laughing as she fished her beeping cell phone out of her purse. Hanging up, she turned to Gayla. "They've finished your dad's surgery."

"He's all right?"

"He's fine. Frank and Dan want us to meet them in the OR lounge. Zach, I guess you've fleeced us as much as you're going to, at least for now. See you Monday." Michelle headed out, leaving Gayla to follow.

"You'll be doing my father's therapy, won't you?"

"Probably. Why?"

Because he was likely to poison everybody against her now, the way he'd done before. Suddenly Gayla's new friendships seemed likely to dissolve. "I just wondered." She wasn't willing to put words to her fear.

Maybe while Eli was confined in a hospital room, Gayla could try again to reach him. She didn't know, though, if she'd be able to handle more accusations from his razor-sharp tongue. As she and Dan drove home, her agitation grew.

* * * * *

Gayla had never before felt like throwing up—not even when she'd been drinking booze by the bottle. Today, though, she'd felt all morning as if she were going to be sick. Trying to ignore her queasy stomach, she attributed it to anxiety about facing her father again.

Here it was, nearly noon. She hadn't eaten a bite since Dan had heated some soup for them after they got home from the hospital last night. There was no reason for her to be sick. None at all. Nobody got sick from canned chicken soup and a handful of salted crackers.

"Want to share this pizza?" Michelle asked as the scent of cheese, tomatoes, and oregano made Gayla's stomach churn faster.

"No, thank you," she managed to say through clenched teeth as she charged toward the rest room. She made it, just barely, before heaving.

Determined to finish her work, Gayla made her way back to her new office. Michelle was there, but thankfully the pizza wasn't. The faint smell that lingered in the room fed her nausea, but Gayla tried to ignore it. Surely there was nothing more inside her that could come out.

"You're sick."

"A little. Don't worry, I don't have fever. It's just anxiety over Daddy, I think. Nothing you can catch."

Michelle raised an eyebrow, as if she didn't believe Gayla's explanation. "When did it start?"

"What?"

"The nausea."

Not anxious to pursue this discussion, Gayla picked up a textbook on aquatic therapy and began to thumb through it. "This morning when I woke up."

"Was Dan sick, too?"

"No. At least he seemed okay when he left for the hospital. I'll be all right."

"Okay, I'll leave you to your misery. I've got a pizza getting cold over in my office, out of range of your tender little nose."

Gayla was beginning to worry about whether that can of soup could have been tainted, so when Dan called her a little later, she asked him if he'd been feeling funny.

"No, princess. I'm fine. What's wrong?"

"I threw up. Twice. The second time from nothing more than getting a whiff of Michelle's pizza. My stomach still feels like something's jumping around inside it."

"I'll come over right now." He sounded unreasonably concerned about her simple little malady.

"No, you have patients to tend. I'm sure this is just a reaction to Daddy's accident."

After a moment's hesitation Dan agreed that she was probably right. "Still, if you aren't better by tomorrow, I want you to see your doctor. And I'll take a look at you tonight."

That last comment made Gayla smile. She felt better, too, as if the nausea was finally settling down. "You look at me every night, Doc. Since when do you need an excuse?"

"It's good to have a reason sometimes. Otherwise you might get the idea you've got me hogtied with your sexy little pussy."

She laughed, then changed the subject. "How is Daddy?"

"Well enough to convene the Death Committee again, from his hospital bed. He refused to postpone the final session, and I refused to let him risk messing up my handiwork by getting out of bed. I'm going to be stuck here again tonight, probably until about eight o'clock." He sounded a little cranky about that.

She'd be finished here by four o'clock and had given her team swimmers the day off from practice. If she went straight to the hospital she could confront her father. Surely since he was well enough to hold a committee meeting, he was in good enough shape for her to beg him one last time for forgiveness.

Telling Dan she'd meet him at the hospital and wait to go home with him, Gayla hung up and turned her attention to adapting therapeutic exercises designed to be done on land for use in the pool.

* * * * *

Dan would rather be dragged through fire than let Ironsides destroy Gayla again. He feared that was exactly what the man would do when she made herself vulnerable by trying again to gain his forgiveness. Still, he could think of nothing he could do to stop her from making effort after effort, until Harris stripped her of everything she'd worked so hard to regain.

Finished with his scheduled cases, he hadn't bothered to change out of his OR greens. Exchanging quips with the nurses he ran into on the way out of the surgical suite, Dan hurried to make rounds. He could have checked on Ironsides first, but he chose to save the worst for last. Preparing himself for an unpleasant encounter having nothing to do with his patient's medical condition, Dan swung open the door and strode into Harris's private room.

"The MRI they took this morning looks pretty good," Harris said by way of greeting.

"Since you had it sent up here instead of to surgery as I had ordered, I haven't had the privilege of seeing it yet. Might I give it a glance?"

"Chart should be in the drawer over there."

"Your chart belongs at the nursing station with all the others," Dan commented as he searched through films and papers for the latest MRI. "It does look good. I did an excellent job, if I say so myself."

"You did. I owe you an apology, Newman. I was wrong when I thought you couldn't handle trauma surgery. You can. Brilliantly, I might add, although it escapes me how you can concentrate and listen to those cowboy songs at the same time." Ironsides grinned. "I wasn't quite as out as you apparently thought when you told the nurse to crank up Garth Brooks."

"Thanks. I think. Are you having a lot of pain?"

"No. If I do I'll just order myself a shot."

Dan resisted a sudden urge to strangle the man. "Any meds you get, I'll order. Don't let your giant ego get in the way of your good sense."

"Or what? You'll get Kelly to knock me out cold again?"

Dan shrugged. "I prefer my patients unconscious while I operate, especially if they think they're going to tell me how to do my job. I'm certain you'd feel that way too under similar circumstances."

"Possibly. Anyway, Newman, I take care of my debts. And I owe you, big time. Name your price."

Setting the chart on the bedside table, Dan met Ironsides' unflinching gaze. "Forgive your daughter."

Suddenly Dan felt as if the air around them had taken on an electrical charge. The silence nearly deafened him. When the older man cleared his throat, Dan felt his own muscles jerk.

"I can't. When she failed herself and shamed her mother and me with her weakness and excesses, she did the unforgivable. Did you know she killed her mother as surely as if she'd put a gun to her head? I think not."

"I don't believe that." Gayla wanted only to love and be loved, never to hurt even those who had done her harm. Dan thought he saw moisture building in Ironsides' small, owl-like eyes, but he couldn't be certain. "Why would you even think it?"

"Because living with the shame of what the girl did ate at my sweet, gentle wife, who never said a harsh word in her life, to the point that she developed hypertension. Within a year after we disowned Gayla, Sylvia died of a massive stroke."

Apparently Ironsides did have some gentler feelings, if only for his late wife. While Dan thought silently that the woman's stress had been caused more by Harris himself than by agonizing over Gayla's sins, he chose not to express his doubt, since his patient appeared to be in danger of hyperventilating.

"We can discuss this later," he said, debating whether he should order medication to bring Ironsides' blood pressure down.

"My answer will remain the same. Take my advice. Get away from her. Someday if you don't, you will be very sorry. She'll shame you as she has shamed me." As if exhausted, Ironsides leaned back against a pillow and closed his eyes.

"I can't do that, any more than you can forgive her." Dan's bubbling hatred warred with his knowledge that this unbending man was a patient in his care and was less than twenty-four hours out of surgery. "Rest. I'll be back at six for the committee meeting." He didn't trust himself to stay, because if he did he was certain his fury would override his good sense.

* * * * *

When Gayla stepped into her father's room, he was sleeping. A good thing, since if she'd walked in while he was awake he'd have had someone rush in and throw her out. As she sat on the chair next to his bed she watched him, intent on planning what she'd say when he awakened.

Instead, her mind wandered. He looked helpless, tethered as he was to the bed with IV lines in one hand and the other, damaged one strapped firmly to an immobilizing board. Asleep, he looked like the man she'd tried so hard to please—his face impassive, his body unmoving.

"Do you remember how proud he was when you won the high point trophy at that meet in Houston?"

It seemed fitting that her mother's spirit had joined her here. Gayla recalled her dad lifting her up and twirling her around when they'd come home from the meet. She'd been eleven years old, and the victory had tasted sweeter because she'd had her daddy to share it.

She remembered times he set her on his lap and praised her for having reached some interim goal they had set, precious moments when he granted her an elusive smile. The occasional holiday he spent at home, looking proudly at her and Tess as they took part in traditional rituals.

The times had been few and far between, but Gayla believed Eli had once loved her. She hoped someday that deep-down love would surface again. Meanwhile she'd only hope for his forgiveness.

"What are you doing here?"

Gayla blinked at the sound of her father's voice. "Sitting with you. Watching you while you slept. Remembering."

"Remembering what?"

"Just things. Little things you used to do that let me know you cared." She wanted to reach out and touch his hand, but she dared not, for fear that when he jerked away he'd do harm to the hand Dan had worked so hard to repair.

"No more. Ever. If you had sobered up and come home before your mother killed herself from worrying about you, my answer might be different."

Gayla blinked back tears. "I didn't have the strength to face you then. I do, now."

"Strength you take from Newman?"

"From me. Daddy, I haven't had a drink or anything else for almost two years now. I still want to, but I haven't."

"Yet there is nothing that says you won't, given the right set of circumstances."

"I know." That knowledge was her Achilles heel, the reason she hesitated to reach out and take what Dan so lovingly offered.

"Get away from Dan Newman. He's a good man, too good to let himself be dragged down by the likes of you. Now get out of here. And don't come back." Turning his head away from Gayla, her father said no more.

* * * * *

Later, after the Death Committee had reprimanded Hap Randall and limited his future surgical privileges, Dan met Gayla in the hospital cafeteria.

"Have you been waiting long, princess?" he asked as he sat down.

"I hate this place!" Shredding her napkin between her fingers, Gayla gave every indication of being close to breaking down.

Dan smiled. "Then let's go home. Feeling better?" From the remains of what looked like tea and toast, Dan guessed her stomach must still be causing her problems.

"No. I wasn't hungry."

Later when she told him about her visit with Ironsides, he had to admire her strength to go on and eat anything at all. Not knowing what to say to ease her pain, he settled for simply holding her in his arms until she slept.

* * * * *

The next morning Gayla's nausea returned with a vengeance. It was all she could do to get into the bathroom before everything in her stomach came back up.

"Gayla? What's wrong?" The loud thud that followed penetrated her sleepy brain. "Oh, shit!"

Not sure she wasn't going to throw up again immediately, Gayla poked her head out the bathroom door, only to find Dan sprawled out by the edge of the bed. "Oh, God, are you hurt?"

A sheepish grin on his face, Dan looked up at her. "Only my pride. I forgot about my leg. Happens sometimes when I've been sound asleep. Are you okay?"

"Better than you, I think. What can I do?"

"Come here and hand me my damn leg." When she did, he grabbed her hand. "What's making you sick, Gayla?"

"Some bug, I guess. Can you put it on with your leg stretched out like that?"

He laughed. "I've done it before. If you want to help, though, come down here and be my guest."

Moving very carefully so as not to trigger another bout with the heaves, Gayla sank to the floor and helped him put on the prosthesis. "There. Think you can get up?"

"Yeah. Thanks, princess."

"You're wel—" The word got cut off when Gayla scrambled to her feet and toward the bathroom. By the time Dan got up and followed her, she had her head back over the toilet bowl.

"Gayla. What's wrong?"

She was in no condition to answer, between fighting dry heaves and darn near choking on the foul-tasting stuff in her mouth. "Go 'way." Vaguely she registered the fact that Dan was supporting most of her weight. "Come on, princess, get it all up. You'll feel better."

Right! Just like she'd felt better yesterday. Gayla hated being sick and fought giving in to illness, but she was about ready to admit she needed a doctor. Slowly she lifted her head, leaning back against Dan's hard body. When he held her like this, she felt almost human, but she didn't dare try to eat a mouthful of the poached egg and toast he set before her after she got dressed.

* * * * *

The smell of coffee brewing in Jamie's lab set Gayla's insides to churning again. Maybe there was something seriously wrong with her. Dragging herself up from the stool where she'd perched to watch the prosthetist assemble the full-leg brace Zach Hamilton would have to wear to do his therapy, she made her way through the gym to Michelle's office.

"Do you think I need a doctor?" she asked after admitting that for the past two days she hadn't been able to hold any kind of food on her stomach.

Michelle looked up from the papers she'd been working on. "I would if I were you. Have you missed any periods?"

Gayla wasn't sure. "I've never been very regular," she replied, sidestepping that question. "Why?"

"Could you be pregnant?"

"No. At least I don't think so. Dan always uses a condom." Suddenly Gayla recalled the one night he didn't. "Usually," she amended.

"Usually?" Michelle's eyebrows lifted, as if she couldn't believe what Gayla had said.

"Every time except one or two."

"Who's your gynecologist?"

Gayla almost named the friend of her father who'd taken care of her when she miscarried. "I don't have one."

"Well, you're going to have mine, at least for a check-up. You'll like Greg Halpern. He's one of the best. Kelly recommended him to me."

The way Gayla's stomach was churning, she wasn't very particular about what doctor she saw, just as long as she could see him or her quickly. "Do you think you could talk him into seeing me today?"

"I can try."

Gayla tried to fight the urge to throw up again while Michelle spoke with her doctor's secretary. When Michelle reported that Dr. Halpern would work her in at four o'clock, she let herself relax.

* * * * *

While she waited in Dr. Halpern's large, comfortable office, Gayla wished she'd asked Dan to come with her. She knew she'd need his strength if she was going to learn she had some dread disease. To take her mind off her worries, she thumbed through leaflets that dealt with everything from uterine cancer to treatments for infertility.

"Congratulations," Dr. Halpern said, his voice booming out as if he loved giving out good news. Gayla could see why Michelle and Kelly liked the man—he was fortyish, almost as handsome as Dan, and possessed of a wicked sense of humor she imagined could bring smiles to the faces of the dead.

"For what?" she asked, happy to be able to assume she was in no danger of immediate death.

"You're pregnant. Would you like to use my phone to tell the lucky father?"

"When?"

"About three weeks ago, give or take a few days. Hey, don't faint on me. It's not good for the baby."

"There's no way." Gayla couldn't believe she was pregnant. She hadn't been sick a day before.

Dr. Halpern's booming laugh reminded her of Dan. "It happens like this. Have sex, and unless there's something wrong with someone's baby-making equipment, chances are good that sooner or later you're going to be a mommy. I assume you *have* been having sexual relations recently."

Gayla nodded.

"Good. I'm not ready yet to believe in virgin births."

Finally she found her voice. "But we used condoms. Almost every time."

"Only takes one time to do the trick. Even if you had used them every time, you still could get pregnant. Condoms, as necessary as they are because of AIDS, are hardly the most reliable form of birth control." He met Gayla's gaze, and his smile disappeared. "Being pregnant isn't a problem, is it?" he asked, his tone suddenly serious.

"Oh, no." No matter what the future held, Gayla wanted this baby. She imagined holding a dark-haired little boy to her breast, and the thought made her smile. "I'm just surprised."

"Understandable. Okay now, let's get down to business. I'm going to run some tests and make sure there aren't any problems we need to watch out for. These are prescriptions for prenatal vitamins and pills to ease the nausea, and a booklet that will answer most of the questions you may have about what you can and can't do while that baby's growing inside you."

Gayla's head was spinning, almost as much as her stomach had been churning all day long. She had to make some decisions now, decisions that would affect not only her but the baby who was still just a tiny speck of cells inside her womb.

"I need the name of the baby's father."

"Dan Newman."

Halpern laughed so hard he nearly fell off his chair. Had the man gone nuts? "What's so funny?"

As quickly as he'd started laughing he stopped and met Gayla's questioning gaze. "Ask Dan when you tell him I'm your obstetrician."

On the way home Gayla decided she had only two choices. She could tell Dan about the baby and agree to marry him. Her other choice, almost too painful to contemplate, would be to leave him and Dallas, go somewhere far away, and raise their baby alone.

If only she could reconcile with her father, her first choice would be so much easier. Gayla didn't need his affirmation to believe in her recovery—but then it had been emotions and not reason that had dragged her down, and other emotions that had let her come back.

Chapter Twenty-Three

The Ghosts

ஐ

"Sylvia, come here. Your daughter has just learned she's going to make us grandparents. Oh, I can't wait. I hope it's a girl. I can buy her little dresses and ruffled socks, and look for some porcelain dolls for her to put on a shelf in her room!"

Sylvia recalled Gayla's other pregnancy that had ended almost before it had begun. Instead of the elation Ruth obviously felt, she had mixed emotions. *"You're certain?"*

"I'm sure. Danny will insist that they get married now. Oh! There he is, getting out of his car. He'll be inside with Gayla any minute now." Ruth paused, as if in deep thought. *"He'll have to get rid of that convertible. Buy something sturdy. Responsible. Maybe a Mercedes sedan? What do you think?"*

"I don't know. Eli has always had one of those. Personally I think Danny's car is just fine."

Ruth's brow wrinkled when she heard Eli's name. *"You know, Ruth,"* Sylvia pointed out, *"Eli will be our grandchild's only living grandparent. Maybe we should wish…"*

"No! Either Eli comes around or he doesn't, but he has to do it on his own. If he wants to hold onto all his anger and meanness, it will be his loss."

Sylvia silently admitted Ruth was right as she glanced at their children. *"Danny's inside now. Do you think she's going to tell him right away?"*

"I certainly would. I wouldn't want it any more obvious than it's already going to be that my baby had been conceived before the wedding."

"Look," Sylvia murmured, her gaze fixed on her future son-in-law—she hoped. "Danny's fixing Gayla a bowl of soup. Isn't he sweet?"

"Hmmm. Can't your daughter even manage to warm up something for them so Danny doesn't have to do everything when he comes home from work?"

That made Sylvia bristle. "I'll have you know Gayla's a wonderful cook. She's not feeling well, that's all."

"How do you know?"

"Because I looked in on her early this morning while you were still haunting your room. Gayla was so sick, she threw up twice. Once before and once after your son decided to try walking without his artificial leg and fell sprawling onto the floor. That, my friend, was a sight to see."

Ruth stood up and stomped her foot. "You think that was funny? You call watching my Danny hurt himself fun?"

"Oh, he didn't get hurt. And he seemed to think the whole thing was pretty humorous. Gayla put all those things he has to wear onto his leg while he lay sprawled out on the floor."

"You sure he didn't hurt himself?"

Whatever bad things Sylvia could say about Ruth, she couldn't fault the woman for not loving her only child. "He was fine. Look at him now. Does he look as if he injured himself?"

"No. He doesn't. You said Gayla was sick?"

"Sick as a dog."

"I don't think you should sound so happy about that, either."

Sylvia smiled. If she were alive, Ruth would probably end up being a model mother-in-law, not the one from hell, as Sylvia had first thought. "For the first few weeks I carried my girls, I was so sick I thought I was going to die. I survived, though, and so did they." She lowered her voice almost to a whisper. "I think she's going to tell him now."

She didn't, though. Sylvia was beginning to worry. Surely Gayla wouldn't...

"She's afraid to tell him," Ruth muttered, a scowl marring her ghostly features. *"Surely she knows he will be thrilled beyond words. Danny loves children. Always has."*

Sylvia's chest constricted as if she still had a beating heart. *"No, I don't think she's afraid Danny will be angry. More likely, she's frightened to death that if she marries him, she'll fall off the wagon somewhere along the way and ruin his life along with hers. Don't worry, Gayla won't be able to deny her baby its father. Not after she's had time to think everything through logically."*

"I hope not." Ruth turned away when Danny and Gayla walked arm in arm into his bedroom, and Sylvia broke the contact with her daughter to protect the other ghost's delicate sensibilities.

"I'd like for them to have a boy," she said wistfully, careful not to phrase the words as a wish. Some things, Sylvia figured, were best left up to nature.

Chapter Twenty-Four

If Dan hadn't known the odds against it, he'd have sworn Gayla was pregnant. She'd tossed up last night's soup and sandwich promptly upon getting out of bed this morning, and when he'd left to make rounds before surgery, she looked positively green.

He trusted her, though, when she told him her doctor had said the nausea was just a passing thing and nothing to lose sleep over. As he drove over to get the verdict from Greg Halpern on just how infertile he might be, Dan tried to recall foods he'd heard would rest easily in a queasy digestive tract. It worried him that Gayla might get dehydrated.

When he got to Greg's office he expected to cool his heels for a while when he noticed a waiting room full of women in various stages of pregnancy. Instead, the receptionist took him to Greg's office and poured him some coffee. A few minutes later she returned, a plate of brownies in hand. "Help yourself. Greg will be right with you," she said, favoring him with a dazzling display of teeth when she smiled. "Your lab results are in that folder. Feel free to look them over."

Suddenly the brownies lost their appeal. Picking up the folder the woman had indicated, Dan hesitated. Figuring Greg wanted to let him down easy, he flipped to the first page of results from the lab and tried to decipher them.

"So what do you think?" Greg asked when he came in and sprawled in the chair behind his desk.

"I think I can read numbers. You tell me what they mean."

"What the hell, Newman. You're a doctor."

His colleague's sense of humor was beginning to run thin. "Can you tell me exactly how to perform a Symes amputation?" Dan paused, as if waiting for Greg to dredge up details he'd learned long ago but never used. "I didn't think so. How in the hell, then, can you expect me to make sense out of a goddamn fertility study?"

Dan was certain Greg's guffaws could be heard all the way out in the waiting room. When he got no response he tried begging. "Come on, it's been nine years since I had to try to memorize this stuff in case they might ask it on the national boards. Pretend I never went to med school and give me the bottom line." He set the opened chart in front of Greg.

"Bottom line? Your count's low, but the little guys have great motility. They've got no genetic problems. If you were anybody else, I'd tell you to go home, flush your significant other's pills, toss out your condoms, and have fun. Good, down and dirty spontaneous fun. It's my considered medical opinion that if your partner has nothing wrong inside, you're going to be buying cribs and strollers and looking into college funds—fairly soon."

"So since I'm me?"

"I'd tell you to get the hell out of here and let me help couples who need help."

That pissed Dan off. "So what have I done to land on your blacklist?"

Greg shot him a puzzled look. "You don't know yet, do you?"

"Know what?"

"You need to talk to Gayla."

Greg wasn't making sense. Or was he? Suddenly Dan remembered Gayla's mysterious nausea. "Are you trying to tell me she's pregnant?" No. If she were, she'd have told him. "It's just not possible."

Shaking his head, Greg fished a chart from his drawer. "I shouldn't do this, but since she said you're the father, I'll do it anyhow. Look. Surely even you can read a positive pregnancy test."

Dan could and did. Shell-shocked, he handed Gayla's chart back to Greg. "Is she all right?"

"She's fine. Sick as a dog from what she tells me, but that's not unusual. She'll probably feel great after a few weeks. I'm surprised she didn't run right home yesterday and tell you. Maybe I shouldn't be, since she seemed as shocked as you do now."

"Shocked isn't the word." Dan had trouble believing the woman he loved was going to have a baby. The baby he'd doubted he could ever give her.

"Like I told you, I don't give guarantees about people being infertile unless the essentials just aren't there. If there's one live sperm and it manages to swim into one fallopian tube that has a ripe egg in it, chances are there's going to be a pregnancy. Remember, Newman, I warned you. So don't go thinking about calling your high-priced lawyer."

Suddenly Dan wanted to shout. He wanted to get down on his knees and thank Gayla for loving him. He wanted to reach across the desk and hug the comedian of an OB-GYN who hadn't had to work his magic so Gayla could have her baby. "I'm more likely to nominate you for sainthood than sue you, Halpern. Thanks."

"Wait to thank me until you get my bill. I assume I should send it to you and not to Ironsides."

"Ironsides? Oh, for the delivery." Apparently Greg didn't know that bastard had disowned Gayla, or that he'd not even give her a chance to get back in his good graces. "Send it to me. That's one bill I'll jump at the chance of paying."

"I take it you're going to marry her?"

"Yeah. I'm going to marry Gayla, even if I have to drag her kicking and screaming down the aisle."

Greg stood up and held out his hand. "I wish you good luck, buddy. You'll need it to stand having Ironsides for a father-in-law. I guarantee you'll go ape over your kid, though. That should be some small solace."

Dan grinned as he shook Greg's hand. Later, while he waited for Gayla to get home, he wondered how long it would be before she decided to tell him about the baby. No way was he going to say a word. He'd just play dumb and let her make the next move.

* * * * *

Gayla clasped her hands over her stomach, imagining that she could already feel the tiny life inside her. Staring up at the new moon in the sky, she tried to clear her mind of everything except the decision she had to make.

It was hard, imagining herself somewhere far from home, alone except for a tiny being who couldn't walk or talk or do anything except sleep and eat for a long time. What would she do? How would she take care of the baby and still manage to support it? Would anybody hire a pregnant swim coach, especially one who had no husband? She doubted it, considering that coaches were supposed to set a good example for kids.

The picture of herself with Dan, making a home for their baby together, came into focus much easier. She saw him, eager to be with them when he came home from a long day of surgery. Somehow she couldn't picture him relegating his child to her and whatever hired help he might provide, the way her father had always done.

No, Dan would be a wonderful father. A wonderful husband, too, one who deserved far more than she could bring to a marriage with him. She'd fallen once, and she had no doubt that she could stumble again, no matter how hard she tried not to.

She shuddered when she thought of her baby having to see her the way she'd been, yet she couldn't fathom giving him up. Recalling the days when she hadn't been able to get up, Gayla wondered what would happen to the child if she should fall back into the pattern of drinking and sleeping, using drugs to wake up and other drugs to stem the feelings of worthlessness she got in rare moments of clear thinking.

If she were alone, the child would suffer, perhaps even die because of her excesses. Could she deny him a father who'd ensure his care, especially when her only reason for doing that would be to protect Dan from what she might do if her world suddenly collapsed again? No. With Dan her world would be secure. He'd love her and protect her, no matter what the tragedies might be that would otherwise send her over the edge.

Then she thought of losing him, not because of anything she could do but by some awful twist of fate. Would she be able to go on?

Gayla sat on a bench in the deserted park and thought of the kids she coached, of Zach Hamilton and the other patients Frank and Michelle truly believed she could help And Dan, who'd had given her love and trust like no one ever had before. None of these people were stupid. They believed in her, saw her as a good person—not perfect but worthy of loving and being loved.

Her father was the only one in her world who expected perfection, the only person who had denied her the right to make mistakes. Why did she keep giving him the power to make her feel like dirt? For as long as she could remember, she'd tried to please him, and at times she'd succeeded. While she wanted to regain his love, not having it hadn't destroyed her. She was still here, still functioning, able to want and love and give of herself to others. She was a good person, no matter what Eli Harris thought.

Yes, Gayla could get along without her father's forgiveness. She could survive alone, but she didn't need to. Dan wanted her, thought she hung the moon. It hurt him when she held back from commitment with him.

Why should she hesitate? Yes, she might slip, but there was at least an equal chance that she wouldn't. Her decision suddenly clear, Gayla laid one hand across her stomach, needing to communicate on some primal level with Dan's baby. "You're going to need your daddy, little one. I need him, too. Let's go home and ask him if he's ready for us to be a family." She patted the spot over where the baby was growing before walking slowly back to her car.

* * * * *

It was nearly ten o'clock, and Dan was beginning to get worried. Gayla had never been so late getting home from the club before. Making a mental note to buy her a cell phone, he gave up on the medical journal he'd been trying to read and started to pace the floor.

Periodically he glanced at the photo that had arrived in today's mail. Black and white, with patterns from leaves of the tree overhead shadowing his and Gayla's faces, it was more a work of art than just another snapshot. The photographer had captured the mood and ambience of new lovers engrossed in each other, so poignantly that Dan could almost replay the accompanying music in his mind.

He remembered having told Gayla he intended to put this picture in the bedroom, but he thought now that he'd seen it that it belonged over the mantel, a tribute to the beginning of their love. Smiling at the thought of someday telling their children about that night by the bandstand, he checked his watch again. Ten after ten, and Gayla was still not home.

When he heard the sound of her key in the front door he took a deep breath. She was home now, and that was all that mattered. She didn't need to know her absence had alarmed him. Seeing her there, looking tired but far healthier than she had this morning, made him ache to take her in his arms.

"I missed you," he said softly as he kissed her cheek. "Look." Handing her the photo, he stepped back so he could see her reaction. "Remember the mariachis?"

For a long time she stared at the images. Then she smiled. "This looks like love."

"The photographer sent a note. Want to read it?"

She shook her head. "Later. Right now we need to talk."

Was she going to tell him about their baby? Finding a spot on the sofa and sitting down, he patted the empty space beside him. "Come sit with me."

Instead of sitting, she knelt between his legs. "Will you marry me?" she asked, her gaze steady as she looked into his eyes.

Dan pulled her up and set her on his lap. "Why, princess? Why now, after you've been putting me off for weeks?" He intended to drag her down the aisle no matter what, but he wanted her to want him not because of the baby but because she loved him.

Gayla blew gently against his neck. "Because Tess and Michelle and nearly everybody I know who ever saw you say you're too big a fish to throw back in the pond. You're silly, Doc. I want to marry you because I love you. And I love how you love me."

"What about your fears?"

"I'm more afraid of losing you than hurting you. I can't make any promises other than that I'll do my best to make you happy." Very gently, as if she were caressing their baby, she stroked the sensitive spot at the nape of his neck.

All Dan wanted was to say yes, get that ring on her finger to stake his claim, and take Gayla to bed—not necessarily in that order. "No one could ask for more." Except the news he wanted to hear from her soft, sensual lips.

"I'm a good person. I know that now. I'm not perfect, though, and I never will be."

He pulled her close and whispered in her ear. "You're all I want, and more. I'm far from perfection myself. Don't tell anybody, though."

"Dan, I'm trying to be serious!"

"Me, too. Tell me, did you manage to get your father to break down and give you another chance?" Dan couldn't imagine any other force that would suddenly have made Gayla feel worthwhile. God knows he'd tried, without much success until now.

"No, but it doesn't matter what he thinks. I'm a good person. I'm doing good things. I don't need his forgiveness anymore. Not if I have your love."

"You'll always have that."

"Will you marry me? Help me take care of you, me, and the baby we've made?" She whispered so softly that Dan could barely make out the words. When he did, it took a moment for him to feign surprise.

"Baby?" he croaked with what he hoped sounded at least a bit akin to shock.

"Our baby."

"How? When?"

"How did you get through med school? We made a baby by making love, and it happened about three weeks ago."

"I meant, when is the baby due?" Dan could figure that out for himself as well, but he wanted to hear it from her.

"Next May. Dr. Halpern said around the tenth of the month."

What was it about hearing the woman he loved tell him she was going to have his baby that brought tears to a grown man's eyes? Unashamed, Dan let the tears flow down his cheeks, holding onto Gayla as though she were a precious, delicate flower. "I'll marry you, princess. Just say when."

"As soon as we can. But, Dan, I want a real wedding. Are you happy?"

He laughed out loud. "Happy" was too wimpy a word to describe how he felt. Gayla was going to be his wife. Miraculously, they had created a child together. Dan wanted to jump for joy, shout out his elation for all of Dallas to hear. He wanted to take his woman in his arms and worship every inch of her gorgeous body.

"We can still make love, can't we?"

"Yes. Oh, yes."

"Then I'm a happy man. Hold on, princess, we're off to bed."

Gayla laughed as he lifted her in his arms and headed for the bedroom. "I seem to recall having done this once before," she told him, her warm breath tickling the skin beneath his ear as she tackled the buttons of his shirt.

"Yeah. We have, haven't we?"

He set her down beside the bed, the way he had that first night. "Pretty soon you won't be able to carry me around like this," she said, her hands already occupied with getting his shirt off.

"Yeah, I will. Unless you decide to get as round as you are tall. Not very far and maybe not all that often, but if you need me to, I'll manage." Without hesitating Dan untied the knot at the waist of Gayla's sundress and unwrapped it from around her as if she were a present sent only to give him pleasure.

Meanwhile she unfastened his pants and let them fall, leaving them both standing there in just their underwear. "I have something for you, princess." He moved to the dresser to get the ring he'd bought weeks earlier, before his fears and hers had nearly wrenched them apart.

When he came to her again, he got down on one knee. Gayla sat on the bed, saying nothing. Her soft, dreamy gaze said everything he needed to hear. "My turn now," he told her as he snapped open the box and took out the ring.

"Will you marry me? Live with me and love me for the rest of our lives? Have my babies and love them the way we love each other? Gayla, will you make me the luckiest man on earth?"

She choked back a sob, and he saw her eyes well up with tears. "Y-yes. Dan, I love you so much."

In slow motion, he slipped the diamond ring onto the third finger of her left hand, taking care not to let the smooth gold band scrape her tender skin. Then, because it seemed so right, he brought her hand to his lips and held it there, tracing the band with soft open-mouthed kisses. There was so much he wanted to say, so many promises he needed to make. He yearned to tell her how she'd filled a lonely void in his soul and made his life complete. The words eluded him, though. A poet he knew he was not.

Still holding her hand, he raised his head. "Thank you for loving me." The words came out so softly he wondered if she could hear them.

"You're welcome, Doc. Now do you think you might let me get a look at the rock that's weighing down my finger?"

"Gayla, you're priceless." Releasing her hand and watching as she held it up to the light, Dan got to his feet and sat beside her. "Well, do you like it?"

"I love it. I love you. What's not to love? I'm going to marry the handsomest, most brilliant, most absolutely fantastic guy in the whole world—and we're going to have a baby."

"Princess, you're going to make my head so big I won't fit through doors." Dan didn't mind, especially tonight when he felt as if he could move mountains if Gayla asked him to.

She held out her arms, inviting him in. "Come here, darling. I want to examine each and every inch of your oh-so-sexy body. Slowly and in excruciating detail. Then I want you to do the same to me. You don't have surgery tomorrow, do you?"

"No. If I did, I'd reschedule it," he said as he deftly unhooked her bra. "Come here."

Chapter Twenty-Five

ಇಾ

Gayla's breasts began to tingle even before Dan tossed her bra across the room. His warm gaze alone had the ability to make them ache for the touch of his hands and mouth. He didn't make her wait. Gently he cradled one breast in each hand and lowered his head, taking first one nipple and then the other inside his mouth. His suckling sent sparks all the way to her toes.

His dark head against the paleness of her breasts reminded her of that night at the concert and the photo that captured so vividly the sensual awareness that had flowed between Dan and her from the moment they met. Threading her fingers through his hair, she drew him closer, letting herself savor the hot passionate need no one else but Dan had ever been able to arouse.

Well-developed muscles in his shoulders rippled visibly as he caressed her breasts, making her itch to touch him, feel his power. She let one hand drift downward to his heavy erection. The reality of his potency held under tight rein flowed through her fingers and into her soul.

He slid one hand slowly down her body, teasing her with feathery touches that could have tickled if they hadn't aroused her so. His finger tracing under the elastic of her panties reminded her they hadn't taken the time to undress completely. She wanted the barriers gone now. All of them.

"Take them off," she whispered. "Please."

"Not yet." For what seemed like hours he used only his hands and touched her only in places she'd never thought of as erotic. Playing her body as if it were a finely-tuned instrument, he built her to a fever pitch of sexual need, then soothed and calmed her, only to build up her passion again. Gayla felt his love in every touch, saw passion in his dark eyes and the tightness of his sculpted jaw.

With her hands she stroked away the tension there. Then she guided his lips to hers. The crisp, woodsy aftershave she loved on him lent a tart, sweet fragrance to the musky smell of their mutual desire. When she traced her tongue along the seam of his lips, he parted them and let her in. Thrust and retreat, ebb and flow. So much and yet so little, compared with what they wanted of each other.

Gayla slid her hand between their bodies in search of his hot, hard cock. Suddenly she wanted to see as well as feel him. Drawing herself up into a sitting position, she met Dan's questioning gaze. "I want to look. See what's going to be all mine."

The tiny lines around his eyes deepened, and the corners of his mouth twitched. "Be my guest. Just don't look too long and hard, or you'll miss out on the main event." He grinned as he lifted his hips and slid his black briefs down, freeing her hand and his extremely enthusiastic cock.

As he'd done to her, she traced her fingertips over his taut, fit body. The silky hair under his arms and the pair of dimples she'd never noticed before at the base of his spine fascinated her, drew extra attention as she explored him. Ignoring his pleas for mercy, she stroked her way down to his toes, stopping when she got there to suck one into her mouth. When she moved over to make her way back up the other side, she burst out laughing.

"You've still got on one shoe."

"Did you forget?"

When she controlled her laughter enough to glance up at him, he looked amused. "Yes. I did."

"Good."

"Why good?" Directing her efforts where they would do the most damage, she ran a finger up the inside of his left thigh and down again until she was touching slick rubbery silicone instead of fit, muscular flesh. "Want this off?"

Dan sat up and put both arms around her from the back. "Good because that thing down there makes so little difference to you that you can forget about it."

"Why should it surprise you that I don't think about it? You obviously forget about it sometimes, too—such as when you get out of bed and go sprawling in a heap on the floor. Come on, future husband. You've got me tingling and aching in spots I didn't know I had. I want satisfaction."

Giving a playful tweak to her tingling nipples, Dan slid off the bed and stood at its edge. "Slide over here, and I'll see what I can do." When she did he slid her panties down and tossed them aside, coming right back to run a finger lightly along her wet, hot slit.

Though she ached for him to bury his long, thick cock deep in her dripping pussy, she also wanted to taste him. When she lowered her head though, he stepped away.

"Not now, princess. Flip over and bring your sweet tush as close as you can get it to the edge of the bed. We're gonna make love a new way. I promise, you'll like it."

Gayla felt awkward, perched on her knees and elbows, her backside in the air. Almost immediately she felt his fingers plucking at her nipples and his throbbing cock nudging her from behind. Her vague discomfort at the strange position soon subsided in a haze of pleasure. "This won't set your tummy off like me being on top of you might," he whispered as he gently thrust home.

He moved slowly, deliciously, stretching and filling her and making every cell in her body sing. His hands roamed, caressing her as though she were a priceless work of art. The tension built inside her, taking her up and making her soar as she never had before.

She willed him silently to move faster, to send her over the edge before she died of ecstasy. His hands slid from her breasts to her hips, and when he had her firmly in his grasp he answered her unspoken plea. Driving deeper and harder, his rhythmic motion building to a crescendo, he led her toward the release she sought. With each thrust, she came closer, sought more desperately for release. As though he knew how much she needed it, he changed the angle of his penetration and caught her G-spot.

That sent her plummeting over the edge just as she felt his semen spurting, mingling with her own hot juices. Wave after wave of pleasure flowed through her body, robbing her strength and leaving her sprawled across the bed in a boneless heap.

* * * * *

Dan staggered backward, nearly landing on the floor. Sooner or later he was going to die, if sex with Gayla kept getting better every time. He was one lucky SOB.

When he sat on the bed, he tried to summon up the energy to take off his prosthesis. Glancing down at the polished brown loafer he rarely took off the prosthesis unless he was planning to wear different shoes the next day, he had to smile. No woman, not even his mother, whose love he'd never doubted, had ever forgotten about his leg. They had tolerated it, ignored it, or tried to deny that it was there. One very strange girl he'd dated in college had even gotten turned on by looking at and playing with his stump. But until Gayla, no one had actually gotten so involved with wanting him that they forgot about his leg.

If it wouldn't have wakened Gayla and scared her half to death, Dan would have yelled out their news loud enough for all of Dallas to hear. He felt as though he could take on the whole world, even though with his leg off now he couldn't even walk. Naked now, he crawled into bed and gathered Gayla in his arms. Flattening his palm across her soft, concave belly, he imagined the thrill he'd get, feeling their baby move inside her as it grew. She shifted her legs, capturing his stump between them, and he tightened his arms around her.

* * * * *

"You awake?" Gayla's soft drawl dragged Dan out of a sound sleep.

"I am now." Suddenly he remembered how sick she'd been the last few days—and that she was carrying his baby. Blinking to focus his eyes in the dark, he noticed she was sitting up. "Are you okay?"

"I'm great." Her fingers traced a path up his leg, and he felt his cock begin to swell as if it knew what was coming. "What you're looking for is about a foot higher up," he told her, his body wide awake even though he was still dusting figurative cobwebs from his brain.

"I know. Lie back and relax."

"Princess, you've got to be kidding." A dead man couldn't relax, not looking at her gorgeous, naked body backlit by the moon—and certainly not while she was running her fingers up the inside of his thighs, just inches from his balls. "Don't stop, though."

Her fingers sank into the tangle of hair at his groin, encircled the base of his cock while she sucked the head into the warm, wet cavern of her mouth. Desire slammed into him. God, her mouth felt good. Too good. She had him so hard he hurt. Silently reciting declensions of Latin nouns did virtually nothing to take his mind off her exquisite torture and what it was doing to him.

He took it as long as he could before gently lifting her away and coaxing her to her back. He slammed into her hard, buried his cock to the balls in her welcome heat. Then he remembered and gentled his thrusts. Stroked her silky hair from her eyes and buried his face against the slender column of her throat. This was Gayla—the woman he loved. The woman carrying his child. Mumbling an apology when he recalled her queasy stomach, he braced himself on his elbows and knees.

"Fuck me, Doc. Don't stop now." When he leaned down to kiss her, she raised up her hips, seated him deeper, drenched his balls with her hot, sweet cream.

"I won't. But princess, I don't want to hurt you." He ground his teeth to keep from pounding into her like the wild beast her loving had unleashed.

He loved how she whimpered and moaned when he fucked her, the eager way she lifted her hips to meet his thrusts. The tight wet glove of her pussy milking him, spasming around him, coaxing out his climax with the waves of her own.

When he came, the pleasure almost shattered him. Each orgasm was better than the last, but no more satisfying, he was sure, than the countless ones to come.

* * * * *

In bed, after showering together and making love again, Dan propped himself up against the pillows and held Gayla. So far this morning, she'd only thrown up once, but he'd still managed to talk her out of going to work at either the pool or the rehab facility.

"You, princess, are a lovely shade of green. Are you going to be sprinting for the bathroom again soon?"

"Shut up. If I don't think about being sick, I won't be sick. Or so I tell myself. Right now I'm admiring my ring. Looks good, don't you think?" She twisted her head, meeting Dan's gaze as she held up her hand for him to see.

"It's almost as gorgeous as you. You just lie still here and admire it some more. I've got to call my office." The ring he'd doubted he could ever get on her finger sparkled at him as he waited for someone to answer the phone. Tired of holding the receiver, he turned on the speaker.

When his nurse Barbara came on the line, Dan told her to let the hospital know he wouldn't be making rounds until after noon and to reschedule all his office appointments for the day.

"Why, Doc, got a hot date?"

Gayla grinned up at him, wiggling the finger that wore the ring. "Yeah, Barbara. Hot beyond belief. You don't know what you're missing out on."

"Get off it. You never cancel appointments. What's going on?" Barbara sounded a little indignant.

"I got engaged last night."

"No way!"

Dan laughed at the funny face Gayla made. "You really know how to hurt a guy. Remind me to fire you when I come in on Monday."

"You wouldn't do that. You might throw a scalpel at me, but fire me? Never."

"Don't count on it. You might, however, keep your mouth shut about this latest bit of gossip—and use your free time to arrange the food and flowers for a little engagement party Sunday night here at my place. For, say, twenty people."

"You aren't kidding, are you? Are you actually going to marry Ironsides' daughter?"

Dan fought down the urge to strangle his nurse. It wasn't difficult, because he was just too damn happy. "Her name is Gayla."

"I know. All the girls who've gone over to the new place this week have met her. Say she's going to do a great job with the new aquatic rehab program. When's the big day?"

Dan raised an eyebrow at Gayla, and she responded with a shrug. "We don't know yet. When we decide we'll be sure to let you know. Now let me go and enjoy my first full day as an engaged man."

When Barbara hung up, Dan turned to Gayla. "How about it, princess? When do we tie the knot?"

"Got a calendar?"

"Here." Digging one out of the drawer, he handed it over.

Gayla frowned. "Sunday. Mom said all weddings should be held on Sunday."

"Okay. If we get the license today, we can do it this Sunday," he suggested, pointing to the Sunday coming up in just three more days.

She looked cute when she pouted, and she was pouting now. "Dan, I'm only going to do this once. I'd like it to be a day to remember, even if…"

"If nothing. You want a three-ring circus, you'll have it. Temple, hotel, country club—whatever you want is fine with me, just so long as we can get it done before Junior arrives. I'm kind of partial to the idea of him coming into the world to parents who are married to each other."

Laughing, she assured him she had nothing quite like a Hollywood extravaganza in mind—more like a quiet ceremony somewhere pretty, with their friends and co-workers there to wish them well. "Tess and Bill had the works—temple wedding, hotel reception, twelve-piece band and five-course dinner. They hardly got the chance to say a word to each other during the entire reception, which by the way went on until three in the morning. One wedding like that per family is more than enough."

Her expression sobered, and Dan wondered again if Gayla could truly be happy without her father's forgiveness. "So how long will this small circus you have in mind take to plan and execute?" He gave her hand an affectionate squeeze.

She pointed on the calendar to the second Sunday in September. "Until then."

"That's the thirteenth. Over a month away." He could tell himself until he turned blue that he didn't care if they waited to get married until the baby was almost due. But he did. He wanted Gayla bound to him as soon as it could be arranged.

"Look. It's only five weeks away. Well, six if you count this week as number one." She grinned. "You aren't superstitious, are you? The thirteenth is the only day in September when we can possibly get married. The sixth is too soon for us to arrange even the simplest ceremony. We can't do it later unless we wait until October, because of the Jewish holidays."

Dan didn't like it, but he had to agree. Sunday was the day of the week that most of their friends would be free, even if he couldn't figure out the reason Gayla's mom had told her weddings had to be held then. Besides, he didn't doubt she'd need at least six weeks to do whatever it was that brides had to do.

"Okay, princess, September thirteenth it is. I'm not superstitious about the number, unless it happens to come on Friday. What say we kick back and take it easy for the rest of the morning? Think your stomach will let you enjoy a little celebratory lunch if we wait to eat until late?"

"I hope so. All this getting engaged stuff takes a lot of energy." Snuggling up to Dan like a friendly kitten, Gayla went to sleep. Getting engaged might be exhausting, but the peace it brought, knowing she'd be his forever...it was worth it. While she slept in his arms, Dan listened to a medical journal on audiotape. For the first time since he'd met Gayla he found himself actually able to concentrate on what the author was presenting.

Chapter Twenty-Six

ಸಂ

When she and Dan came home from shopping Sunday afternoon, Gayla barely recognized his condo. A waitress in a short black uniform scurried about, setting out bowls of nuts and candy, and a tuxedoed man with a twirly mustache stood behind the bar apparently assessing Dan's liquor supply. From the noise that came from the kitchen, she assumed that at least one more person was out there, doing something to get ready for their engagement party.

He hadn't let her lift a finger, other than to go with him this afternoon to buy her a new dress. She didn't mind. Parties had always been more her mother's thing than hers. She did wonder, though, if he intended for them to entertain like this after they were married. If so, she'd better re-think her tentative plans for a pretty but very informal wedding.

Idly she picked up a blush rose from the bouquet on the table in the foyer, inhaling its sweet perfume. "Do you put on a bash like this very often?" she asked Dan as they walked back toward their bedroom.

"I've never put on any kind of bash before, unless you count me having the partners over and setting out beer and carry-out pizza for them to drink and eat. Barbara took care of arranging this party. I wanted it to be special."

"Barbara?"

"My nurse Barbara. The one you listened to the other day when I told her to have someone do a party for about twenty people." Dan brushed his lips across her cheek as he took out her dress. She watched him lay it on the bed along with the shirt he'd bought.

"I guess we should get dressed before these people start arriving." Kicking her sandals off first, she pulled her knit shirt over her head and shimmied out of her jeans, her gaze on Dan as he did the same.

"Quit looking at me that way, princess, or our guests will be enjoying our party all by themselves." Although he sounded serious, she could tell by his quirky grin that he was only kidding.

His gaze told her she looked good in the lime-colored linen sheath with its scooped neckline and tiny cap sleeves. Turning her back to him, she waited for him to zip her up. "Thanks."

"Any time. Want to straighten my tie?"

Standing on tiptoe, Gayla ran her finger under the collar of his shirt, smoothing the back of the tie against the soft cotton fabric. "I've never seen you wear a tie before, except with your tux." She admired the jade, beige, and dark brown one that went perfectly with his beige shirt and olive green dress slacks.

"I hate the things. Do my best to avoid wearing them."

"You look good enough to eat." Teasing him, she licked her lips as if anticipating a feast.

He leaned down, nipping lightly at the slight cleavage the dress revealed. "You know what, princess? So do you."

The doorbell rang, effectively ending a delightful romantic interlude. Smoothing her dress down over her hips and slipping her feet into high-heeled white sandals, she followed Dan to the door.

One by one all of Dan's co-workers and their significant others showed up, along with Tess and Bill. Gayla kept smiling, trying to keep everyone's names straight while the guests made themselves comfortable and kept the bartender busy fixing drinks. Only Jim and Jamie opted for mixed drinks, she noticed with hardly a twinge of envy—and as many of the others asked for soft drinks as for the white and red wines in their crystal decanters on the bar.

When the doorbell rang again, Dan had gone with Frank to his study to show him something or other, so Gayla answered it alone. "Dr. Halpern," she exclaimed. "Come in."

"Sandy, honey, this is Gayla Harris. Gayla, my wife, Sandy. For God's sake, call me Greg. Hey, there's Tess. She's got to be your sister."

Gayla recognized the stunning blonde from the studio portrait she'd admired in Greg's office. "Sandy, I'm glad to meet you."

Greg had rushed into the living room and was crushing Tess in a bear hug. Not knowing exactly what to say, Gayla smiled at Sandy. "He must know Tess from somewhere," she observed, knowing she must sound like an idiot.

"Greg knows everyone. Loves people. He's one of the most genuinely caring guys I've ever known. He tells me you and Dan are going to have a baby."

Gayla smiled. "Yes, we are. I understand you have a brand-new baby boy and that he's the most miraculous child ever born."

"Tyler's great. Not as exceptional as Greg thinks he is, but he's my little darling. This is the first time I've left him to go anywhere except for my checkups." Smiling, she reached in her purse and produced a stack of snapshots.

"Tyler must be your first baby," Gayla commented. Surely no two people who had produced children before would be quite as obsessed with their newborn as Sandy and Greg appeared to be.

"My first. Greg's second. His daughter is thirteen, going on thirty." Sandy thumbed through the pictures. "Here she is, holding Tyler the day we brought him home from the hospital."

"Sandy, come here," Greg called, his booming voice causing almost everybody in the room to look up from whatever they were doing. "I want you to meet my old buddy Tess."

Just then Dan came up behind Gayla and put his arms around her. "You okay, princess?" She imagined he expected her to be sick again at any minute.

"Hey, Newman, stop that. Don't want you getting in trouble, playing it hot and heavy with a pretty lady." That was Jim, keeping up the good-natured razzing he'd started almost before making it through the door.

Greg laughed. "Too late for Dan to close the barn door, Jim. Cow's already out. You know, you guys are great for my business. You're paying for my son's first year in college with this baby boom of yours. Sandy, don't you think they deserve our thanks?"

"Oh, Greg. Quit teasing." Sandy's adoring expression when she looked at him took the edge off her words.

"You're hardly one to talk, Halpern. Married just a year and already you're changing diapers," Frank observed.

"Hey, enough of this! When are you two getting married?" Jamie asked.

Gayla smiled. "September thirteenth. If we can find a place to do it."

"You mean you haven't booked a temple?" Tess sounded scandalized. "You'll never get one now, or a decent hotel for the reception, either. And you can't put it off much longer than that."

Frank laughed. "Dan can get the hospital chapel almost any time. Worked fine for Michelle and me."

"What's the name of that place where we got married, honey?" Greg asked Sandy. "We managed to get in without booking a long time in advance."

Sandy named a restored Victorian house that had been converted to a wedding hall. "It's gorgeous. So romantic. They provide everything, even the most divine cheesecake wedding cake you ever tasted."

It boasted astronomical prices, too, or so Gayla had heard. "I'd thought maybe the country club where I coach would do. It's pretty out by the pool."

Tess looked as if she were about to faint. "Outside? In September? You can't be certain of good weather."

Gayla nodded. She hadn't thought of that. "I guess we could have it indoors."

Her head was spinning. Maybe Dan's suggestion was the best one after all. "We could just go find a justice of the peace and avoid all this hassle."

"You wouldn't like that." He clapped his hands, and everyone quit chattering and turned to face them. "We're getting married September thirteenth at Bluebonnet Country Club. Outside if it's nice weather that day, inside if it isn't. You're all invited, and we'll let you know the time and whatever else you need to know later. Now let's have a good time."

Putting his arm around Gayla's waist, Dan gave her a subtle squeeze as they headed for the food.

* * * * *

A week and a half later, Dan hung up the phone in his office and scratched out another line on the list of things he had to do before the wedding. After making a dozen or more calls in search of someone to officiate, he remembered Dave Karp, a former patient of his who just happened to be a circuit judge over in Fort Worth and who appeared delighted to help Dan get himself married off.

He glanced at the clock and smiled at the picture of Gayla that he'd blown up and put in a silver frame. Standing at that scenic overlook where they'd stopped and stretched their legs, she looked as if she were remembering some distant but pleasant event. Dan smiled. Somehow having her picture here, where he met with patients, made their commitment seem very real. It added a personal touch, too, that the simply furnished room had always lacked before.

Turning back to his desk, he thumbed through Eli Harris's chart. Tuning out his personal feelings for the man, he studied scans, comparing the ones taken yesterday with those that had been done before and immediately after Eli's surgery. The hand was healing well enough for him to start rehabilitative therapy.

"Dan, Dr. Harris is here."

"Okay. You can bring him in here, Barbara." No need to annoy Ironsides by herding him into an examining room when it wasn't necessary. Dan stood to greet his patient.

"Well, what's the verdict?" Harris asked, settling carefully onto a chair.

Dan met his gaze. "The hand's healing well. I want you to start physical therapy tomorrow, three days a week."

"At your fancy new facility?"

"Michelle's the best therapist around. You're welcome to choose your own, though, if you prefer. I'll have Barbara give you the prescription on the way out."

"I'll go to her. May as well help swell your wallet. I hear you're going to need it. Drug and alcohol rehabilitation centers are expensive."

Ironsides' oblique reference to Gayla's past problems incensed Dan. "I'm not anticipating needing their services."

"Then you're a fool. That fact, of course, is evident in that you are actually planning to marry her." Harris's gaze settled on Gayla's photo, then shifted to Dan. "Mark my words, you'll regret that decision."

"What do you plan to do about it?"

"I could ruin you in this town, Newman. Make sure you and your partners don't attract the first paying patient. Get your staff privileges revoked."

When Ironsides paused, Dan interrupted. "Do your worst. Gayla and I are getting married, and we're going to stay in Dallas. In the first place, I don't believe you would stoop low enough to undermine mine or my partners' careers because of a personal vendetta. Anyhow, my ego is healthy enough to believe you couldn't succeed even if you tried."

That brought a smile to Ironsides' thin lips. "You're smart. Damn smart. How in the hell can you do something so stupid as marry a woman like her?" He glanced at the picture again, as if trying to reconcile his prejudices about Gayla with the impression she gave in the photograph.

"I've said it before. I love Gayla. I'm going to marry her. She has reconciled herself to the fact that you won't let her into your life. It's you who will lose if you don't. Do you really not want to know your grandchildren?"

Harris stood and focused his gaze on something outside the window behind Dan's credenza. "Grandchildren?"

"Yeah. Gayla's pregnant. Our baby's due early in May."

Whirling around to face Dan, Harris stopped just inches from his chair. "You've made my daughter pregnant? And you have the goddamn audacity to stand there and tell me about it with a silly grin on your face?"

"Yeah. I do. I couldn't be happier."

"I ought to castrate you! How dare you take my child to bed and not even bother to protect her? I'm going to run you out of town, the same way I did that bastard Marc Solomon."

"I thought he was your fair-haired boy. So does Gayla. You stood by him, as she sees it, while you tossed her out like garbage." Dan tried to squelch his anger with her father by imagining Gayla stretched out across his bed, naked and wanting him.

Harris picked up the picture of Gayla, studying it as if he expected to have some profound revelation. "It took me nearly two years, but I got rid of him. Caught him violating one of the terms of a ten-year contract with seven left to go—the contract I'd given him and Gayla as an engagement present."

"Well, I'm not going to run out on your daughter. I love her. I'm sorry if it offends you that we've slept together, but I'm ecstatic that she's going to have my child. If you want to be a part of his or her life, you're going to have to forgive Gayla. She belongs to me now. I won't stand by and let you hurt her."

Harris stood up, apparently at a loss for words. Setting Gayla's picture back on the credenza, he turned toward the door.

"The wedding's September thirteenth at Bluebonnet Country Club. Six o'clock. Don't come unless you want to share our happiness and be part of Gayla's life again," Dan told Ironsides as they parted.

* * * * *

"Sylvia, our baby's getting married."

Awkwardly, Eli knelt down and touched the simple, flat stone that marked his wife's final resting place. It had been so long since she'd been with him, making their home a peaceful haven instead of the luxuriously furnished void he came home to now after a long day's work. He glanced down at his right arm, securely tethered to his body in a sling to protect the hand Newman had patched together. The thought of not being able to go back to surgery ate at him, largely because he didn't know how he'd fill the empty hours and days if he couldn't work.

"What should I do?" he asked, and he felt Sylvia's gentle presence almost as if she were really here. Tracing the raised letters on the marker, he strained to hear her soft, soothing voice.

An image came to him, of the stricken look on her pretty face when he'd decreed that from the day when they had found Gayla strung out and incoherent, she'd be dead to them. Had she wanted to protest?

That day had marked the beginning of Sylvia's illness. Eli knew it as certainly as he knew how to patch up hearts. While she'd kept on as always, making their house a home and carrying on with the volunteer work he'd encouraged her to do, Sylvia had quietly killed herself with worry. Worry over the daughter who hadn't lived up to their bright expectations.

What would Sylvia have told him if he'd been able to get to her bedside before she died? Eli would never know for sure. Recalling his wife's generosity and sweetness, he had to believe she'd have wanted him to forgive and forget. She'd loved both her girls, but Gayla had been her baby. While he'd focused on his career, she'd focused on him — and, his hopes and dreams for their children. When his plans for Gayla had gone up in smoke, Sylvia's disappointment had been a mirror of his own instead of the expression of her own disillusionment.

Why had he never realized this before? Standing and staring across the carpet of grass dotted here and there with colorful bouquets, Eli tried to remember one time during all the years they were married that Sylvia questioned one of his decisions. Surely he hadn't been such a tyrant that she'd been afraid to voice her opinions. Or had he? Eli would never know. He was very certain now, though he didn't know why, that Sylvia had wanted to help their daughter. Not throw her out, and certainly not deny her existence.

"Why in the hell didn't you open your mouth? I'd have given you the moon, sweetheart. What did I do to make you so goddamn afraid of me that you wouldn't even stand up for what you wanted for Gayla?"

Eli stood there for a long time. It was true, Sylvia hadn't had the strength to stand up to him. But he was the one who deserved most of the blame. He cursed his own ego that had balked at accepting his child whose actions had been so much less than perfect. When he turned and walked away he knew what he had to do.

What he didn't know was whether he could summon the courage to do it.

Chapter Twenty-Seven

❧

Between occasional bouts of morning sickness, her coaching, and her work with patients at the rehab facility, Gayla barely had time to catch a breath, much less plan a wedding. In the few moments when she could spare a thought, she wished her mom could be there on her big day.

"I'll be with you, baby, even though you won't be able to see me."

Other than the one time in Dan's bedroom, Gayla had never been able to see her mother, but still she looked around the car. Not even a shadow suggested Sylvia's presence, but Gayla felt it all around her. "I know you will, Mom. I love you." A teardrop made its way down her cheek, coming to rest in the hollow of her throat.

"And I love you. Dry your eyes, honey, and tell me about your wedding. This should be the happiest time of your life."

Smiling through her tears, Gayla described her off-white Mexican wedding dress with its handmade lace and elaborately patterned embroidery. Her mom assured her that Dan was going to love it.

"I wish you could borrow my pearls," Sylvia said, her tone conveying a world of regret.

"That's all right, Mom. I'm borrowing a locket from Tess. All I need now is something blue."

As she drove into the parking garage, Gayla sensed that her mother had floated away.

* * * * *

"How's my baby feeling?" Dan asked when Gayla got home. He wished she'd pare down her hectic schedule, or at least let him do more to help.

"He's fine. I'm beat. Haggling about food and flowers for the wedding is more exhausting than doing ten thousand yards in the pool. We're using mums instead of carnations, and I decided it was easier to do a buffet supper than have World War III over whether the consultant could bring in her own banquet servers to do the sit-down dinner. How was your day?"

He grinned. "Probably a lot less hectic than yours. I had four surgeries, all of which went uneventfully. Made rounds. Hamilton, by the way, said to tell you hello. We're sending him over for therapy tomorrow."

"Then the cast is off his leg?"

"Cut it off myself this afternoon. Come on out to the kitchen, princess. I grilled chicken breasts and made a Caesar salad."

"Good. You know, you're a pretty swell guy to live with. I think I may have to keep you."

"Glad to hear it. I've gotten kind of used to finding you snuggled up to me when I wake up every morning."

Dinner settled fairly well on Gayla's stomach. Maybe the nausea was going to go away. Comfortably curled up on the sofa beside Dan while he read some medical journal, she let the sound of his favorite country singers lull her off to sleep.

* * * * *

The next morning they left together. Gayla watched Dan drive away after dropping her off at work. She wished the contractor would finish soon so his office would be close enough that they could see each other occasionally during the day.

Inside, she concentrated on getting ready for Zach Hamilton. Of all the patients she'd met, he touched her heart with his good humor and optimism. Like Dan and so many others she'd only noticed recently, Zach had taken tragedy in stride and was determined to succeed in spite of it—the way she was doing, though on a smaller scale.

Figuring Zach should be in Jamie's office, Gayla headed that way. "Morning, Jamie. Zach."

"I'll have him ready for you in a few minutes," Jamie said, not looking up from her work. "Zach, I'm sorry, this may hurt a bit."

"Go on. Anything if it will help me get vertical." He didn't make a sound, but judging from the expression on his face, whatever Jamie was doing caused Zach a lot of pain.

Gayla noticed the bandage on his hand. "Is that going to stay on?"

Zach grinned. "Dr. Newman's coming to take it off. He said he wanted to check the fit on the glove Jamie made, but I think he wanted an excuse to come see you."

"Probably." Gayla returned his smile. "Shall we get you over to the pool now?"

When Dan arrived Zach had just finished doing his leg exercises. "How's it going?" he asked.

"Fine. It feels great to stand up, even if it is in water."

"You'll be getting around on land sooner than you think. Let's go down to the lab and unveil your hand."

Dan stayed while Gayla put Zach through his exercise routine. While they waited for the van to take Zach back to the hospital, they talked.

"When's the happy day?"

Gayla turned to Zach. "Next Sunday—September thirteenth. We'd love for you to join us."

Zach's expression clouded over, then brightened. "I'd love to, if Doc springs me from the hospital by then."

Later as they shared lunch, Gayla asked Dan if Zach had suffered some personal trauma other than his injuries.

"His partner died in the explosion—and he just went through a divorce. He got the final papers a day or so after he woke up, or so one of the nurses said."

"He looked so sad for a minute, after I asked him to our wedding. I just wondered…"

"You did right, princess. It will be good for him to get out and socialize." Reaching across the table, Dan squeezed Gayla's hand.

Chapter Twenty-Eight
The Ghosts

ೕ

"I had sort of hoped she'd keep her own name," Sylvia commented.

Ruth shook her head. She'd been listening to the other ghost whine about that ever since Sylvia realized that Gayla intended to take Dan's name. Frankly Ruth thought the girl would be crazy to want to keep Eli's after the way he'd treated her. *"Enough already. The guests are starting to arrive."*

"I hope it doesn't start raining."

"Sylvia, take a look up at that sky. Tell me, does it look like rain?" A bright Texas sun shone against a background of brilliant blue as wispy white clouds floated by, obscuring it momentarily every now and then.

"No, but I would never have chanced doing a wedding outside. You just never can tell..."

"Quit kvetching and watch. How many ghosts get to watch their children's weddings?" Ruth could practically smell the hundreds of roses that covered the huppah and filled crystal bowls on each of the round tables set up for the guests. The riot of color, from pure white to deep burgundy with every shade of pink and red in between, worked beautifully despite what Ruth had thought when she heard Gayla describe what she wanted. *"I was wrong, thinking the colors would clash. Aren't the flowers beautiful?"*

"Yes. I told you they would be. See how the fern and baby's breath pull it all together?"

"You're right." This was her son's wedding day. Ruth wasn't going to let anything spoil her good mood. Not even having to admit to Sylvia that she'd been wrong. *"Look!"* she exclaimed. *"There's Danny."*

Her boy looked wonderful in his tux, with a blush-colored rose in the lapel—and so happy it nearly made her burst with joy. When Sylvia gushed on and on about how great he looked, how brilliant he was, and how lucky her daughter was to be marrying such a paragon, Ruth refrained from reminding her she hadn't always felt that way.

"*I wonder where Gayla is,*" she said, certain that the girl's mother was itching to get a glimpse of her baby in her wedding gown. "*Why don't we try to find her?*"

"*We'll miss seeing the guests arrive.*"

Ruth concentrated until an image of her future daughter-in-law materialized in a room somewhere inside the club. "*Look. I've never seen Gayla look so beautiful. Bernie's going to be sorry he went fishing instead of staying with me.*"

"*Ruth, you're going to make me cry.*" Sylvia's watery gaze focused on her daughter and Michelle. She imagined the other ghost was wishing it could be she, not Gayla's friend and coworker, arranging the gossamer lace veil over her daughter's glossy dark hair. "*I wonder if Eli will be there.*"

Chapter Twenty-Nine

ಬಿ

"Scared?" Jim asked Dan as they took their places under the canopy of roses and baby's breath.

Dan smiled. "I don't know why I should be. I'm getting the woman I love beyond what I ever imagined in my wildest dreams. Do you have her ring?"

Jim patted his pants pocket. "Right here."

"What about the check for Judge Karp?"

"Got that, too. Relax. We've got this under control."

"All right. I just have the feeling something's missing." They had rehearsed the ceremony Dan wanted to be all Gayla had ever dreamed of, but he'd sensed last night that she was missing something besides the traditional processional. While deceased parents certainly couldn't be expected to join the bridal party, Eli Harris was very much alive. Dan's jaw tightened when he remembered Gayla's sad expression when she'd asked Frank and Michelle to escort her down the aisle.

A soft prelude Dan couldn't recall the name of soothed him as he took his place to the left of Judge Karp. The tables, he noticed when he glanced around the deck, were nearly all full. But he didn't see the one person he hoped, for Gayla's sake, would come.

Tess and Kelly joined them under the canopy, and the volume of the music started to build up. Gayla stepped out of the club building, a determined smile on her face as she took her place between Frank and Michelle. As they took the first step onto the white runner, Dan's breath caught in his throat. The music's volume dropped to a mere whisper.

Ironsides had showed up after all. His heart beating in double time, Dan strained to hear what he was saying.

"That's my job, Grogan."

Just four words, but Dan was certain that to Gayla they meant the world. While Frank circled the crowd to make his way to the huppah, the musicians began the processional once again.

On her father's arm, a brilliant smile on her face, Gayla came to Dan. Eli gave Dan her hand without a word. The older man met Dan's gaze as if warning him to take care of the precious gift he'd been given. Then he stepped to the side to stand as witness to the marriage.

Only after the vows had been made, the crystal wineglass crushed under his heel, and congratulatory shouts of the guests acknowledged did Dan find time to thank God for whatever He'd done to bring his bride the only present he hadn't been able to provide.

* * * * *

Gayla loved Dan. She loved her father. Today she loved everyone. She ate and chatted and danced with Dan and with her dad, then with Frank and Jim. Though she hadn't spied her mother, she'd felt her loving presence, smelled the haunting fragrance of her favorite perfume.

The sun shone brightly on her wedding day. It was silly, but Gayla sensed that Dan's parents, too, were somewhere up there rejoicing in their happiness.

"Ready to go, princess?" Coming back from dancing with one of the guests, Dan whispered to Gayla as he nuzzled at her neck.

"Not yet. Look at Greg and Sandy. They make such a stunning couple."

"Better than us?"

"Never. I meant to tell you before now. I have a feeling I have you to thank for getting Daddy here." Smiling, she watched Eli waltz by with one of the nurses from the hospital.

"He came because he can't deny any longer that he loves you. At least that's what he told me after warning me I'd better take damn good care of you."

That sounded more like the man she'd grown up around than the father who today had begged her to forgive him and let him be part of her life once more.

Her gaze settled on Zach Hamilton. "Dan, is Zach in pain?" she asked when she noticed how he was sitting alone, staring at the bouquet of roses on the table next to his wheelchair.

"Let's go see." His arm around her, he maneuvered between the dancers, pulling back a chair for her at Zach's table. "How's it going?" he asked, still standing behind her.

"Fine. Great wedding. You two make a good couple."

Zach sounded tired, or maybe disillusioned. "Are you feeling all right?" Gayla asked.

"Not bad. Just a little down, sitting here watching folks do what I can't manage yet."

Dan squeezed Gayla's shoulders, as if telling her to let it go. "You're coming along fine. Just give your body time to heal. We're glad you could come and share our big day. See you in two weeks, after we get back."

As they walked back to the head table, Gayla suddenly couldn't wait to be alone again with Dan. "Come on, Doc, let's sneak out of here and get on with the honeymoon."

"One honeymoon coming up."

Frank laughed. "Not until your beautiful bride tosses her bouquet to some hopeful female—and not until you take that garter off her leg and throw it to some hapless bachelor."

That particular ritual had slipped Dan's mind—understandably, since his mind was focused on escaping well-meaning friends and making love with his brand-new, beautiful wife. Telling himself it wouldn't be much longer, he watched Gayla throw her flowers into a groping sea of female hands. When the commotion died down, Jamie had the flowers.

Grinning, he went down on one knee and lifted the tiered skirt of Gayla's wedding gown. The prize was there—a lacy blue garter that he slid down her leg. Standing, he heaved it high in the air. When it came down, it caught on the arm of Zach's wheelchair.

"Jamie's getting married in December, so I guess there must be something to that thing about catching the bouquet," Gayla said later as they were putting their things away in the bridal suite of the same Galveston hotel where they'd been when Dan got the call about her father.

"Zach got the garter," Dan reminded her.

"So, that means he's going to find someone to love again soon. Dan, did you notice how Frank was looking at Michelle?"

He certainly had. In the past few weeks his partner had been acting strangely like a man in love, not a guy who had married his good friend just to provide a home for their baby. "Yeah, princess. He was looking at her the way I look at you."

Desire, bubbling barely below the surface since Dan had gotten the first look at his bride coming down the aisle, came to a sudden boil. "Come here. I want to make love with my wife."

Epilogue

Seven months later

ಐ

"*You're sure we can do this?*" Bernie sounded skeptical, but Ruth quieted him with a glare.

Sylvia had never felt more confident. "*Wild horses couldn't keep me from going down there to see little Bernie and Sylvia Ruth on Mother's Day. If you want to go with me, hold onto my hands.*"

Concentrating harder than she ever had before, Sylvia's spirit transported them back into the world of the living. The first thing she saw on the polished walnut coffee table in Gayla and Dan's living room was the photo album, opened to a page filled with brand-new snapshots.

Gayla, Dan's arms protectively around her as she held her twins. The babies, together and apart, naked as the day they were born and clothed in the latest fashions for baby boys and girls. Eli with the babies and with Gayla and Dan.

Suddenly Sylvia couldn't wait any longer. She had to see the babies—and her own baby girl, all grown up and a mother herself this year. Getting up quickly, she floated toward the bedroom wing of this new, roomy house.

"*Sylvia, no! They may be...*"

"*Don't be silly, Ruth. The babies are only three days old. Surely you don't think we're likely to walk in on anything we shouldn't see.*" Pausing until Ruth caught up with her and Bernie, Sylvia set off again to find the master suite.

"Mom!" Gayla exclaimed as they floated through the door to her bedroom.

"What, princess?" Dan glanced up from the tiny bundle he held in his arms. Sylvia wished she had a camera to record the expression of wonder on her son-in-law's handsome face. "Mother? Dad?"

"Is that really you? Danny, let me see my namesake." Bernie hunkered down by Dan's chair, his gaze unbelievably tender. *"Boy, you've done all right for yourself. Don't sit there gaping. Introduce your mom and me to your pretty wife and daughter."*

Ruth was uncharacteristically quiet as they looked at the baby girl in Gayla's arms. *"This is Dan's mother, Ruth, and his father, Bernie. Oh, Gayla, I'm so glad you took my advice. Didn't I tell you Dan would be perfect for you? You make beautiful babies together."* She'd never seen her daughter look so content.

Moving over to the bed, Dan sat down beside Gayla, his son snug in his arms. "You told Gayla what?"

It was Ruth who answered. *"That you two would have a marriage arranged in heaven, Danny."*

"You mean…"

"I'm afraid she does, son. You know how your mom is when she sets her mind on something. She and Sylvia here got together and decided you and Gayla needed each other, so they plotted and schemed from before you two met until the day you married."

Bernie paused, taking a closer look at his granddaughter. *"Looks like the four of you are doing all right."* He stepped back and looked at them, his eyes full of wonder.

"Yeah, Pop, we're doing fine. But—"

Sylvia smiled. *"Don't be angry, Danny. You and Gayla fell in love all by yourselves. Your mom and I just set it up so you'd meet, and you took it from there. Be happy, my darlings, and give my love to Eli."* She felt herself beginning to fade away, but before she did she heard Ruth choke back a sob and wish Gayla many happy Mother's Days.

"I can't believe that," Dan muttered as he settled Bernie and Sylvia into their bassinets after the ghosts disappeared as suddenly as they'd materialized. "My mind must be playing tricks on me."

When he came back and joined Gayla on their bed, she snuggled in his arms. "I can."

"How so?"

"Mom started talking to me not long after you and I met. It was almost as though I'd wish for her and she'd be there. Not for long. I actually saw her only once before today. But I believe she's been looking down on us. From what your dad said, your mother has been doing the same thing."

If Dan hadn't seen and talked to the ghosts, he'd have thought the ordeal of having the babies had addled Gayla's brain. But he had, and suddenly the whole preposterous yarn his dad had spun didn't seem so far-fetched after all. "You're probably right. I don't like it, though—thinking we got pushed together because our mothers couldn't stop their meddling even though they're dead."

"I don't know, love. I kind of like the idea of having a marriage that was—what was it your mother said?"

"Arranged in heaven."

Gayla hugged Dan hard, then lay back and shot him a silly grin. "That's it. God, but I love you. And our babies. Today I love the whole world, I'm so happy."

"No matter what our moms may have cooked up for us, it's you who has made my life heaven here on earth. Happy Mother's Day, princess."

And Happy Mother's Day to you, too, Mom—and Sylvia. I owe you, big time, wherever you are.

Why an electronic book?

We live in the Information Age—an exciting time in the history of human civilization, in which technology rules supreme and continues to progress in leaps and bounds every minute of every day. For a multitude of reasons, more and more avid literary fans are opting to purchase e-books instead of paper books. The question from those not yet initiated into the world of electronic reading is simply: *Why?*

1. *Price.* An electronic title at Ellora's Cave Publishing and Cerridwen Press runs anywhere from 40% to 75% less than the cover price of the exact same title in paperback format. Why? Basic mathematics and cost. It is less expensive to publish an e-book (no paper and printing, no warehousing and shipping) than it is to publish a paperback, so the savings are passed along to the consumer.

2. *Space.* Running out of room in your house for your books? That is one worry you will never have with electronic books. For a low one-time cost, you can purchase a handheld device specifically designed for e-reading. Many e-readers have large, convenient screens for viewing. Better yet, hundreds of titles can be stored within your new library—on a single microchip. There are a variety of e-readers from different manufacturers. You can also read e-books on your PC or laptop computer. (Please note that Ellora's

Cave does not endorse any specific brands. You can check our websites at www.ellorascave.com or www.cerridwenpress.com for information we make available to new consumers.)

3. *Mobility.* Because your new e-library consists of only a microchip within a small, easily transportable e-reader, your entire cache of books can be taken with you wherever you go.

4. *Personal Viewing Preferences.* Are the words you are currently reading too small? Too large? Too… ANNOYING? Paperback books cannot be modified according to personal preferences, but e-books can.

5. *Instant Gratification.* Is it the middle of the night and all the bookstores near you are closed? Are you tired of waiting days, sometimes weeks, for bookstores to ship the novels you bought? Ellora's Cave Publishing sells instantaneous downloads twenty-four hours a day, seven days a week, every day of the year. Our webstore is never closed. Our e-book delivery system is 100% automated, meaning your order is filled as soon as you pay for it.

Those are a few of the top reasons why electronic books are replacing paperbacks for many avid readers.

As always, Ellora's Cave and Cerridwen Press welcome your questions and comments. We invite you to email us at Comments@ellorascave.com or write to us directly at Ellora's Cave Publishing Inc., 1056 Home Avenue, Akron, OH 44310-3502.

The
✢ Ellora's Cave ✢
Library

Stay up to date with Ellora's Cave Titles in
Print with our Quarterly Catalog.

To recieve a catalog,
send an email with your name
and mailing address to:

CATALOG@ELLORASCAVE.COM

or send a letter or postcard
with your mailing address to:

Catalog Request
c/o Ellora's Cave Publishing, Inc.
1056 Home Avenue
Akron, Ohio 44310-3502

Now Available
from
CerriOwen Press

Keeper of the Spirit By Ruby Storm
Book 1 in the Keeper Series

Minnesota lumber baron Tyler Wilkins knew he needed to come to grips with the death of his wife. Little did he understand that his business trip to New York would be the beginning of a journey to find peace within himself and a love that sometimes happens twice in a lifetime.

Beautiful Emma Sanders has her entire world mapped out. Being the daughter of one of the richest shipbuilders in New York in 1880 guaranteed her a life of leisure. It also guaranteed the option she'd chosen—to remain single and manage her father's company someday. That is, until Tyler walked into her father's study and turned her world upside down. Crossing paths with this one sad man would change the course of her life forever.

The mysticism of an old Indian brave…a forgotten evil that lurks in Emma's past…one tragic hour in their lives, will all combine to lead them to a future filled with trust and understanding…and the discovery of peace and love that a man and woman can share.

Cerridwen, the Celtic Goddess of wisdom, was the muse who brought inspiration to storytellers and those in the creative arts. Cerridwen Press encompasses the best and most innovative stories in all genres of today's fiction. Visit our site and discover the newest titles by talented authors who still get inspired - much like the ancient storytellers did, once upon a time.

Cerridwen Press
www.cerridwenpress.com

Discover for yourself why readers can't get enough of the multiple award-winning publisher

Ellora's Cave.

Whether you prefer e-books or paperbacks,

be sure to visit EC on the web at
www.ellorascave.com

for an erotic reading experience that will leave you breathless.